We hope you enjoy t...
renew it by the

Loan

D1188790

THE SPIDER'S WEB

A HARVEY STONE THRILLER

J.D. WESTON

WESTON MEDIA

THE SPIDER'S WEB

To catch the spider, he must become the fly...

PROLOGUE

A gloved hand pushed a single photograph through a letterbox early one Saturday morning in 2001.

The moment it touched the hallway carpet, the lives of hundreds of people altered forever.

When the intended recipient heard the letterbox slap against the door, they padded into the hallway. For that individual, the world stopped right there and then.

The young girl in the photo smiled for the camera with a confidence that only children seem to bear; adults somehow lose that beautiful gift to life experience.

The image showed nothing untoward. Only the recipient's own cheerful daughter. It would have been innocent, had the photo been placed on a mantlepiece, beside a bed, or framed on a wall. But lying face-up on the hallway carpet, it was far from innocent, and when they turned the image over, three words written in black ink struck terror deep in their heart.

You cannot run.

PART ONE

ONE

"I have eyes on the target, sir," said Detective Sergeant Hawes, as Detective Inspector Mark Debruin entered the dark room. It was what Debruin had been waiting for. He knelt beside Hawes at the window.

"Get TSG on full alert," he replied. "He's not getting away this time."

"Tactical Support Group, this is command. We have eyes on the target. He's approaching the east entrance on foot. Give me Hammersley's location."

"Hammersley is behind the reception desk. Hasn't moved a muscle."

"Good. Wait for the command."

TSG confirmed the communication and the jabber of radios quietened as the two detectives and twenty-five tactical support operatives waited. Debruin and Hawes were positioned in an empty office space above a warehouse. The lights were off, and they peered through a grimy window at a dog food factory on the far side of the empty road. There was nothing special about the factory. There was nothing special about the owners or management of the factory.

What was special was the night-time security guard. Wayne Hammersley had a series of sex related convictions and a history of mental health problems.

"How the hell did Hammersley get a job as a security guard anyway?" asked Hawes. He spoke low as if he was voicing his thoughts and expected no answer.

"He's not a thief, he's a convicted sex offender. I can't think of any place less enticing than this, can you?"

"Well, yeah, I guess the smell is hardly an aphrodisiac, is it?" said Hawes, then he raised his radio and addressed the entire team. "Target is at the east entrance. We'll lose visual in five, four, three, two—"

The target, who seemed to be waiting by the entrance, slipped through the doorway and into the dark of the night. Debruin could just make out the lithe shape of the man as he took care to close the door behind him without making a noise. He seemed to just stand there. A faint outline of a man waiting in the shadows.

"What's he doing?" asked Hawes.

"He's waiting."

"What for?"

"I don't know. It's all part of his control. He waits. Maybe he's getting a feel for the room? Maybe he's listening?"

A full minute passed, then the dark shadow that was the target slipped from view.

"Target is in the building," said Hawes into the radio. "We've lost visual. TSG to follow on camera."

"Roger," came the reply from TSG command, Sergeant Gavin Spencer, a confident and able man who had made his mark in the force and now commanded the delicate operations that required brute strength and precision. The role was a fine balance of control, ruthlessness, and risk awareness. Not every man demonstrated the skills required. But Spencer was in full control one hundred percent of the time. Debruin had seen his team take down targets in busy train stations, crowded streets, and even a football stadium. All with minimal fuss and, even better, minimal media sensation. The use of firearms in a public place requires a commander to own every aspect of the scene. Any man can give the order to shoot, but most men would give the order to restrain for fear of entering the slippery slope of disciplinary action following an internal investigation. Spencer had that balance. He had the balls to go ahead and take a target down and he knew the limits. He was a safe pair of hands for Debruin to put his sting operation into.

"We have eyes on the target. He's moving along the east corridor. No weapons as yet."

"Roger that," said Hawes, then he lowered his radio and spoke to Debruin. "How do you think he'll do it?"

Hawes was referring to the man's MO. Most serial killers had a preferred method of carrying out their kills. But this particular killer had used a variety of methods, making it hard to pin crimes on him. He'd burned a man alive, he'd glued a man's mouth and nose closed, and he'd strung another up, slitting his throat to bleed out.

"He won't get the chance. We've got a tiny window of opportunity, Hawes. He's inside the building, but that's not enough. We need to catch him in the act. We need to catch him on camera."

"That's the easy part, sir."

"What do you mean?"

"Once we have him on camera, we actually need to catch him."

"That's why TSG are here. We've got a helicopter in the air, the streets are closed off, and we've got a dog team standing by. All we need is for Hammersley to give the signal."

"You have to admit," said Hawes, as he peered through the

binoculars searching for TSG who were waiting in the shadows ready to pounce, "it's a good deal for Hammersley. A new identity. A new house in a new town. Not to mention the clean slate."

"You don't think he deserves it?"

"I'm not sure my opinion counts much. But no, sir. No, I don't. He's ruined the lives of at least five young girls. He deserves to rot in prison."

"He's done his time, Hawes."

"Oh, come on, sir. We both know he'll do it again. New identity or not. He won't be able to help himself."

"He's putting his life on the line here. He's risking a lot so that we can catch this man."

"The suspect hasn't hurt anyone that didn't deserve it, sir."

"Sorry, Hawes?" Debruin was riled by the flippant comment. He understood where Hawes was coming from. But to voice the opinion was to go against everything the force stood for. "Are you saying that we should let this man carry on killing people because he's only killing perverts and sex offenders?"

Hawes said nothing.

"Are you saying that we shouldn't give Hammersley a tiny bit of credit for risking his life?"

"I'm just saying—"

"I know what you're saying, Hawes. And for the record, you need to keep those thoughts to yourself in future. We're catching a vigilante here. The last thing I need is for my DS to be rooting for the target. I need to know you've got my back."

"I've got your back, sir," Hawes said after a brief pause for contemplation.

"Good. Well, let's keep it that way," said Debruin. "Get me an update from TSG."

"TSG, come back."

"Command."

"Sit rep?"

"Target is in the blind spot. He'll be moving into the reception area shortly and we'll pick him up on cameras seven and eight."

"Keep us updated, Spencer," said Hawes, then mumbled to Debruin. "I do, you know?"

"What?" said Debruin, his tone sharper than required.

"Have your back, sir. I know this is important. I'm all for it. I don't know why I said what I said."

"You said what you said because you have a daughter, Hawes. Because you're a father, as am I. But, to do what we do, we have to leave that father at home. We have to be the law and nothing else. Our opinions, as you said, don't really count. We're an extension of the law and that's that. Right or wrong. I've been chasing this man for six months and right now, this is the closest we've been to getting him. Do you know what I'm going to do when we have him in custody and he's charged with three counts of murder?"

"Go on, sir."

"I'm going to go home and pour myself a scotch and sleep the sleep of the dead. When I wake up, my daughter will be awake and having her breakfast, as will hundreds and thousands of other daughters. I'll be her father then. When it's over." He raised his binoculars and peered through the window at the teams he had prepared. It was the largest sting operation he had managed in a long time and all the wheels were in motion. "And then I'll go back to bed and sleep for a thousand years, Hawes," he said.

"We have to catch him first, sir," said Hawes, and he raised the radio. "TSG, any visual?"

"Negative," said Spencer. "He's still in the blind spot."

Debruin turned and sat on the floor with his back against

the window. He closed his eyes and tried to channel the negativity from his mind.

The sound of the east door slamming was loud in the silence of the night and Debruin glanced up at Hawes whose body had stiffened.

"TSG, target has left the building through the east exit. Do you have eyes on Hammersley?"

"Hammersley is at his desk at reception. Do we move in?"

"No," said Debruin, and he snatched the radio from Hawes. "TSG, do not move in. We don't have anything to hold him. Something has spooked the target."

"Hammersley is on the move. He heard the door slam," said Spencer.

Debruin knelt beside Hawes and watched the target slip from view into the shadows between adjacent warehouses.

"Hammersley is approaching the east corridor," said Spencer.

"What's in that blind spot?" said Debruin to Hawes. "You did the survey. What rooms are there?"

"Hammersley is in the corridor. He's trying doors," said Spencer, relaying the man's every move over the radio.

Hawes unfolded a piece of paper and shone his small torch to reveal a floor plan of the building. The east entrance corridor had several rooms off either side before the reception.

"Stationery cupboard, first aid room."

"This one. What's this room here?" said Debruin, pointing to the largest of the side rooms.

"We've lost visual on Hammersley," said Spencer. "He's in a side room, north of the corridor. It's too dark to see what he's doing."

"That's the boiler room, sir."

"The boiler room?" said Debruin, and he sat back against the wall with the map in his hands. "Stop him," he called, just as a flash of brilliant orange lit the night. Less than a second later, the windows imploded. The blast sent Hawes crashing across the room and the sound of the gas explosion seemed to echo on for eternity.

More than twenty seconds passed before Hawes' radio crackled into life and Spencer's commanding tone came through loud and clear amid the shower of debris. The bright orange flame that had lit the sky was replaced by thick, acrid smoke that billowed from what had been the east end of the factory.

"We've lost Hammersley," he said.

"Any other causalities?" said Hawes, as he scrambled to his feet, slipping on the carpet of shattered glass and dust. He fingered a small slice on his face that had been made by the shattered glass and inspected the blood on his finger.

"Minor. We're dealing with it."

"What about the target?"

Debruin's head dropped in defeat. He knew what was coming next.

"Negative. We've lost him."

TWO

From an open window, birdsong announced the morning. From the open doorway at the end of the room, the hiss of a shower accompanied the warm steam that flowed through in clouds.

The light was bright against Harvey's eyelids. The sun was up, and the walls of the bedroom were brilliant white, alive with the warmth of summer.

But for Harvey Stone, the sun shone cold, and its light was tainted by the shadows of the previous night. He stretched and checked the time. It was gone seven a.m. He rarely slept past five or six, but the night had been long, and his mind was busy trying to make sense of the events. The distant helicopter, the dog units, and the two vans that had been parked in the corner of the car park.

He sat up in bed and rubbed his face. For a moment, he considered joining her. A hot shower might help to clear his mind. But his thoughts were elsewhere. In a few moments, he had dressed and was peering through the venetian blind to where he had parked his motorcycle. The room was clean. He liked that. The order and balance of the space appealed to his senses. A tall, potted spider plant occupied one corner. Fitted wardrobes of light oak filled one wall, and the large bed with its Egyptian cotton sheets was the only sign of disarray. He pulled the duvet back into place, then tugged at each corner. And all was in order again.

A brown, leather handbag was on the floor beside the bed. It was the type that women slung over their shoulders, with large, hooped handles, and gold-coloured buckles. Her purse was inside; it was large and matched the handbag in colour and design. With intrigue, Harvey reached for it, knowing nothing about her other than her first name and address. There was also a makeup bag, a mobile phone, and a notepad. He unzipped the purse. The contents were sparse for its size, just a bank card and her driving license, which he studied and became closer to her by a margin.

Alice Valentine.

The picture must have been old because her hair was a different length and colour. It was like looking at a different person.

The hissing shower stopped and footsteps padded across the tiled en suite. He zipped up the purse, dropped it into the bag, and stood beside the window.

There would be questions as to why he was there. Of that he was sure. His opportunity to leave was waning with every passing second.

But he owed her more than that.

He turned away and peered down to where he had parked his motorbike. A young couple were leaving the apartment block. The man wore smart shorts, a loose-fitting linen shirt, and loafers, and the girl wore a blue summer dress with a ruffled hem that flowed with the morning breeze, offering a tantalising taste of her fine, tanned thighs.

"You're awake."

Her voice was one of her most alluring qualities. It was

sweet and innocent, yet her tone was defensive. He remained facing the window, allowing her a few moments of privacy to dress. But she lingered. The white towel that covered her in his peripheral fell away. Her flesh was perfect in every way. He didn't have to look to know it was.

"It's a beautiful day," he said.

He watched the young couple flag down a taxi and Harvey was pleased to see the man hold the door for his wife or girlfriend, or whoever she was to him.

A fresh fragrance drew near; her shampoo, or maybe just her natural scent.

"There's something on your mind," she said, and her soft, fleshy chest pressed into his rigid back. Her slender arms slid beneath his, and inquisitive hands explored.

"No," he replied. She would never understand. Nobody would. "Not really."

Her head lay flat against his shoulder and her warmth matched the rays of sun on his face. A tentative digit raised the hem of his t-shirt, and delicate, wandering fingers traced his core. She sighed.

"This is the second time you've come to me in the middle of the night."

Her other hand slipped beneath his shirt and they rose in symmetry, searching and groping at his chest.

Harvey didn't reply.

Her hands, which were small and fragile, found his wrists. Her grip was tight and persuasive, and she led his hands to her hips, before returning to tease at the prickles on his skin.

"I don't let just any man into my apartment, you know?"

Her hands wandered down. Her fingers walked to the button of his cargo pants. And she kissed his shoulder.

He didn't reply.

Her flesh was soft and smooth beneath his fingers, and he

wanted so much to explore. He wanted to reach further. He wanted to turn around to witness that perfect body.

But she was innocent. Her sweetness was alluring, and to touch those parts of her that few men had would be to taint the image of her.

And she gripped him, her fingers splayed across his groin, and her breath warmed his back.

He pulled away and moved from the window.

"I'm sorry. I should go."

He expected her to cover herself, to make a show of being embarrassed, and he was thankful that she didn't. But her disappointment was evident in her eyes. Those round gems of azure seemed to question him, while her full and perfect lips remained half-open. Her unspoken words held Harvey where he stood, as if she had scolded him.

But she hadn't. She was perfect, adorable, and she had probably never scolded a person in her life.

"It's not you. You're..." He paused. "You're perfect."

"So, why don't you touch me?"

The warmth in his loins voiced its response, but only Harvey felt it.

"Can we take it slow?" he said, and she laughed. Her laugh was short, and she realised how her amusement may have hurt.

"I'm sorry," she said, still as naked as the day she had been born and with the confidence of a child. "I've never heard a man say that before."

"I'm not most men."

"That's why I keep letting you in." She inched closer. "Do you have someplace to be? A wife?"

"No," said Harvey.

She took three strides towards him and those parts of her that weren't taut and toned swayed, stirring Harvey's carnal instinct. She stopped before him and held his face in her hands, searching his eyes for some kind of emotion.

Once more, she took his hand. He offered no resistance as she spread his fingers across her chest, interlacing hers behind his, and she gave a gentle squeeze. Her body hardened at his touch. Her eyes closed and those sweet lips parted as she exhaled, soft and warm.

"Take your time," she said, holding his hand in place. For a girl as tender and pure as she was, she carried a confidence, a sincerity that Harvey admired. She stared into his eyes, unwavering. "Talk to me when you're ready. Or don't talk, if you prefer. Just treat me well."

Harvey didn't reply. The heat of her body beneath his hand enticed him to go further. But he stopped.

"Do you know why I come here?" he said, and with his free hand, he let the back of his fingers graze the skin on her shoulder. Softly, he plunged his fingers into her hair.

"No, but I'm glad you do," she replied. Her hands lay flat against his chest and she leaned into him.

The mirror on the dresser revealed her in all her natural glory. He released her, and cool air found the moist skin on his palm. Then he held her. Her slight frame was perfectly in proportion. In the mirror, his hands traced the outline of her spine then stopped above her perfect cheeks. His fingers splayed and he pulled her into him. Her body pressed against his and his male arrogance.

She smiled but made no attempt to tease him into anything further.

"So, you *are* human."

"Last time I checked," he said.

"You didn't finish what you were saying."

"No," he said, and he pulled her away just enough to admire her form.

She turned away from him, and her hand slid the length of his arm, hanging onto his touch, stealing a few more seconds of tenderness. Then she let him go and his hand fell limp to his side.

"You can buy me breakfast," she said. "You owe me that much, at least."

She sauntered into the dressing room, running her fingers along the walls. Harvey stared after her, lost in thought. For a few short moments, he had put aside the memories of the previous night. The distraction had been more than welcome. It had been enjoyable. And, for the first time in as long as he could remember, the smile that formed on his unshaven face was broad and true.

"Alice?" he said, and she turned to face him unabashed, offering one more full view of her exquisite body in all its glorious beauty. She deserved something in return for her patience, her understanding, and her charm. She deserved more than what Harvey had offered, but maybe that would come. Harvey's life was far from normal. On the surface, he was a true man with unbreakable morals. But when the surface was scratched, there was a life that nobody, not even the pure and sweet Alice, would understand. He had to hide that hidden world from her. He couldn't allow her to find out. The news would break her, crush her, and destroy that beautiful confidence.

And it was that confidence, along with her sweetness and innocence, that drew him closer.

She deserved better.

"Thank you," he said.

THREE

A vertical slice of bright sunlight found a tiny gap between the drab curtains. It pierced the otherwise darkened room, lighting the pile of clothes on the carpet beside the bed and the figure that lay entangled in the cotton sheets. Minutes rolled by and as the earth moved around the sun, and the man's dreams ventured from chase to chase, the slice fell upon his eyes, as if the heavens were calling him.

He rolled over away from the light, but it was too late. The dreams of an endless chase were no longer quarantined to his sleep. They were alive in his conscious thought.

Debruin stared across the room. It was a hovel. There were used tissues on the far bedside table, and the cheap wardrobe doors were open, revealing the empty space where the pile of laundry that had gone untouched for weeks would one day hang.

One day, when he managed to get past this abominable period of his wretched life.

"Are you awake?" said a voice from downstairs, and his chest tightened at the thought of her. "Mark? You'll be late. Are you awake?"

"Well, if I wasn't, I am now."

"Do you want a tea?"

"Do I want a tea?" he mumbled to himself, as he dragged his legs out of bed and searched for his slippers. He continued the mumbling until he found his old moccasins and bent to pick them up. "I want a bloody good lie in is what I want."

"I said do you want a tea?" she called up again.

"Of course I want a tea. When do I ever not want a tea?" he called back, then returned to mumble to himself. "Make me bloody beg for a tea."

He stood, sighed, and then dragged the curtains open. The light was brighter than he had considered, blinding him long enough for him to kick the bed post. The pain was sudden and sharp. He fought not to unleash a string of verbal abuse and leaned against the wall. The pain subsided and he stumbled across the room to where his dressing gown hung on the door. He tossed his slippers to the carpet, slipped his feet inside, and pulled his dressing gown over his t-shirt and shorts.

Above the toilet, his wife had hung a small, framed sign that was designed to be humorous. *Stand closer, it's shorter than you think.* He ignored the sign, as he had for the past four and a bit years, and then he ignored the mess he'd made on the rim of the toilet, as he had done for the past four and a bit years. He flushed. At least *he* always flushed afterwards. He thought about the sign he'd considered adding to the humour wall for the past half a decade. *Flush the toilet, you disgusting pig.*

Whatever bitter humour the thought provoked was numbed when he walked into the kitchen and saw Julie feeding Grace.

"You're running late this morning," she said, as he hit the switch on the kettle. "Your tea is on the side."

A cup of hot tea was less than two feet away.

"You're still half asleep. Why don't you call in today? I have to take Grace for tests. You'll have the house to yourself for the morning."

The mention of the tests did little to lift Debruin's mood. He crouched beside Grace, who smiled up at him, oblivious to her condition that hung over the household like a brooding, dark cloud.

She was two years old, and by rights should have been running around, picking things up she shouldn't, opening cupboard doors, and falling over. Instead, she was restricted to minimal exercise. Only enough exercise to aid her development, was what the doctor had said, which Debruin deemed as ridiculous. Running around, picking things up, and falling down was part of any child's development.

"No. I'll go in," he said finally. He wanted to tell her about the explosion. He wanted to tell her how the powers that be will be grilling him for wasting police resources, and how he had to get through it. He had to keep going to give Grace a chance of a life. "Any news on the diagnosis?"

"Same as before," said Julie. "The same as it'll be tomorrow and the next day."

"It's been six months now and she's not getting better. Surely, they can see that? All they do is take test after test, Julie. I'm not a doctor and even I can see she's not right."

Julie's head dropped and she turned her face away. It was the onset of a breakdown. He'd seen it countless times before.

"I'm sorry. You don't need me to state the obvious."

"Just go, Mark," she said, her voice thick with tears. She raised her head and continued to help Grace feed. His little girl wore a banana like lipstick and face cream, and she seemed pleased with her efforts.

"I'll find the money, Julie," he said, just as he had said for the past six months. "We'll go private."

Julie said nothing.

"When this case is over, I'll take some time. Maybe we can go somewhere? It would be nice to get away for a week or two."

"And what about Grace?" she said. It was just like Julie to find the negative spin on anything he said. "She has to have tests every week to make sure she isn't deteriorating."

"Then we'll work it around the tests, Julie." He placed his hand on her shoulder and she flinched, then warmed to his touch. "This is going to be hard to hear, but if there's a chance she won't–"

"Don't say it, Mark."

"If there's a chance she won't be with us for long, then let's give her the best life we can."

Grace stared up at him, waving a piece of mulched banana and laughing. Julie hid her face from him, stood, and walked out of the room. The bathroom door slammed shut a few seconds later. With banana all over her face, Grace cocked her head as if she was studying him. He pulled a face at her, mimicking the cartoon trolls he'd seen on one of her programs, accompanying the expression with a low growl. His troll took an interest in the banana on the tray on front of her. He bent his hands forward and, in the voice of the idiot troll he'd seen, made snorting noises to accompany his actions.

Grace laughed. She kicked her feet as he collected a piece of banana and touched it against his tongue pretending he'd never tasted banana before. He ate the banana and crouched down beside his daughter, smoothing her fine hair from her face.

"Nana," she said, in that smooth and innocent tone that could raise a smile on his face regardless of anything his job might throw at him.

"You're just a normal kid, aren't you?" he said, expecting no reply. He leaned in close and whispered, "Daddy's going to get you fixed, okay? You just hang in there. I'm going to get you fixed if it kills me."

FOUR

"So, what is it you do, Harvey?" she asked, as she closed the café menu, folded her arms, and stared at him from across the table. "Don't you have to be somewhere? An office maybe?"

Harvey leaned back in his chair and waited for a couple in their mid-thirties to pass. They were both dressed in business attire and walked with purpose. The area was pedestrianised with young trees sprouting from spaces in the pavement. The buildings had that clean and new feeling still, even after fifteen years. The café was named Leonardo's, and the owner had gone to great lengths to give the place a Mediterranean feel, despite it sitting in the heart of London's Isle of Dogs.

She waited.

"I'm freelance," he replied. He had spent a long time developing a story that didn't involve being dishonest. The truth has many faces; it all depends on perspective. "I choose my hours."

"Good for you. And what is it you freelance in?"

"I'm a security specialist. Boring really. How about you?" he asked, turning the focus away from himself. He couldn't see her as an employee of a corporation. It wasn't that she lacked any traits. It was more that she hadn't been worn down, hardened, or ruined by office politics, low pay, and the daily fight.

"I work in art," she said.

"You paint?"

"Mostly. I like to create through any medium I can."

It suited her. A career in creativity somehow matched her soft tones and tender personality. Her life seemed to happen in her own time, and she danced from event to event in a swirl of sweet summer dresses.

"It suits you," he said.

A waiter stopped beside their table. He wore dark trousers, clean shoes, and a pressed, white shirt that hugged his body. He wore his dark hair cropped and had the cleanest, whitest teeth Harvey had ever seen.

"Are you ready to order?" he asked, dragging his gaze from Alice to Harvey with his eyebrows raised in expectancy.

"After you," said Harvey.

"Just coffee for me, please."

"Two coffees," added Harvey.

The waiter smiled out of politeness, retrieved the menus, and sped back into the restaurant.

"I don't normally do this," said Alice.

"Do what? Have coffee?"

Her cheeks folded into dimples when she grinned. It was a wonderful sight. She checked over her shoulder to make sure she wouldn't be overheard.

"Hook up with strange men. And I especially don't let them into my home in the middle of the night." She studied him. "Tell me why you come. Honestly, or I'll know."

It was a question Harvey hadn't expected right there and then, and a suitable response eluded him.

"Harvey? Why do you go silent sometimes? It's like a wall goes up. I can't get in."

He stared at her. He had to say something. She would just get up and leave him there. The truth was that he had been close to being caught. He had walked straight into a trap, knowing the police were there. He'd spent his entire life avoiding the police, taking precautions and planning in meticulous detail every single move he would make.

But the fact was that he had enjoyed it. He hadn't felt the adrenaline surge through him like that since he was a young boy, since his first kill. It would have been better if he could have been more hands on. If he could have slit the man's throat or squeezed the life from him. But the risk made up for the lack of sensual pleasure.

He had needed to lie with her. Just to share her space. To feel her calm presence. To breathe the air around her. To smell her. But not touch. Not yet. To touch would have crossed a line. To touch, at this stage, would only end in her heartbreak. He couldn't bear to think of her in any pain that he had caused.

"I'm not very good at this," he said at last.

"You're doing great from what I can see. You just need to talk to me. That's what people do, isn't it? Talk."

"I don't know."

"You've never done this?"

Not with somebody so pretty. So pure and innocent.

"Of course. But it rarely starts like this."

"How does it start, then? Normally? How do you meet a woman and get close to them normally?"

I don't. Women are a risk. They don't understand. They don't have empathy. Not like you.

"I haven't been with many women."

Her eyebrows belied her silence.

"Honestly," he said. "I don't normally put myself in social situations."

"Why? I would have said you could have any girl you want."

I don't want any girl. I want you.

"Work. I get busy. I work strange hours and I'm often gone for days or weeks at a time."

"And the girls you've met before can't handle that?"

He nodded.

The few girls that Harvey had met before, in his search for normality, had raised too many questions. They had been needy and narcissistic. The world had revolved around them, or so they had thought. But Alice was different. Different in every way. The questions she asked were out of curiosity, and she never pushed for answers when Harvey failed to respond.

"They didn't understand, that's all. I don't blame them."

"And that's why you like to take things slow? Because you feel that if you take, or if *we* take the next step, you'll somehow be locked into something that's harder to get out of?"

The waiter returned holding a tray. He placed a small pot containing sachets of brown and white sugar in the centre of the table, then set their coffees down, Alice's first.

"Madam," he said, with a smile that was bordering flirtatious. "For you, sir," he finished.

Alice offered her thanks, and the man left as quickly as before, adjusting a few chairs on nearby tables as he passed them.

"I just want to do the right thing."

"Are you worried you'll hurt me?"

I'll destroy you. I know I will. I can't let it happen.

Harvey didn't reply.

"Or maybe," she said, as she sipped at her coffee, "maybe you're worried *you'll* get hurt."

She studied his face for a reaction.

"I'm right, aren't I?" She gave a childish giggle that was as alluring as those big, round eyes.

"I just want to do the right thing. I want to make sure you understand who I am."

Although you'll never truly understand.

"I think I have a good idea. From the very first moment I saw you in that bar, you intrigued me. You were sitting alone, and you seemed lost in thought and concentration. You frown, Harvey. It's as if your mind is in perpetual thought."

It had been late evening when Harvey had followed his target to the bar, and he had been thankful to find an empty table in the corner, from which he could sit and watch him. The man had been wealthy, confident, and connected to the right people, who, in turn, had managed to have a series of sexual assault charges dropped and ensure the news was swept under the carpet that was high society.

"Can I let you into a secret?" she said, and she could have told him anything at that moment. He would have swallowed any sentence that those soft, sweet lips said. She bit her lower lip and those dimples formed in her cheeks. "I have never ever approached a man like that before. I don't think I've ever even approached a man."

"Why should you?" he said. "I imagine you have men approaching you all the time."

"Rude, crude, lewd, slimy, over-confident, and desperate." She nodded her agreement to his comment. "To the point where a girl finds herself questioning if she should even go out to meet friends. The cheap bars attract cheap men, who think a slap on the backside is enough to prompt a conversation. But the conversation rarely extends further than them trying to learn where you live. The expensive bars garner men with a different style. But listening to them talk about hedge funds and how they like to spend their money can be just as tedious as having your bum slapped. They all want the same thing, and, according to friends of mine, they're all just as bad at it as each other."

It was Harvey's turn to smirk.

She had been a distraction at first, and for a few moments, he had lost sight of his target in the crowded bar. But as the girl in the flowing, white summer dress had begun to speak, Harvey had found him in a group, toasting his release, no doubt.

"But you were different. You *are* different. I can't quite put my finger on it. When I got home, I lay there wondering if you would come. I wondered if I had done the right thing by giving you my address. I waited for hours in hope. I thought myself stupid. Just a dumb girl who should have listened to a man boast of his wealth and let him take her back to his place for ten minutes of..." She made quotation marks with her fingers. "Pleasure. Why did you wait so long to come?"

Because I found a man with more money than morals. I followed him home and strung him up by his ankles. He begged me, Alice. He begged me to let him go, right up until the point I nicked his jugular with the tip of my knife.

"I was working."

There was a silence between them, and Harvey took his first sip of coffee. It was good. Rich and strong, the way a coffee should be.

"And then you came."

I had to. I had to be with you. There's something about you that I need.

"You came and you told me about your home, your life, and your foster-father. Not once did you touch me, Harvey."

"What did you want me to do? Slap your arse or tell you how rich I am?"

"Neither," she said, revealing her dimples. She stood and waved at the waiter for the bill. "This girl happens to like the strong, silent type. She happens to admire the respect you have for women." She bent and leaned into him, delivering a kiss on his cheek. "But don't make her wait too long."

FIVE

The first-floor meeting room at Barking Police Station, according to one of the many health and safety signs on the wall, had a capacity of twenty-eight people. Debruin counted thirty-four, including himself and Hawes, who was standing beside him sipping at a take-away coffee with a plaster on his cheek from the previous night's blast.

There was hushed mumbling as the various teams waited for the meeting to begin, and as Debruin gazed around the room, he locked stares with Spencer. Neither man smiled, nodded, or offered any form of greeting, and neither expressions were accusing, suspicious, or malicious. But there was a message in that stare that Debruin was failing to translate.

"Did you get much sleep, sir?"

Hawes' question distracted Debruin from Spencer, and by the time he looked back, Spencer had turned away.

"A little," he replied.

"My ears are still ringing. I've never seen anything like it. I'm sure I dreamed about it too." Hawes followed Debruin's eyes and caught his attention again. "Sir? Are you okay?"

"Do you know what we're doing here, Hawes?"

"It's a debrief, sir. Lessons learnt. A few pats on the back for morale purposes and then my guess is that Barnes will cut the team in half."

"That's my guess too. How would you feel if you were moved onto a new case?"

"To be honest, I'd be gutted. I've put a lot into this case."

"Well, be ready for it when it comes and try not to show any emotion. If you get moved on, accept it with grace."

"Do you really think I'll be moved on, sir?"

"It's just a case, Hawes. Remember that. It doesn't matter who we're hunting down, as long as we're hunting somebody. If you get attached to the case, you'll end up going bananas."

"Yeah, I get it. Still, I want to stay. I want to see this guy brought down."

"Do you?" Debruin questioned, lowering his voice to an inquisitive grumble. "There's not a little part of you rooting for him?"

"What? No." Hawes sighed. "I didn't mean what I said last night, sir."

"I know. I know. But look at his victims. They aren't exactly the salt of the earth, Hawes."

"They're human beings, sir."

It was Hawes' turn to lock stares with him, but this time the expression was accusing, suspicious, and incredulous.

"Just checking," said Debruin, and he winked at the man who had stood by his side for the last three years. "Because there's someone in this room that doesn't want him to stop."

Hawes was about to voice a question when the double doors burst open and DSI Barnes entered, along with two men in their late forties.

Thirty-five, thirty-six, and thirty-seven. Health and safety would have a field day.

Barnes carried a thin, blue file that lacked the usual dog-ears and creases of the files Debruin usually worked with. Such were the joys of a desk job. Debruin imagined the file on Barnes' desk, placed neatly in the corner, symmetrical and uniform.

The hushed murmur ceased as Barnes stepped up to the front of the room. The associate to his right was greying and his face bore the tell-tale lines and creases of a seasoned officer. His suit was cheap, but in Debruin's experience, that didn't necessarily mean the man was of low rank. Debruin knew many senior officers who cared little for their appearance. The job was everything to them.

"That's DI Carver," whispered Hawes, and he nodded toward the man to Barnes' right. "I worked with him at Romford nick. Organised crime. Knows everybody. He's as much of a criminal as they are."

Debruin opened his mouth to reply, but Barnes commanded silence.

"We have a leak," he said. His opening statements were often less than gracious. Every man and woman in the room had spent their evening holed up waiting for the target to strike. A little thanks would have gone a long way. "But the good news is that we have a development. I'll start with the leak. The only people who knew about the sting operation last night are in this room. TSG, field ops, support, and the detectives assigned to this case, led by Detective Inspector Debruin."

All eyes fell on Debruin, and he absorbed the stares. It wasn't his first rodeo.

A TV on a stand, which Debruin hadn't spotted before, turned on, and a junior officer Debruin had seen but never spoken to handed Barnes the control. He hit play. There was never much fluff in replays of footage and the filming was far from Hollywood grade. The scene had been shot in night-vision and was a post-apocalyptic green and black.

"One-eleven a.m., the target is seen approaching the east

entrance. Notice he isn't looking around. He's not searching for cameras, and most interesting of all is the casual manner in which he is walking. He opens the door and slips inside. Before we move to the next angle, notice that from where the target has approached, he had no view of the TSG units parked in the corner of the north car park. The only way he could have known we were there is if he had been told beforehand."

He hit play on the VHS and the angle changed to the corridor security camera. The lens was wider to cover as much area as possible, and the green and black changed to a dull monochrome.

"One-thirteen a.m., the target is in the building. Notice the clock in the corner of the screen. He waits a full minute. He doesn't move a muscle. Why is this?"

"Maybe he's listening," said a voice from the far side of the room.

"Maybe," said Barnes. "We'll voice our opinions after the debrief."

He hit play again. The man walked slowly and quietly along the corridor until the camera no longer covered him. The video had been cut to show the view of the next camera. Barnes hit stop.

"At this stage, the target is just fifty metres from Hammersley. He could easily walk up to him and do what he had to do. But he doesn't. He's waiting in the blind spot. How does he know the blind spot even exists? Has something spooked him? These are the questions we need to be asking. The video rolled but showed nothing except an empty corridor.

"At this stage, the target is inside the boiler room. We now know that he loosened a pipe connection and filled the space with gas."

The video returned to the original corridor camera. The

target was walking as casually as before. The only difference in his exit was that he let the door slam.

"That's his trigger. That's what gets Hammersley's attention," said Barnes. The screen flicked back to green and black and showed the man strolling away from the building as if he'd borrowed a book from a library. "He's not rushing. He knows Hammersley will attend to the noise. He knows he'll smell the gas. He knows he'll open the door and flick on the light. And he knows the blast will destroy the building and Hammersley with it, and that the blast will affect the heat cameras on the helicopter. He didn't run. He walked. And by the time we reacted to the blast, he was away."

Barnes stared at everyone in turn.

"Now, you tell me that that wasn't the work of a man who knew he was being watched. He doesn't have a defined MO, but we do know that he likes to get up close and personal. He strangled one man. He stripped another and hung him upside down to bleed out. He knew we were there, and he knew that we couldn't do a damn thing about it until we had him actually committing a crime. So, we know that he knew we were there. What we don't know is who told him."

Thirty-three faces glanced around the room, as if the culprit would be reddening, sweating, and shaking in his or her boots. They found nothing. Debruin stared dead ahead at the man to Barnes' left.

"That's why I've invited Detective Inspector Hargreaves to join us," said Barnes, and he presented the stranger. He was the younger of the trio that had entered the room. He wore his dark hair in a neat side-parting and his skin was as smooth as the skin on Grace's backside. "DI Hargreaves will be conducting an investigation. He'll begin by interviewing each and every one of you. At this point, need I remind you that it is your duty to attend when asked. It is your duty to be honest and to provide all pertinent information. Failure to do so is a criminal offence and may indeed be used against you. If you have nothing to hide, you have nothing to fear. This is an internal investigation and is standard operating procedure."

He changed arms to present the other man in the cheap suit.

"However, the investigation must go on. The case was brought up in yesterday's board meeting before last night's incident and I have reason to believe the case may be linked to an organised crime syndicate. Detective Inspector Frank Carver leads the regional organised crime unit, so he'll play a passive role in the investigation and, with any luck, he can shed some light on our suspect. In the meantime, DI Hargreaves will be scheduling interviews with you all and reporting back to myself."

He held the file to his side and offered one final statement. He left the formal tone behind and adopted a serious, warning grumble that each and every person in the room tuned into.

"As I said, if you have nothing to hide, you have nothing to fear. And I hope DI Hargreaves finds nothing to incriminate this department. But if any one of you knows anything, has said anything to anybody outside of this room, or even suspects a colleague, now is your time to say. Or God help you."

SIX

Her beauty was all natural, and her innocence was as addictive as a drug. Her hips swayed as she walked away, but not like the hips of the girls Harvey had known before. She wasn't trying to entice him or tease him. She was just walking the walk of a girl who had nothing to lose and not a care in the world. She was free, and he envied her freedom.

He sipped at his coffee and paid the bill. The waiter paid less attention to him than when Alice had been there, and offered a curt, "Thanks," despite Harvey's generous tip, then walked away.

Harvey sat in silence while commuters came and went. Some stopped for a take-away coffee, some hurried, speed-walking to meet their trains, and others ambled past. But it was the few who wore casual clothes that interested Harvey. They strolled with all the time in the world and peace on their faces. Harvey guessed that some of them would work from home, their homes being similar to the luxury apartment that Alice owned, with a nice view across the river and nobody leaning on them to work harder, faster, and later.

He took another sip of his coffee and sat back, acutely aware that for the first time in a long time, he had found a small slice of peace. It wasn't his for the taking, not yet, but maybe Alice could lead him to it. The world in which he was sitting was normal. There was no ill-feeling in the air. People weren't looking over their shoulders. It was a normal life, and for a man who had spent his life on the wrong side of the law, it was as alluring as the feminine sway of Alice's hips and the velvet, soft down on her face that was invisible to the eye until the sunlight framed her in its halo.

The normal lives that people led were clean and simple. Most had likely never even struck another and would shy from danger, whereas Harvey had spent his life learning how to walk into it. He'd waited in shadows to slit a throat, to clamp his hands around a neck, or worse, to keep somebody on the precipice of life, in agony and fear until they revealed their secrets.

There were two types of men that Harvey had killed, although the numbers were too great to recall. The first were at the request of his foster-father, who, on the surface, was a serious businessman, ruthless in his dealings. But if somebody were to scratch that surface, they would reveal the criminal empire that John Cartwright had created from the blood of others. And it was often Harvey or his mentor, Julios, that spilt the blood.

The second type of man that suffered Harvey's wrath existed at the very pit of society. The bottom feeders of existence. They preyed on the young and the vulnerable, destroying lives and minds for a few moments of satiation and sexual gratification. It was these types of men that had killed Harvey's sister when he was just a boy. It was these types of men that had destroyed his own life, steering him onto a path from which his efforts to deviate were perpetual and often futile.

Men like Hammersley.

It was the dreams that provoked the actions that stirred the beast inside. The dreams of running with his sister on an endless beach, two children with their lives ahead of them. It was always the same dream. The long grass where the beach met the fields was always the same. The flowing dress she wore was always the same. And every time he reached for her, every time he came close to grabbing her hand so they could roll to the ground in laughter, she vanished. Always out of reach.

Culling the bottom feeders was the only way to quieten the dreams. Sometimes he could keep the dreams at bay for months. At other times, it was just a week or two. The process had gone on for so long that he saw no light at the end of the tunnel. He often wondered if one day he would find the right man, the man whose crimes were so heinous that the incessant dreams would stop at the exact same time as the man's heart pulsed for the final time. Harvey could be free. He could live a normal life like those around him.

The café was growing busier. A queue was forming inside, yet few sat outside. There was a scrape of a chair behind him, and the leathery scent of a man's aftershave blended with the coffee aroma. It reminded Harvey of his foster-father who commanded his illegal empire from behind his walnut desk in the cushioned arms of his leather Chesterfield captain's chair. The walls of John's office were oak-panelled and the herring-bone parquet flooring in the hallway outside spread into the office, like the blood of so many men, beneath John's leather-soled shoes.

It was from that leather chair that John instructed Harvey to carry out his work; a hit, a murder, unspoken commands. He was intelligent enough to rarely incriminate himself. He chose his language wisely and relied on Harvey's intelligence to fill in the blanks, often referring to the victims as a risk, as enemies, or a means to deliver a message to a warring faction who John wanted to put back in their box.

There were times when John's anger would overcome his calm and confident persona. His rage would be evident in the shape of his narrowed eyes, the spittle that flew from his lips, and his cherry-coloured cheeks.

Whichever method John chose to instruct Harvey, the message was always clear. He left no room for ambiguity. There was always an admiration in John's expression. Harvey always felt John's eyes bore into his back when he left his foster-father sitting behind his desk. Save for the modern tailored suit and shirts, and his handmade Italian shoes, John, sitting in his office, was the epitome of wealth and class from an age long ago. A landowner perhaps? Or a lord. That was how John saw himself, of that Harvey was sure.

But he was a lord of nothing but a criminal empire, and his world was so far from the normal that Harvey yearned for, the difference was black and white.

He set his coffee down and was considering what he might do. He should go home, shower, or even go for a run to quell the hunger for a life that could never be his. But not yet. He would savour this slice of normality for as long as he could, even if he was the wolf in sheep's clothing.

"Don't turn around," said the man sitting behind him. The man with the leather scent. His voice was low and rough with age and smoke, and the beast inside Harvey stirred at its tone. "I've got a job for you."

SEVEN

It was normal for officers who were leading a case to be interviewed first. It was normal even for the interview to be recorded so it could be used as evidence at a later date. What wasn't usual, in Debruin's experience, was to be treated as guilty. Not in the first round of interviews. The initial round of interviews was a process designed to weed out the impossibilities, much the same as a criminal case.

But Hargreaves made it clear from the moment he set his coffee down and hit record that Debruin was his number one suspect.

He introduced the interview, stating the date and time and the attendees.

"Detective Inspector Debruin, you're aware that you are entitled to invite a peer in for the purpose of being a witness? That witness may not be involved in the investigation in any way. You are, of course, also entitled to legal representation if you so wish."

"A peer that isn't involved in this investigation?" said Debruin. "There are more than two dozen officers involved. There can't be many officers who aren't."

"Are you revoking that right?"

"Am I what?"

"Are you happy to proceed without a witness or legal representation?"

Debruin had never met Hargreaves before. Most internal investigations were handled by third-party units. They worked for the force but were far from revered.

"I think happy is a strong word, Hargreaves."

"For the duration of this interview, I'd appreciate you referring to my rank. To benefit the recording, you understand."

Debruin nodded.

There were various types of police officer, in the same way there were various types of criminals, and the lines between them became blurred with age and experience.

There was the easy-going type. The type of individuals who had succeeded at most things in their lifetimes and who breezed through life with charm and wit and were fortunate enough to be admired by both peers and senior officers alike. It was these individuals that climbed ladders at a steady pace. Then there were the cowards. The individuals that were happy to stand on the progress of others in return for a glimmer of recognition. They would be the last to raise their hand, often introverted, and would be the first to have a quiet word in the ear of a superior officer to land a colleague in trouble.

Finally, somewhere in the middle of both, were the rule-books. No deviation from any rules no matter how slight. They didn't need to stand on colleagues to rise through the ranks but lacked the personality to shine among peers. It was pure dedication to the rulebook that took these people forward, and the path they trod often led somewhere close to where Hargreaves existed.

"For the record, DI Debruin has nodded, confirming his

consent to continue in the absence of a peer or legal representative."

It was going to be a long interview. Debruin sat back, hoisted his leg onto his knee, and took a deep breath.

"DI Debruin, can you confirm that you were present in the debrief that took place this morning, during which DSI Barnes provided video footage of a sting operation carried out last night, on July twenty-first, two thousand and one? A sting operation that resulted in the death of one Wayne Hammersley, the destruction of a factory, and which led to the escape of a serial killer."

Debruin, shocked at Hargreaves' insinuating and condescending tone, nodded.

"For the tape, please," said Hargreaves.

"Yes."

"And what is your appraisal of the events that took place last night?"

"My appraisal is that the suspect knew we were there, altered his MO, and escaped. How he knew we were there, I don't know."

"Have you, DI Debruin, been in contact with the suspect and were you responsible for informing him of our presence?"

"It was my operation. Why would I do that?"

"Answer the question please."

Hargreaves refused to look Debruin in the eye. He looked up on occasion but spent much of the interview tending his notes.

"For the record, Detective Inspector Hargreaves, I have not been in contact with the suspect and I was not responsible for informing him of our presence."

"Do you know the suspect's identity?"

"No. That's why I'm referring to him as the suspect, and not using his name."

"So, you know it's a *he*? You know the suspect is male?"

"It's an educated assumption based on the suspect's size, weight, strength, speed, and profile."

"Speed?"

"I was close to catching him once."

"You're referring to the murder of Jack Slater?"

"I am."

"As I understand it, Mr Slater was killed in his flat in Barking three weeks ago. I didn't realise you were planning a sting operation on that occasion."

"It wasn't a sting operation. I was visiting him."

"For what purpose?"

The visit had been off the books, off the cuff, and out of line. Debruin had known that before he'd even been to see him, and Hargreaves knew too, although finding a claim to a crime in the fact would be tough, even for him.

"He was a recently released sex offender living in an area where an individual, or individuals, were and still are targeting and murdering habitual sex offenders."

"And you just happened to be there at the right time? At the time when he was murdered?"

"Pure coincidence."

"I understand," said Hargreaves, with all the disingenuity he could muster. "And you were going to warn him, I presume?"

"I was going to tell him to be careful."

"Is there any record of your intention prior to your visit?"

"No. Why would there be?"

"I don't know. Perhaps you might have had a conversation with DSI Barnes or DS Hawes? Perhaps you mentioned your intentions to one of them?"

"I didn't. It was out of hours. I was going to ask him if he'd seen anybody suspicious. If he was being followed at all."

"And you didn't mention it to DS Hawes?"

"Come to think of it, yes, I did. But nothing concrete. We had been discussing other potential victims, trying to get a head start on the suspect. Slater was ear-marked as being the most likely given the local media coverage of his release."

"But you hadn't planned a visit? At this stage, Slater was just a possibility?"

"Yes. Just a name. You have to understand. We have nothing on this guy. A head start can be a game changer."

"Your intentions, in light of there being only one witness, could easily be misinterpreted, DI Debruin."

"That's right."

"Were you alone when you visited Mr Slater?"

"I was, yes."

Hargreaves took a few seconds to make notes. The silence was an indication of the man's thought process and the deductions he was making.

"I was not setting the victim up in a trap, if that's where you're going with this."

"I didn't say you might have been."

They locked stares across the desk.

"Tell me about last night. Where were you during the operation?"

"I was east of the factory in the first-floor office of the adjacent building."

"And who were you with?"

"Detective Sergeant Hawes."

"Anybody else?"

"No."

"Did either yourself or DS Hawes leave the room at any point during the evening?"

"Yes. I had a bathroom break. Would you like to see the note from my mother?"

"That won't be necessary," said Hargreaves. His face was

unmoving as he scrawled notes. "At what time was this and how long were you gone for?"

"It was a bathroom break for crying out loud. I don't know."

Hargreaves waited, pen poised.

"It was about ten minutes before the suspect arrived. Do you want to know if it was a number one or two?"

"That won't be necessary. How long were you away from DS Hawes?"

Debruin shrugged. "Five minutes. Maybe ten."

"And during this time, did you see or speak to anyone else?"

"We had an armed officer outside the door to the office in which we were waiting. He'll confirm how long I was gone for."

"Who was it?"

"I'm not sure of his name. He was TSG. He wasn't under my command."

"I'll be talking to everyone who was there. I'm sure they'll identify themselves. Did you see or speak to anybody else?"

"If you mean, did I see or speak to the suspect, no, I didn't."

"You didn't speak to anybody at all?"

The line of questioning was tedious, but Hargreaves was covering all angles.

"No. I went to the bathroom, I did what I had to do, and I returned."

"Okay," said Hargreaves. "Let's move on. Let's talk about the explosion. You say you were with DS Hawes during the operation."

"That's right."

"In a first-floor office?" Hargreaves flicked through his paper-work, making a show of checking his notes, but it was just a ruse. The man couldn't look Debruin in the eye. He was weak and the power his role gave him was the only authority he had. He was married; the ring on his finger was dulled with time. Debruin imagined he was far from authoritative at home. Under the disapproving eyes of an unsatisfied wife, he would slink from room to room, seeking a place to hide. "Detective Inspector?"

Debruin blinked away his daydream to find Hargreaves with his brow raised, waiting for a response.

"That's right," he said. "The first-floor office opposite the east entrance. It was about one hundred metres from the factory."

"I imagine you were watching through a window. Or was there a live feed you were monitoring?"

"There wasn't time for a live feed. Hammersley had reported that he was being followed. Somebody had been in his flat. He reported that he didn't feel safe. We had to act fast."

"One hundred metres, you say?"

"That's right."

"Close enough for the blast to shatter the window."

"And throw Hawes across the room."

Debruin recalled the moment. The force had been immense. The power had been devastating.

"I noticed that DS Hawes was treated for minor cuts and abrasions."

"That's right. He was at the window when the blast happened."

"I see. So, where were you? Why weren't you injured? And for the purposes of the recording, we're talking about the very moment of the explosion. You had both seen the suspect approach the building. You had seen him enter the building. After that, you were relying on Sergeant Spencer to relay information back to you by radio. You heard the information that the suspect was moving along the corridor. You heard the report that the suspect was in a blind spot between two cameras. At that point, where were you exactly? Why is *your* face not cut to ribbons, as DS Hawes' is?"

Hargreaves looked up from his notes, his face confused. He

rested his hands on his lap and waited patiently. Debruin knew his answer would only add to the evidence against him. It was all perception. The spin that Hargreaves was putting on everything Debruin had said was a guilty stance.

He took a breath and exhaled long and slow.

"Detector Inspector Debruin?" prompted Hargreaves.

"I was sitting on the floor away from the window with my back to the wall."

Hargreaves feigned a surprised look but retained the confused tone in his brow.

"You were sitting on the floor with your back to the wall, away from the window?"

"That's right," said Debruin, waiting for Hargreaves to voice his assumption.

"At the very peak of the operation, you were sitting down? You weren't even watching?"

Debruin said nothing. He closed his eyes and tried to find that thought of the subservient Hargreaves with his domineering wife. But the image was lost.

"Can you see, Detective Inspector Debruin, how this might lead an investigating officer to believe you knew the explosion was going to take place?"

EIGHT

Harvey pushed back his chair, preparing to stand.

"I wouldn't do that if I were you," said the voice. "Don't stand, don't turn, and don't talk. Face forward and listen to what I have to say."

Harvey stopped. What seemed like a thousand thoughts ran through his mind. He scanned the pedestrianised square in front of him, isolating anybody that appeared to be out of place. Two men were loitering on a corner forty yards away. They were dressed in jeans, smart shoes, and casual t-shirts. But there was something about the way the men were standing. It was unnatural. They seemed unnerved. The shorter of the two glanced in Harvey's direction every few seconds, while the taller man, who wore a thick beard and shades, looked in the other direction, presumably watching for the arrival of police. The shorter man locked stares with Harvey. He seemed troubled. He mouthed something to Harvey, then looked away as the taller man saw him.

It looked like he was mouthing the word 'Run'.

On the far side of the square, on a road created for delivery trucks to service the outlets, was a black van. It was unmarked, clean, and looked like anything but a delivery van. There was a driver in the front, and he seemed to stare across the square at Harvey.

Harvey pulled his chair back in and folded his arms on the table, using the cover of his left arm to reach for the knife in his jacket.

"I wouldn't bother searching for a weapon," the man said. "We know you keep a knife inside your jacket. If so much as a hint of steel shows itself, you'll see what we're all about."

"Who are you?"

"It doesn't matter who I am."

"So, what do you want?"

"Like I said, I have a job for you."

"I have a job. Why don't you try the classifieds?"

The man was relaxed and confident enough to offer a laugh.

"You work for John Cartwright," he said, and an image of the man began to form in Harvey's mind. He was mid-fifties, judging by his gravelled tone and the way his saliva popped when he spoke. He was tanned with skin like leather. He wore expensive clothes, probably a nice watch too. "You ride a BMW motorcycle, and you've killed more men than you can remember, which isn't bad for a man in his early twenties."

"Early twenties? That's vague."

"You're a hard man to track. In fact, you don't seem to exist at all. We established your approximate age from the grave of your sister. We know she was a few years older than you, and we know when she died."

"So, you're a mathematician?"

"No, Harvey, I'm so much more than that. But what I am to you all depends on your outlook. Right now, you are at a crossroads in life. Take the wrong turn, Harvey, and the rest of your short life will be a torturous misery. Turn the other way, however, and life will go on as usual."

"You seem to have the wrong man. I'm just a guy enjoying a coffee."

"You found our little note last night."

Harvey didn't reply. To admit that he'd found the scribbled note with the initial 'H' on the front would be to incriminate himself.

"Apologies for the crudeness of our methods. The police operation was a last-minute thing. By the time the information was fed through to us, we had little time to act."

"Why?"

"Why did we help you? That's easy. We want you on our side, Harvey."

"How did you know I would be there?"

"Because we've been following you for weeks. We know everything about you."

"There's nothing to know. I'm just an ordinary guy."

"Precisely. That's what makes you perfect for the job we're planning."

"I told you, I have a job."

"What can we do to convince you? You don't need money, but we can offer freedom. We can place you at the bar where you met your friend. We can place you entering a block of apartments a few hours later, the same block of apartments where a man was found hanging upside down and drained of blood. We can place you at the factory last night. We have enough photographs and security footage to have you locked up until the day you die." He spoke those final three words with immaculate articulation, as if he was savouring the moment.

Harvey said nothing.

"Ah, the silent man," he said. "Sadly, silence won't get you off this time around. So, you see, we can make it so that you never breathe fresh air again. Freedom is the one thing we all want, and we have yours hanging by a string."

Harvey identified more men in the square. Among the sour and focused expressions of the commuters were idle faces. Faces that did not belong.

"If you're thinking of running, we have every corner of the square covered," said the man. It was as if he could read Harvey's mind. "You won't make thirty steps."

Harvey searched the windows of the apartments that overlooked the square, but the sun's reflection was bright. It was the perfect set-up, done with almost military precision.

"Who are you?"

"It's early days, Harvey. One thing at a time. All we want is a little cooperation. Show us that, and we'll show you a little mutual respect."

There it was again. He used *we* in place of *I*. He wasn't the boss. He worked for somebody. Judging by the amount of men Harvey had spotted, not to mention the ones he hadn't spotted, the organisation was one of means.

"Who do you work for? Tell me. I want to speak to the boss, not some old puppet."

"You'll meet the boss. I'll see to that."

It was as if the man's grin was audible. Harvey could hear it in his voice.

"What happens if I say yes?" said Harvey, buying time for a plan to formulate. But other than a surprise bout of violence and speed, he had nothing.

"If you say yes, we'll leave you to finish your coffee and we'll contact you when we're ready."

"And what happens if I refuse?" said Harvey, continuing his search for a sniper on the rooftops in the square.

It was then that the waiter returned. He set the menu booklet down in front of Harvey once more, then retreated. Harvey hadn't asked to see the menu. He hadn't asked for coffee. Harvey studied the waiter. He wasn't a large man, but he was toned. His tight shirt revealed a muscled chest and shoulders. He avoided Harvey's stare and stood beside the door with his hands folded in front of him. He scanned the square as any waiter might, enjoying the sunshine and fresh morning air.

"Open it," said the man behind Harvey.

His options were few. He had to admit they had covered every angle. There were two ways out of the situation. The first was to run and fight. But he would be gunned down in seconds. He couldn't outrun a sniper, and even if he could, every exit of the square had been covered.

The second option was to refuse. He didn't have to run. No doubt the police would arrive in moments and Harvey would spend the rest of his life behind bars. The menu booklet likely contained the photos the man had mentioned earlier. Photos of Harvey at the bar, the apartment block, and the factory. Not ideal.

He stared at the menu. It was the same as the menu he had used earlier. The options weighed heavy on his mind. John Cartwright owned one of the largest criminal organisations in London. There was only one, perhaps two others that had similar resources. But the operation was too slick. The set-up, the van, the men, they were all too organised for anyone but the government. The whole thing stank of government, right down to the smarmy waiter. Who else could have known what he was going to do last night and warn him?

Harvey tore his eyes from the menu to analyse the waiter, but he was gone. He looked up at the corner where the two men had been standing, and they were gone. The van was gone. The men on the far side of the square were gone. He spun, only to find the table behind him empty with no sign of even a coffee. The table was set ready for customers to sit down and enjoy the sunshine.

Harvey stood, and his chair fell to the ground. A passer-by

glanced across at the distraction then continued on her journey. She was a commuter. He scanned everybody he could see but found no sign of anyone but ordinary people.

He hadn't imagined it. Of that he was sure. His heart raced and his palms were slick with sweat.

The only indication of the discussion was the menu. It stared at him, enticing him, calling him, and beckoning him. But he found himself fixed to the spot, unable to flex his fingers or think of anything but the menu.

He took a breath, reached out, and placed his hand on the faux-leather booklet.

And he opened the cover to find a single photograph. It was tacky, as if it had just been printed. But the image it showed rocked Harvey on his feet.

It had been taken from inside the back of the black van Harvey had seen. The van walls and floor were covered with black carpet. And at the far end of the space, with her feet and hands tied, her mouth gagged, and her pleading eyes wide with fear, was Alice.

NINE

"I'm a suspect?" said Debruin, as he marched into Barnes' office without knocking. "Me? I'm leading the investigation, and I've spent the last thirty minutes being accused of leaking information to the killer."

Barnes was his usual calm self. He stopped what he was doing, replaced the lid on his pen and set it down on his desk. He steepled his fingers and sat back to wait for Debruin to finish.

"I don't know who this guy is, and I understand why you brought him in, but if he talks to everyone the way he's just spoken to me, we're going to have a mutiny."

Barnes was silent. He peered past Debruin at the door, a silent request for privacy before the discussion began. Debruin turned and closed the door and by the time he had returned to where he was standing, on the guest side of the desk, he felt both his temper waning and embarrassment for his outburst.

"I shouldn't have spoken to you like that. Apologies, gov," he mumbled.

If he had been wearing a hat, he would have held it in both hands and fidgeted with it. Instead, he stared at his shoes, waiting for Barnes to say something. But, Debruin's mind was working overtime, and he filled the space with his own thoughts and questions.

"Do you have someone in mind, sir? Or am I the lead suspect?"

Barnes was crafting his words in his mind. He chewed his lip as he thought, a sign that he had a lot to say on the subject and that the delivery of his opinions would be tailored to the individual, unemotional, and backed by proof.

"It could have been any one of Spencer's team, sir. I don't see it being one of ours. We've all worked too hard on the case. If Hargreaves wants to point the finger at me, then so be it. I haven't told a soul. I know I'm innocent, you know I'm innocent, and everyone out there knows I'm innocent. But all the same, I'd appreciate you having a word with him. I was three minutes into the interview when I wanted to walk out. He could have got the same information without being so vindictive and sanctimonious."

"Have you finished?" said Barnes. They were the first words he'd spoken, and his tone was as sharp as a razor.

"Yes, gov."

Barnes nodded.

"Good. Do try to keep your emotions at bay, Debruin."

He stood and walked to the door, leaned out, and muttered something to somebody. By the time he had returned to his seat, the man who been standing beside Barnes during the debrief, was in the room. He closed the door and took the seat by the desk without being asked, turning it side-on to face Debruin and Barnes like an independent adjudicator.

"Detective Inspector Mark Debruin," said Barnes, by way of an introduction, "this is Detective Inspector Carver. He runs the—"

"Regional organised crime unit," said Debruin. "Yes, sir. You mentioned in the debrief."

Debruin offered his hand, which the man shook with a firm, professional handshake. "Frank," he said.

"DI Carver has some news that I think you might find interesting," said Barnes, and he nodded to Carver for him to take over.

Carver met Debruin's stare. He was a hardened man, unflinching and confident, the way men in their forties who have seen and done it all, often are.

"Five years ago, we identified a group of individuals," he began, and Debruin tuned into his voice. He had the remnants of a Scottish accent that had faded with time in London, Debruin guessed, like a lady's perfume that fades with the day and is only evident in close proximity. But once smelled, the scent becomes alluring, and Debruin heard nothing but the man's voice. "These are bad men. The nastiest you can imagine."

"I don't see what this has to do with a serial killer. Our suspect is operating alone."

"Not for long," said Carver. "I believe the organisation is recruiting him, shielding him from us to demonstrate their competence, then they'll entice him in."

"Entice him in?"

He nodded.

"They are planning something, but we don't know what."

"If they're criminals, why can't you build a case against them?"

"To build a case, we need evidence."

"But they're too good?"

"Something like that."

"And you say they've been doing this for how long?"

"We've been onto this particular group for five years, on and off. Who knows how long they were operating before we got wind of them."

"How do you know so much about them?" asked Debruin. "I mean, you're talking about a significant operation here."

"Two years ago, we sent a man in undercover. DS James Butler. Thirty-five years old, single, London born and bred."

He handed Debruin a photo of a man with a full beard, dark eyes, and cropped hair. He was a good choice for an undercover unit. He looked more baddie than cop to the point that Debruin couldn't even picture the man in a uniform.

"We think he's gone rogue," said Carver. "He's been feeding us information that leads nowhere. Every time we set up an operation, they strike elsewhere."

"Diversion tactics?" said Debruin.

"He's smart. But we have nothing on him. We can't pull him out. We can't even reach him. He comes to us when he has news and all we can do is act on his information. What we do know for sure is the group comprises some of the worst men you can imagine. At least one of them is a known killer. I suspect there's more."

"They're recruiting killers?"

"Not just killers. Drivers, bankers, lawyers, engineers," said Carver, with admiration in his tone. "Whatever they need, they recruit. We track them and do all the hard work. The information is fed to Butler and the organisation snaps them up before we can put them away. Then they just disappear. The leak isn't from us to your suspect, DI Debruin. The leak is to DS Butler. *He's* the connection."

"So, you think my suspect is being recruited by this group?"

"It would explain how he knew you were at the factory."

"And how does this fit in with me being the leak?"

"If Butler learns that we know there's a leak, he'll go underground. However, if he learns that we think the leak is you—"

"Which it isn't," added Debruin.

"He'll continue as he is. He'll think he's safe."

"So, we find Butler and we catch the suspect," said Debruin, nodding as the plan began to form in his mind.

But Carver shook his head, and Debruin looked to Barnes for an explanation.

"We find the suspect, and we find Butler," he said. "Then we shut the whole thing down."

"We work together," Carver chimed in, offering a sweetener to Debruin, who felt his expression drop in dismay. "And we get them all."

"We let Hargreaves pursue you as lead suspect," said Barnes. "The real leak will carry on talking to Butler while Hargreaves pulls you apart. Do you think you can handle it?"

"Is Hargreaves in on this?" asked Debruin.

"No. He's genuine. He's fast-tracked to bigger things. It takes a certain type of individual to do what he does."

"I'm guessing *you* led him to believe that I'm the prime suspect?"

"Everyone in this station is, or at least should be, wary of Hargreaves. The leak will be watching him, reporting his investigation to DS Butler."

Debruin understood. "So, if the real leak is compromised, Butler will go underground."

"That's why we need him to think that you're the leak. It sounds complex, but it really isn't. We've positioned you as the leak. Hargreaves is like a dog with a bone, he'll pull your life apart searching for something to nail you with."

"He won't find anything material."

"Precisely. Which means we have until Hargreaves finds you innocent to find the killer and Butler."

"Who's the man behind it all? Who's the ringleader?"

"Ah," said Carver, and his lips formed a perfect horizontal line, neither a smile nor otherwise. "Nobody knows him. Nobody sees him and nobody hears him. Before Butler went rogue, he gave us a rundown. There is one man who runs the show. He reports into the unknown ringleader via text messages on a mobile telephone, and even he doesn't know the true identity of the boss."

"Can't tech trace mobile phones?" said Debruin. "It's two thousand and one. Why aren't we bringing them in?"

"They can trace a phone if they know the number. We've got nothing."

"So, if nobody knows who is behind all this, the highest up the food chain we can go is whoever takes the orders and dishes them out?" asked Debruin. "We need to find him. Who is he?"

"Ebenezer Bloom, early fifties, began his career robbing banks in the seventies. He's spent more time inside than out. He's a dangerous man, or at least he *was*. Now all he has to do is click his fingers and his band of men will do whatever he tells them to. His last sentence was fifteen years in Belmarsh for three counts of murder."

"Fifteen years?" said Debruin. "Is that all?"

"He struck a deal. Gave up some names and was released."

"So, he has no loyalty. Can we use that?"

"If we could find him maybe," said Carver. "We're not talking about your everyday criminals, Debruin. These are dangerous men. Smart and connected. They're not afraid to do whatever it takes to get their own way."

"So, we have one man who we know is a criminal, an undercover policeman who we're not sure is rogue or not, and a bunch of specialists," said Debruin, admiring the set-up.

"And the ringleader," said Carver with distaste etched on his face. "The boss. The head honcho."

"What do we know about him?" said Debruin. "Anything at all?"

"Nothing," said Carver, as if the word was on the tip of his tongue and was poisoned. "Except that he's referred to only as

Spider. We were close to catching him five years ago when all of this began. We even found the warehouse from which he operated."

"What happened?"

"We struck with every man we could find. Roadblocks, helicopters, you name it, we had it. The place was empty. He disappeared for a while, but it wasn't long before we recognised the signs and saw the same familiar pattern. Spider is a devious man. He needs to be stopped."

"The spider's web," said Debruin, and pictured the set-up with fascination. "It's brilliant."

"It's over is what it is," said Barnes.

"So, how do we catch him?" said Debruin. "It's not like we haven't been trying."

"Ah," said Carver. His eyes darted to Barnes and back to Debruin. He adopted a grave expression and lowered his voice to a low grumble. "That's where we need to cross a few grey lines. If we're right, and Spider has recruited your man, every effort will be made to have us believe he is acting alone."

"You think my suspect will carry on killing?"

"He has to. It's no longer a killing game. This is a game of wits," said Carver. "The way to win a game of wits, Debruin, is to carry on as normal. Maintain the status quo. We've all read the psychiatric profile on your killer. Why does he kill?"

"He's drawn to his victims," said Debruin. "He targets sex offenders, yet none of his crimes are sexual. He has a deep-rooted hatred of the men he kills. It's like scratching an itch."

"And did last night's explosion scratch that itch?" said Carver, leading Debruin through his own thought process.

"No. He gets up close and personal. He's hands on. The explosion was more of a getaway for himself. He killed Hammersley, but not the way he wanted to."

"What does that tell you?"

"He still has an itch that needs to be scratched. He'll strike again soon. Tonight maybe?"

"Do you know where?" asked Carver.

"Every one of his targets has been in the media at some point. That's how he finds them. Across Britain there are hundreds of released sex offenders. The media only finds out about a handful of them. We used that information to build a list of his potential local targets."

"How long is the list?"

"Well, last night there were two," said Debruin. He spoke as if he was thinking out loud, and Carver was his subconscious prodding his thoughts in the right direction.

"So, there's one left."

"Samuel Norris."

"That's where he'll strike," said Barnes.

"I can talk to Norris. Get him on board. Does he get the same deal as Hammersley?" asked Debruin.

"Clean slate and a new start," said Barnes.

"Tempting for a man in his position, I'm sure," said Carver.

It was a good deal. Debruin couldn't argue with it. It had been agreed in principle for Hammersley, whose offences had been worse than Norris' and who had received a unanimous guilty verdict in contrast to Norris, who had been close to getting off due to a lack of evidence.

"That'll be all, Debruin," said Barnes. "Make your plans. You have my clearance for TSG."

Debruin's mind was deciphering the information. He ambled toward the door, perplexed at the day.

"Oh, and one more thing," said Barnes, and Debruin stopped at the door. "If you fail, if you let him get away again, I'll be left with little choice but to assume Hargreaves' theory is right. Everyone is a suspect. Don't let me down."

PART TWO

TEN

Harvey dizzied at first, then was breathless. He clutched the photograph seeking any detail, no matter how small. But there was nothing. It was just a photo of the inside of a black van, with black carpets, and Alice, pleading for her life.

He searched the square again. The buzz of commuters was waning, and the masses had thinned. There were no men on the corners, nobody appeared out of place, and the van had gone. All he had was a photo that offered no clues. He flipped it, more out of desperation than anything, and on the back, written in neat capitals, were three words.

You cannot run.

The door to the café opened and Harvey spun, ready to attack. But it was just a waiter, different from the original guy who had served them. He jumped at Harvey's sudden movement, then muttered something under his breath as Harvey dropped his arms to his side.

Harvey walked away. The two hundred metres to his bike passed in a blur, a haze of questions with clear answers that his conscience refused to believe. Alice had been taken and her life was being used to blackmail Harvey into doing a job. His stomach lurched, as if something inside stirred. The beast. The rage-filled being that drove him to do the terrible things he did, clawed at his insides.

Then he was riding. He had no recollection of putting on his helmet or starting the bike, and he couldn't recall checking for traffic. He recognised the street and the bridge he was crossing. He was leaving the Isle of Dogs. He knew he had to find Alice before it was too late.

But he had no place to start.

He followed the slip road onto the East India Dock Road, a five-lane highway out of town. The opposite lanes heading into town held slow moving trucks, vans, and cars jostling for position. But the road out of town was empty enough for him to clear his head and make a plan.

They had known he would be at the café long enough for them to place the fake waiter. Which meant they had known he would go to Alice's apartment, and had known that she got her coffee from that place every morning. It also meant they had followed him from the factory.

But he hadn't seen anybody. His escape had been as clean as his entrance. He had walked and ran a mile to where he had parked his bike. He hadn't seen a living soul.

You cannot run.

The writing on the back of the photo. It was the bike. They were tracking the bike somehow.

The realisation opened possibilities. He'd gone from having no clue as to how to find them to knowing how they would find him. He pulled off the main road, followed the slip road into Canning Town, the heart of London's East End, and into the Royal Docks, Silvertown. It was one of his favourite places. Decades before, it had been bustling docks with cargo being loaded from all reaches of the British Empire. Spices, silks, timber, and crates of anything the Victorian man desired. But as the ships were replaced by larger vessels that were too large for the inland docks, the area became derelict. It became the breeding ground for men like John Cartwright and his fore-bearers to rise. A scene where battles were won and lost, and where bodies were loaded with rocks to lay beneath the blanket of water for all of time.

The warehouses, offices, and holding pens had been flattened since those days. All that remained were the tall, black cranes that stood like soldiers on the waterside, a testament to what made Britain great.

Most of the area had been pedestrianised. Where rows of warehouses once stood, an exhibition centre had been built, and where the offices from which strong leaders had run the docks once stood, hotels had been put up. The area was clean, modern, and fresh.

Along the waterside, beneath the giant cranes, benches had been installed. Harvey parked his motorbike beside one, switched it off, and stowed his helmet in the top box. All the while, his eyes scanned the neighbouring roads for signs of the black van or a slow moving vehicle. He ran his hand beneath the mud guards, the rear number plate, and the bodywork, searching for something out of place. He found it beneath the top box. A small, circular device two inches in diameter. It didn't beep. No lights flashed.

It was an inanimate object that gave him no further clue, except that it shouldn't have been there. He replaced the device, feeling the strong magnet cling to the box's steel frame.

Another scan of the surrounding area showed no signs of the man or his men.

Harvey could wait. He was good at waiting. It was an art, he found. He wondered how long he had sat, or lain, or stood in the same place, watching his victims over days and sometimes weeks. Watching for patterns. Watching for habits. Finding weaknesses that he could exploit, like plunging a pick into a hairline crack in the ice. Once he'd found that weakness, and he was inside their minds, he left only devastation.

But the game began with waiting. The view from the bench was of new-build apartments on the far side of the water with landscaped gardens and balconies. Traffic flowed along the roads, but there were no black vans or slow moving vehicles.

The wind was blowing toward him, forming tiny crests of white on the water's surface. It was mesmerising to watch, but each time he tracked a single white cap, Alice's face came to him in torturous flashes, stirring the beast he'd calmed.

"There's only two ways out of this, Harvey," said a voice. *The* voice. He wore a long woolen overcoat, the type that businessmen wear. It hung above his knees and his hands were lost in the deep pockets. The breeze flicked at his flock of white hair as he stopped to block the view with his back to Harvey. Then he turned away from the water that had entranced Harvey, and said, "But I'm sure you know that already."

"Is she okay?" said Harvey, offering no sign of anything but deep-rooted malice and contempt.

"I like it here," he said, as he took the place beside Harvey and ignored the question. He pulled his hands from his jacket and interlinked his fingers on his lap. "It's peaceful."

Harvey interpreted his comments as a sign that Alice was okay for the time being, but those circumstances might change depending on the outcome of the meeting.

"You've got two minutes to make your point," he said.

The comment washed over the man the way the incoming tide covers a rock, then falls away.

"Then what happens?"

"I walk away. You don't."

"And Alice?"

Harvey didn't reply. He'd find her, although he knew his chances of finding her in time were slim to none.

"You're not in much of a position to be offering threats, Harvey," said the man, as he heaved one leg onto the other and settled into the hard bench. "But I like your tenacity. It's one of the reasons why we chose you."

"You say *we* a lot. Who's we?"

"The team."

"Vague."

"Are you in? Do say yes. Alice wants you to."

"Let Alice go and I'll think about it."

"It doesn't work like that."

"So, tell me how it works."

"You say yes, and Alice lives."

"And if I say no?"

"Alice dies and you face one more choice."

"Die or go to prison?"

"Something like that."

"What's the job? What do I have to do?"

"What you do best."

"And the team?" said Harvey, inhaling a lungful of air to quell the stirring beast. "Who are they?"

"The best. We have the best minds in crime and all the resources we need."

"All the resources you need to do what?"

"To be the biggest criminal organisation that Britain has ever seen," said the man, matter of factly. And for the first time, he turned to look at Harvey, revealing ice-blue eyes that seemed to glow against the bright and featureless sky behind him. "Are you in?"

ELEVEN

"Hawes," Debruin called across the open office, "get Spencer and meet me in the meeting room."

Giving Hawes little time to raise any questions, Debruin crouched beside Charlotte White, a young, keen, and intelligent girl who worked in support. It wasn't her intelligence Debruin was interested in.

"Hello, Charlotte," he said, and received a pleasant smile in return, although she didn't look at him. She continued to type.

"I am listening," she said.

"I need you to pull some files for me."

"Okay," she replied. "What type of files are they?"

Charlotte White was a cool character. Debruin couldn't remember a time when she had been flustered, upset, or even mad, despite being the go-to girl for any kind of research. She knew her way around the new computer system better than anybody in the office.

"Anything you can find."

"I mean, are they the type of files that will land me in Barnes' office? Or are they the type of files you can find yourself?"

She was sharp. The only reason Debruin asked her for anything was either because he didn't have access and the information he sought was above his access level, or because he was just too lazy to search for it himself.

"Like I said," Debruin reiterated. "Anything you can find."

She stopped typing, picked up her pen, and waited, poised to write the names down.

"Samuel Norris."

"Okay," she said, as she wrote the name in large, rounded letters. The 'i' had a little circle instead of a dot. The writing was neat and uniform. "Anything else?"

"James Butler," said Debruin.

Again, she wrote in rounded letters, taking her time to write in a neat fashion that matched her personality.

"Detective Sergeant James Butler," said Debruin, and watched her expression falter for a moment before her professionalism pushed her through. "How long?"

"I'll see what I can find."

"You're a star," he said, as he stood. He leaned in and lowered his voice. "I'll be in the meeting room. Oh, and if anybody asks—"

"If anybody asks, sir, I'll be sure to recite the confidentiality clause."

She didn't look up. She didn't even smile. She just continued with her document.

Debruin found the meeting room door open and walked in to find Hawes sitting down and Spencer leaning against the wall.

"Sergeant Spencer, how fast can you enable your team?"

"On-duty can be ready in under three minutes. Off-duty takes a little longer, as you can imagine. It all depends how many men we need."

"I need a dozen."

Spencer nodded. "Just say the word. I'll need sign off from DSI Barnes."

"Not a problem," said Debruin, and he turned to Hawes. "We're going after Samuel Norris."

"Samuel Norris, sir?" said Hawes. Hawes knew of the man. They had discussed the killer's potential victims at large and Samuel Norris had been identified as the most likely to be next, given his location and the publicity the man's conviction and subsequent release had attained.

"I think the killer will strike tonight. It's our only chance to stop him. Tonight, or tomorrow. I'm sure of it."

"With the best will in the world, sir," said Spencer, as he pushed himself off the wall and folded his arms, "I can't have men on surveillance all day and night until the killer strikes. We're under enough backlash as it is from last night's cock up."

"He'll strike soon, Spencer. We need to be ready."

"How do we even know that Norris will be next?"

"It has to be Norris. In the past six months, four local sex offenders have been released from prison. Norris is the last one."

"I can't have a dozen men out on the whim of a–"

"Of a what, Sergeant Spencer?" said Debruin, reminding him of his rank.

Spencer averted his eyes, gathered his thoughts, then turned to stare at Debruin with narrowed eyes.

"Twelve men?" he said, opting not to venture down the route of discussing his opinions on the leak, choosing the path of least resistance.

"Twelve men. That's all we need," said Debruin. "One night. If our man doesn't show, then we have a bigger problem than a serial killer."

Hawes' head perked up at the comment, and Debruin turned his attention to him.

"We'll need an ambulance on standby, eyes in the sky, and

road traffic units ready to shut the roads down. I'll be going to see Norris in a while to line it up. We'll offer him the same deal as Hammersley."

"Oh right, because that turned out well," said Spencer.

Debruin ignored the comment, despite his own retort that was coiled like a spring on the tip of his tongue. Hawes noted down the request. They both waited for the crucial piece of information, until Charlotte White gave a gentle tap on the door and entered. She held out two files for Debruin to take. They were both thin, but if he knew White as well as he thought he did, they would contain every piece of available information on both Norris and Butler.

He opened the first file and found Samuel Norris' profile. It detailed his name, age, address, and convictions. He snapped the file closed and handed it to Hawes.

"Make copies," said Debruin. "I'll make a plan while I'm visiting Norris and I'll feedback locations of the various units. I want everyone in place for seven p.m."

Hawes and Spencer moved toward the door and White waited.

"Is there anything else you need, sir?" she asked. Her voice was professional, yet innocent. He liked her. She would go far on competence alone. He followed Hawes to the door, then closed it and turned to her.

"Yes," he said. "Yes, there is something you can do."

TWELVE

"Where is she?" asked Harvey, as he climbed into the back of the Audi that had pulled up behind the bench. The rear windows were tinted, the seats were leather, and the interior had that new car smell. The man with the blue eyes climbed in behind the driver. He closed the door, and the driver pulled the car away.

Harvey's question went unanswered for a while, and the man seemed to muse at the world they passed. He was playing the silent game now that he had Harvey where he wanted him. Harvey could be silent too. That was his game.

The driver was a lean man with short, dark hair. He held the wheel with a light touch and drove smoothly. Not once did he look up and find Harvey in the rear-view mirror, even though Harvey stared at him, saving every detail to memory. His narrow, brown eyes, his straight Roman nose, and the dark layer of growth on his face. The driver read the traffic well, seeming to know what the other drivers would do before even they did, changing from lane to lane to maintain the speed limit.

Harvey watched the road, wondering how far they would be going, knowing that at some point he would need to get back to his bike. His bike was everything to him. His pride and joy. It was nothing much to look at, not like a Harley or a super-bike. But the BMW R1200GS had gotten him out of more tight spots than he could remember, and nothing matched the feeling of opening the throttle up on an open road. It was stable, fast, manoeuvrable, and off-road it topped most other bikes, hands down.

But somehow, even though he hadn't known her long, Alice's life was more important. A bike could be replaced. The girl's life was in his hands. She was perfect in every way and if she were to die because of him, he would never forgive himself.

"She's okay," said the man, after a twenty-minute silence.

Harvey didn't reply.

"But the decisions you make from this point on can change that." He turned away from the window to look Harvey in the eye. "Make the right choices, Harvey."

They were heading out of town. Trees and forests soon replaced the concrete and brick buildings, and before long, they were driving through Epping Forest. The road cut through the trees, snaking towards Epping. It was Harvey's neighbourhood. Just a few miles from his house. Just a few miles from John Cartwright, his foster-father and all his resources.

But even John's power and influence couldn't help Harvey. The organisation was so slick that Harvey had thought they were government of some kind, one of the many undercover operations that Harvey had read about, carrying out unofficial work on behalf of the state.

He couldn't have been more wrong.

He was on his own. If he even tried to bring John into this, the outcome could be disastrous. But one thing was for sure. There was a chance Harvey wouldn't see him again. Harvey's bike might be found beside the water, and someone may come to the conclusion that his body was resting with all those souls of old, so often lost when the docks were the battleground of the rising empires.

"You're an interesting man," said Blue Eyes. "We've been watching you for some time."

"You should find a hobby," said Harvey, and he stared out of the window as they pulled off the main road onto a lane. There were fields on either side, and they were a mile from Epping town centre. Harvey could find his way home blindfolded if he had to. He had used the lane a number of times and he recalled the few expensive and secluded houses, wondering if they were heading to one of those, and if so, which one.

But their destination was not any of the multi-million-pound homes, and Harvey saw the true reality of who he was up against when the car stopped outside an ancient looking building named Dukes Hall, and those blue eyes turned to see his reaction.

"Impressive, eh?" he said.

Harvey knew of the old house. It had been empty for some time. There were local rumours that beneath the old house, a network of tunnels and secret rooms played host to devil worshippers. But, to Harvey, it had always just been an old building. Impressive, yes. But he gave no weight to the rumours, and he offered the man no sign of his thoughts. He climbed from the car, closed the door, and waited, staring across the fields towards home.

"The original house was built in the twelfth century, you know?" he said, and for a moment, Harvey heard John giving his favourite talk on his own house, which was also twelfth century. John's favourite anecdote to impress admiring guests was that Henry the Eighth had planted one of the great oaks on his land. "It was originally built as a hunting lodge for Henry the Second, and some three hundred years later, it was given to Henry the Eighth."

There it was. Of all the things the man could have said about the house. It was like he could read Harvey's mind, or that he'd witnessed John giving one of his own immodest speeches.

"Of course," he said, as Harvey turned to look him in the eye, "it's changed somewhat since those days. Shall we go inside?"

Harvey turned to take in the old building. It was as wide as five or six average houses and just as deep. The two ends of the house were additions, and the roofs were modern in comparison to the central section, with its ancient double-fronted doorway and tall, narrow windows. But the main feature of the house was a single, circular tower that rose from the centre of the building. It was, Harvey thought, as if the house had been built around an old castle.

The man waved his hand for Harvey to enter first, and he obliged, listening for the footsteps behind him to gauge the distance. Although a surprise attack from behind was unlikely, Harvey couldn't help but be on full alert. The two front doors were large and opulent. They were arched at the top and were painted black to match the rest of the woodwork. Dukes Hall was a three-storey building above ground, with the tower adding a fourth level. Harvey was keen to see if the legends of the basement rooms and tunnels were true.

The inside of the building was where the image of opulence and grandeur fell away in tatters of moth-eaten curtains and carpets. Bare, wooden floors that had once gleamed and shone were a dull matte, like the withered skin of an elderly woman.

The walls, which had once been a rich burgundy, were featureless, dark, and foreboding, with light spaces where Harvey imagined great paintings had once hung. To the rear of the hallway, a central interior feature was an old staircase that led up to the tower room.

"We still have some work to do," said Blue Eyes, as he stepped in behind Harvey. "This way, please."

He led the way into the east corridor, where parts of the floor were missing. He traversed a single plank of oak floor, navigating the ruined walkway with confidence, then turned once more. They were following the shape of the house and heading toward the rear. The walls were still faded, chipped, and marred, and in the places where the floor was intact, it was dulled, warped, and loose. They turned once more and entered what Harvey imagined was a large kitchen.

"Fit for a king," said the man. Then he added, "At least, it *was*."

Stone steps led from the kitchen to a cellar. The man began to descend the steps. Harvey checked behind him to make sure nobody was following. He sniffed, finding the stench of stale air and damp. Then he followed.

The ceiling in the cellar was higher than he was expecting. It was at least twice as high as the cellar in John's house. The walls were of stone and formed a corridor fifteen feet across and as long as the building, perhaps one hundred metres or more. The steps led down into the centre of the cellar and the corridor led left and right. In front of Harvey, the stone wall was featureless, save for some old wrought iron hooks and chains where tools had once hung, and there was a string of lamps along the wall that cast a yellow light across the stone floor. Along the back wall was a row of large alcoves divided by stone walls and with iron bars at the front. They resembled prison cells.

Blue Eyes followed his stare.

"It's an old house," he said. "In the days of old, the workers that ran the house would have stored various goods in each alcove; grain, wheat, barrels of wine and beer."

Each alcove was deep enough for two men to lay head to toe and just as wide. Harvey wasn't convinced of their purpose.

"As the years passed," continued Blue Eyes in the same historical lecturer tone he had used outside, "and the house stood from age to age, the purpose of the alcoves altered to suit the times. They might look like ancient prison cells, but instead of keeping people in, they had originally been installed to prevent theft. Their purpose is altogether different now."

There were at least ten cells to the left of the stairs, and the same number to the right. Harvey prepared himself to be locked inside an empty cell. He prepared himself to fight.

The man, who in his smart and modern clothing seemed so out of place against the medieval scene, was no longer smiling. He eyed Harvey with caution. He was standing beside the driver of the Audi and he addressed him with the authoritative tone of a man with something to prove.

"Fetch Mrs Giggs," he said, and he watched the driver march away up the stairs and disappear from view, before turning his attention to Harvey. "We strive for a perfect world, Harvey. We don't ask for much."

Harvey didn't reply.

"Follow me," he said, and he turned and walked away with his hands behind his back.

Harvey followed at a distance. It was the third alcove on his left that caught his attention. The space was filled with a mattress, a table, and a small tray with an empty plate. There was a man on the mattress who hugged his knees close to his chest. His eyes were reddened by tears. The man with blue eyes stopped and turned to face the man in the cell. The prisoner flinched at his stare and backed into the corner, drawing his knees up once more. It was a primal reaction to danger and helplessness that Harvey had seen before, but only when he had demonstrated his capabilities and his victim was emotionally broken.

There were so many questions on the tip of Harvey's tongue. But he said nothing. The answers would come soon enough.

And they did.

The driver returned, dragging a woman by her arm. She was pretty, but her beauty was marred by the fear that seemed to tug at her features, pulling them down into a grimace. She wore jeans and a loose sweater, the type somebody might have worn to lounge around the house. Harvey tensed at the sight, but his reaction was quelled by Blue Eyes' light touch to his arm.

"You need to see this," Blue Eyes muttered, as he produced a mobile phone from his pocket. He flipped the phone open, and the light from the screen cast a green glow over his face. He read a short message, then snapped the phone closed before Harvey could see what it said.

The woman, when she saw the prisoner, ran to the bars of the cell. For a short while, she smiled and seemed spirited at the sight of the man. The prisoner held her hands through the bars and began to shout, anger replacing his fears. It was then that Harvey recognised the man. It was the man who had mouthed something to him in the square. But he refused to look Harvey's way.

"Let her go," the man called to Blue Eyes. "She has nothing to do with this."

"What's happening? What is this? Why is he in here?" she called.

Blue Eyes unlocked the iron gate and stood back. She brushed past him, ran inside, and hugged her man. But as they broke away, the prisoner, who wore a blood-stained shirt, jeans, and smart shoes, pulled her behind him.

"It's over," said Blue Eyes, and he smiled that tight-lipped smile. "We're done with you."

He stood back as if to accentuate the point, and the man in the bloodied shirt led his wife from the cage, edging toward the cellar steps.

"Do you remember what I told you, Giggs?" said Blue Eyes,

and Giggs stopped and turned, waiting for Blue Eyes to continue. "Nobody can ever know what we do. We're watching everything you do."

Giggs nodded.

"You made a serious error today. One that could have been detrimental to our plan." Blue Eyes spoke loud and clear, articulating his words and projecting his voice like a stage actor might, so that those in the cheap seats could hear.

Again, Giggs nodded. It was only slight, but his face was a picture of fear. Blue Eyes moved forward with his arms behind his back. He seemed to pace the floor, taking time with each step. The heels of his expensive shoes clicked on the flagstone, and Giggs' eyes followed him, his body frozen with terror. Blue Eyes circled the couple and stopped before the woman.

"And you, young lady," he began, "do you understand the rules?"

She shook her head and backed up against Giggs. "Let us go. What is this?" She turned to her husband. "Who are these people?"

Blue Eyes seemed keen to hear Giggs' description, and Harvey tried to read the scene, ready to react.

The woman backed up against Giggs. The move was futile. They were defenceless. Blue Eyes held his hand out and the driver placed a small handgun butt-first into his palm.

"No," said Giggs. "It was a mistake. It won't happen again. I'm sorry—"

But his words had barely left his lips when the gun recoiled, and the air was filled with a fine mist of red spray.

THIRTEEN

The Hillview Estate in Harold Hill, Essex, comprised of three tower blocks and a large car park, surrounded on all sides by a strip of green grass. To the untrained eye, the estate was peaceful, though a little run down.

But to a man like Debruin, the estate was a hive of illegal activity. He could remember when the estate was new. He had been young, and the local residents had been in uproar at the unsightly, concrete block that tainted the horizon. If those residents had known what the place would become, they would have moved out before the first spade hit the ground.

The local council had filled the flats, all one hundred and forty-four of them. On each of the thirty-six floors were four flats, two lifts, one fire escape, and a garbage chute. Not all of the occupants were criminals of course. But even those law-abiding citizens that called the place home were embittered with the card that life had dealt them. He recalled a time when he had been a uniformed officer, just twenty years previous. He and another officer had been called to the flats to break up a party that had gotten out of hand. Just two officers against a dozen drug-fuelled punks. It had been late, gone midnight, and the Sex Pistols were blaring through the open front door. They hadn't taken a single step inside and they had witnessed a female, with her hair dyed orange and formed into neat spikes, swallow two pills and wash them down with a bottle of Vodka. Then she turned and froze when she saw Debruin and his colleague standing in the doorway in all their uniformed glory.

She dropped the bottle on the floor and the glass shattered.

The Sex Pistols continued to scream.

Cause I wanna be–

"Pigs," the girl had yelled, and a dozen heads, shaved, Mohicans, dyed, and just downright ridiculous, had turned to find Debruin and Davis entering the flat, truncheons raised and ready to do battle.

Anarchy–

Some of them tried to swallow everything they had. Some bolted past Debruin and Davis and ran for the fire escape. The brave few stayed and seemed to enjoy the fracas. They threw wild punches, kicked, and used anything they could find as a weapon; a bottle, a chair, and at one point, the tallest of the bunch even had Davis in a headlock and was hitting him with his own helmet.

Two officers against a flat full of punk rockers who were high as kites were never going to walk out with half-a-dozen arrests each. Debruin cuffed a man's hands behind his back, and Davis, whose nose was bloodied, had a girl who kicked and spat like a trapped, wild cat. By the time the piss-puddled elevator reached the ground floor and they each shoved their arrests into the cold night, they had found their police Rover vandalised. The windscreen had been smashed in with bricks. The word 'SCUM' had been spray-painted on the bonnet, and, 'FASCISTS' had been sprayed across the driver-side doors.

That had been twenty years ago, and the estate had been spiralling downward ever since. Not once in all Debruin's life could he recall a time when any effort had been made to clean the image up. He parked his Ford in the car park, locked it, checked the doors, then walked to the main entrance of Saxon House, the centre of the three blocks. He was mildly surprised that the elevator was no longer graffitied. Instead, crude pictures had been scrawled with permanent markers. There were pictures of ejaculating genitalia and women's breasts that could only have been drawn by an individual who had been exposed to too much pornography and not enough real-world experience.

He pulled his sleeve down over his thumb to hit the button for the fifth floor, hoping to avoid contracting any diseases or germs. The doors closed with a long and drawn-out squeal as if they knew where they were going and did so with reluctance. They opened quicker than they closed, and Debruin stepped into the fifth-floor landing. Even if Charlotte hadn't given him the exact address, he was sure he would have found the right flat.

The door to the right of the elevator had a door mat and a small, potted plant. The flat opposite had an extra security lock at both the top and bottom of the door. The flat to the right of the elevator also had a door mat that looked as if it had been there since the days when Debruin and Davis had taken on a dozen punk rockers with just truncheons.

But the last door had a decoration quite unique when compared to the others. It was definitely the flat he was looking for. The decoration came in the form of thick sprayed letters in red paint.

'NONCE'.

Debruin knocked and stepped back, allowing the occupant to view him through the peep-hole.

There was no answer, so he knocked again. He peered

through the letter box and saw a shadow moving against the far wall.

"Mr Norris?" he called.

There was no reply.

"Mr Norris, I know you're in there. I can see you. I'm Detective Inspector Debruin. I'd like a word with you if you don't mind."

He let the letter box fall into place and stood back. There followed a series of clicks and the rattle of a chain as Norris unsecured the front door. It was like a fort.

A bald head and an aged eye appeared in the gap as the door opened, and Debruin flashed his ID.

"I won't take too much of your time."

Norris opened the door a little further and leaned out into the landing to check the blind spot to the right. He eyed Debruin with caution and then relented.

"You'd better come inside," he said. His voice was soft, gentle, and articulate.

Debruin had seen the man's profile. In a previous life, he had attended school in West London and lived off a dwindling inheritance. He had lived such a quiet life that his identify was almost unknown, save for a driver's license, passport, and a bank account. He had the appearance of a man who dined in the upper echelons of society, at the finest of restaurants, and it was easy to imagine him, Debruin thought, in a smoking jacket sitting in a wing-back Queen Anne enjoying a glass of port and listening to Bach.

Instead, Debruin found him in a pair of old suit trousers that may have once been teamed with a matching, tailored suit jacket and waistcoat, and a crumpled shirt. And in place of the chesterfield wingback was a settee that looked as if it had been found in the car park five floors below.

The once admirable Samuel Norris had fallen from grace

and been reduced to near destitution. But he was not a broken man. Somehow, he'd been through hell, survived prison, assaults, insults, and lost everything he had, and still retained a fragment of his former self. He refused to let his shoulders hunch, his back remained ramrod straight, and he peered down his nose at Debruin before he closed the door behind them and slid the multiple locks into place. Hanging in the hallway was an old, green jacket. It was the waterproof kind that Debruin had seen wealthy men wearing in films while shooting clays, a waxed Barbour jacket with a corduroy collar.

"I imagine you've come to rub salt into my wound, have you?" he asked, as he shuffled past Debruin into the dull living room. "I suppose I'm required to attend a meeting of some sorts to talk about how I'm coping and to prove I'm following the parole requirements."

Debruin said nothing. He followed Norris into the living room and found him staring out of the balcony window. The door was closed, and the curtains were tied back to the walls with ties in the form of old manila rope. The balcony floor was littered with half-full plastic drinks bottles, probably belonging to the same teenagers who had decorated Norris' front door.

"Well, I won't," said Norris, voicing his adamant position on the subject of parole responsibilities. "I'll go and see them if I must. Once per week is what was agreed, and I committed to that." His head nodded as he voiced his own thoughts. "But I shan't commit to any more than what's required. I was promised a home. I was promised a new start." He turned to Debruin. "And this is what I got."

It was at that moment that the letter box flapped open in the hallway and a prepubescent boy's voice called through, "Paedo scum!"

There was laughter and the fire escape door slammed shut as the boys retreated.

Debruin turned his attention back to Norris and found him staring beside the window.

"Every day. Every day it happens. It'll never stop. I know it won't. Those children will grow older and the ones that follow in their footsteps will hear the stories. This is my life now. This is what I've become."

Again, Debruin said nothing. A life in the force had taught him long ago to remain impartial. A convicted criminal who is either serving or has served their sentence should be treated as any other member of society. The rules became more challenging on the second, third, and fourth offences. A recidivist deserves to be treated as such. Norris, however, had been convicted once. It had been his first offence for anything. But the crimes for which he was charged were of such severity that society found it difficult to fortune him a graceful retirement, despite the lack of substantial evidence. He hadn't run from his crimes. He had handed himself in to the police in an effort to prevent a media frenzy. And despite his legal advisor's protests, he had pleaded guilty, welcoming the punishment for his crimes.

Another plastic bottle clunked against his window but bounced back and down to the ground five floors below.

"So?" he said. "What is it you've come for? You've disturbed the hornet's nest. No doubt the little bastards will hound me for the rest of the day now. It's a wonder I'm not back inside, detective."

There was no denying it. The man was handling the abuse and the insults, on the surface at least. But what was happening inside his mind? How long would it be before he did something he would regret? A small part of Debruin felt for the man. It was hard not to. His case hadn't been open and shut. The guilty verdict had been disputed on many occasions and over-ruled each time. The proof that had convicted him was not, as

Debruin would have hoped it would have been, black and white. He could be staring at an innocent man who had lost everything and pleaded guilty to prevent a gruelling trial. Debruin wondered if he would have coped so well had he been through the same trauma. The man was embittered, and rightly so, but strong beyond belief.

On the other hand, from where Debruin was sitting, he could see only one side of Norris. There was a chance, and a good chance at that, that he was staring at a sex offender. A man of the most despicable kind.

"I've come to offer you a way out of all this, Mr Norris," he said, then gestured at the old, grubby sofa. "Why don't we sit down?"

FOURTEEN

The gunshot in the confined space left Harvey's ears ringing. But he stood stoic and unmoving, showing no signs of weakness.

Blue Eyes handed the weapon back to the driver and returned his hands behind his back, leaving Giggs to drop to his knees cradling the body of the woman. Blue Eyes stepped past Harvey, unmoved by his own actions, and continued along the corridor.

"I'd like to show you something," he said, and Harvey followed beside him, matching his slow steps with cautious paces of his own.

Another gunshot rang out and Harvey turned to find the driver, gun in hand, and Giggs lying motionless over his wife.

"We do not tolerate mistakes, Harvey," said Blue Eyes. "That's the secret to our success."

They approached the last of the cells, and Harvey had an idea of who might be inside.

"We have rules, Harvey," said Blue Eyes, as he turned to face him and folded his arms. "It's our rules that make us unstoppable. Stick to them and we'll all walk away from this. Break them and people die."

"And him?" said Harvey. He gestured at the mess in the corridor behind them but didn't turn to see.

"He made a mistake." Blue Eyes stared hard at Harvey. His eyes seemed never to blink. "Rule number one," said Blue Eyes, ignoring Harvey's expression as it tightened into a scowl. "You do not talk to anybody about us. If you're planning on bringing in the big guns, I can assure you, John Cartwright and all your friends are being watched. Do you understand?"

Harvey didn't reply.

The man waited. He stared at Harvey, refusing to proceed until he had his response.

"I *will* have your cooperation. I can stand here all day. And I can promise you that every time you refuse to answer me, her life will become more unbearable. I can understand you want to make life difficult for me, but if you have any feelings for her at all, then I suggest you answer me when I speak to you. The silent man act will not wash with me."

His expression was one of a man who thought he was untouchable. In Harvey's experience, no man was untouchable.

"Do you understand?"

The driver now stood beside Blue Eyes. He held the gun by his side. Harvey gauged the time it would take to get to him and disarm him. But he was too far away.

Harvey nodded.

"Just tell me what it is you need me to do."

"That's easy. You're a killer, Harvey. You prey upon convicted sex offenders, is that right?"

Alice emerged from the shadows in the end cell and came to the bars, her face a picture of bewilderment.

Harvey said nothing. Blue Eyes was correct, but he would never voice a confirmation and incriminate himself, ever.

"I'll take that as a yes," said Blue Eyes. "You hunt them. You watch them. You learn them. We've been hunting, watching, and learning you, Harvey."

The beast in Harvey's gut stirred at the thought.

"You research your victims through the media and the news. You use public libraries to access archives. But the thing that strikes us about you is how good you are, how calm you remain, and how ruthless you can be."

Blue Eyes paced the room, seeming to enjoy the clicking of his heels on the flagstone floor and the disappointment on Alice's perfect face. He stopped beside her, and she moved away from the bars, slipping into the shadows.

"You have a list, Harvey. A list of men who..." He paused, searching for suitable words. "Meet your requirements. Men who prey on the vulnerable. Men who abuse women. Rapists and bullies, and especially those who enjoy the taste of young flesh."

Alice's face was lost to the shadows. Harvey searched for her but felt her chagrin in the stale air.

"Who's next?" said Blue Eyes.

Harvey said nothing.

"Oh, come on. We know all about it. There was Slater and Hammersley, and I can't imagine how many before them." He met Harvey's stare and offered a knowing smile. "I know who's next and you know who's next. I want you to find Samuel Norris, and I want you to do what you do. It's quite simple. If you get caught, she dies. If you try to hide, she dies. If you try to get help, she dies. And if you talk to the police, Harvey, which I'm sure you won't, I'll kill her myself in the most inhumane way I can think of, and I have a pretty damn good imagination."

"Is that it?" said Harvey. "Then you'll let her go?"

"That's it for now." He raised his sleeve to check his watch, then pulled his cuff down and smoothed his jacket. He retrieved his phone from his pocket again, flipped it open, and read a new message.

Harvey searched the shadows in the alcove but found only two pale glints of watery eyes.

"It's midday," said Blue Eyes, snapping the phone closed. "You have nine hours."

FIFTEEN

"I suppose you want tea," said Norris, when Debruin had outlined his plan and the subsequent reward.

"I want to talk about saving your life, Mr Norris. Time is short."

"My life is beyond saving, don't you think?"

"Have you seen the news?"

"I've seen what the news can do to a man, detective. It was the news that swayed my conviction. Of that I'm sure."

The man was bitter. And rightly so if he was indeed as innocent as Debruin suspected. The rules of the legal proceedings suggest that until such a time that a man is found guilty of a crime, the media should refrain from shining him in a less than favourable light. Debruin remembered the newspapers. There were images of him scowling at the camera. It was common practice for newspaper photographers to goad a suspect, then capture him in a state of frustration or, as in Norris' case, aggression. He had lashed out and the scene was captured for all the world to see, along with a headline that was designed to stir public tempers.

The result had been devastating for Norris. Angry parents

had demonstrated outside his house, he was spat on, and if it hadn't been for police arriving on the scene, he would have been lynched.

The newspaper with the offending photographer had issued an apology, as was standard practice, but by then, the damage had been done.

By the time the court proceedings had taken place, public perception of him had been in the gutter, and regardless of the lack of substantial evidence, a guilty verdict had been close to unanimous.

Norris nodded. "We can talk over tea. All the best decisions are made over a pot of tea."

There was no avoiding it. Such was Norris' ways that he wasn't going to sit down and listen to any more of Debruin's plan without a cup of tea.

"One sugar," said Debruin, and he checked his watch. It was twelve-fifteen. If the killer was to follow his usual MO, he would strike in the dead of night, when the shadows would conceal him.

Norris fumbled around with cups in the kitchen, while Debruin studied the sparse flat. It was hideous. The wallpaper was peeling, the paint was flaking, and the ceiling was yellowed with nicotine from previous tenants.

The kettle was being filled. The pipes in the ceiling rang and shook, then shuddered, and the kettle's metal lid clanged into place.

Debruin imagined the Norris of old. He was the type of man to cling onto the old ways. If, for some reason, Debruin would have had reason to visit him before the court case, before the man's life had been stripped away, Norris would have emerged from the kitchen with a tray. There would have been two china cups on saucers, a little matching bowl of sugar with a spoon, and a small plate with a modest amount of plain biscuits, two each. It was how Debruin's grandmother would have served tea. There was something about the style that was almost ritualistic. It made having tea an event.

He stood and moved to the balcony door. The outer wall was glazed from floor to ceiling, which, in the designer's mind, must have been modern and sleek. But the reality was that the local council had performed cost-saving exercises on every single material used in the build. The cheapest kitchenware had been installed, the cheapest bathrooms fitted, and of course, the windows that had been chosen were anything but modern and sleek.

Debruin pushed the handle and stepped outside as the kettle in the kitchen began to rattle with fury. The image of the raging water was synonymous with Norris. Debruin couldn't help but feel for the man. There was a chance he was innocent. The legal system, and everything men like Debruin stood for, had failed him. The man had been reduced to misery. The drinks bottles on the balcony floor, the graffiti on the front door, and the lines that were etched into his face were just surface results.

The real damage had been done deep inside the man's heart.

Debruin peered down to the ground below, leaning on the balcony wall. The teenagers had gone. They had done well to get the bottles so high. Each of the plastic containers were half-filled to give them the weight they needed to travel far enough upwards. It was then that Debruin noticed that it wasn't drink that filled them. The bottles, regardless of what it said on the label and the brand, contained a deep, amber liquid.

"Scum," said Debruin, and he felt for the man inside even more.

He hoped the boys tried to throw more while he was there.

He would be happy to collar one of them. But he knew that would do little to make Norris' life any easier.

But right there and then, as Debruin looked down to the ground floor car park and the surrounding roads, a few boys making Norris' life a misery were nothing compared to the beast that would visit him that evening.

The killer would arrive on foot, as he had done with Hammersley and the others. That meant he would park nearby somewhere. A side road maybe? Up to a mile away. A mile would be far enough away to avoid his car being identified. There was no way Hawes would convince the road traffic police to block all the roads in a mile radius. At best, they would block the road outside the flats, if they were asked nicely.

There were three blocks of flats. Norris' was at the front of the central block, which meant that none of the other flats over-looked his. Debruin, Hawes, and Spencer's team would need to use parked vans on the far side of the road. One perhaps in the car park wouldn't draw attention, but any more and the killer might be spooked. Adjacent to the entrance to the flats was a side road. Debruin knew it from his days on the beat. It was a dead end road and from memory it was two to three hundred yards long and lined with trees.

It would be the perfect place to sit in the back of one of Spencer's TSG vans to wait. He made a mental note of the team positions, leaving men spare to cover the rear.

But the thoughts of Norris that he tried so hard to move past became barriers. He couldn't see the operation with any clarity. He wondered if Norris was indeed innocent. He wondered what he had been through in prison and since. The family he had lost, the home, the life, and the wealth. Society was cruel.

But the killer was worse.

Maybe Norris would be happy to endure what the killer had in mind for him if the result was the end of his life. To be switched off. For most, death was to be feared. People are rarely ready for it and those around them must learn to adjust.

But for Norris, death would be welcomed. It was a wonder he hadn't launched himself from the balcony already. Five floors, sixty feet onto the grass below. Death wasn't a certainty. He would likely be crippled with nobody willing to look after a man who served a sentence for the types of crimes that Norris had been charged with.

Maybe he was guilty? Maybe his confession had been accurate and the life of squalor he now led was somehow justified and deserved.

He shuddered a little at the thought of what was to come, forcing himself to focus on the outcome. Debruin stood straight and leaned on the balcony, taking one last look at the grounds below.

He stepped back inside and closed the door. The smell of damp hit him first. The whoosh of air quietened, and the raging kettle whistled to announce it had boiled.

"Mr Norris?"

He moved into the hallway and, in an instant, all his plans tumbled like a house of cards.

The front door was wide open, and Norris' green Barbour jacket was gone.

SIXTEEN

The ride in the Audi was smooth. The engine was quiet and when the driver pulled out of the lane onto the main road towards Epping, the power was impressive. He drove well. His eyes darted from mirror to mirror, not to look at Harvey in the back seat, but to register the cars behind.

"What's your name?" he asked.

Harvey didn't reply.

The driver took the silence well, but it was clear his efforts to get Harvey to talk wouldn't stop there.

"You'll have to show me the way," he said, forcing Harvey to engage.

"Don't you know where we're going?"

"I was told to drive you. That's all I know."

"Gallows Corner," said Harvey, referring to a major junction of the A12 into London. "I'll guide you from there."

The command gave Harvey at least twenty minutes to think. He was capable of doing what he had to do, but it was the first time he had ever been under instruction, and he would have preferred to carry out his work in his own time. He lived by a mantra that he had inherited from his mentor, Julios. Patience, planning, and execution. It was the key to his success.

The hit was on Samuel Norris. Harvey knew the address; it was imprinted on his memory. The man had been on his list since his release, and Harvey had been waiting for the dreams to spark the desire. The planning allowed the beast inside him to savour every stroke of his knife when the moment finally came, by which time Harvey would have learnt the man's movements, learnt his habits, and could time his execution with precision.

But to strike on demand would require Harvey to break every rule Julios had ever taught him. The risks were high. Julios' rules were in place for a reason, to save Harvey from being caught and spending the rest of his life in prison. But Blue Eyes' rules contrasted the practice. The way in which he had dispatched Giggs and his wife hit home that Alice's life was in severe danger.

He considered the option of slotting the driver. Harvey could easily reach up and cut his throat. He would wait until the car was on the faster roads, when the driver had little chance of fighting back. He could take the car back to the old hall, walk in there, and take the man down.

But he stood little chance of doing so before Alice was killed. That much had been made clear.

His thoughts turned to the darkest of places, a place his mind rarely ventured. If he was caught, killed, or even maimed, Alice would die. Her parents would never know what happened. They would be left wondering what had happened to their precious daughter for the rest of their lives. John and Julios would suffer the same fate with Harvey. But the road Harvey trod was filled with danger. They all knew that one day one of them wouldn't make it back from someplace. It was a fact that each man who was embroiled in the world of crime to the levels they were, understood, accepted, and tried never to think about.

But Alice would be sitting in that grimy cage without reason, experience, or even the understanding of how to close that part of the mind off. She would be terrified.

He had seen it in her eyes when the man had spoken of what Harvey had done. He knew that she would never forgive him for lying. Even though he hadn't technically lied. She wouldn't see it that way. Even if by some miracle Harvey was able to get her out and to safety, she would run from him. She would think of him as she thought of the man with those cold, blue eyes.

He could live with that. He pictured himself watching her in years to come. He saw her walk through the square and sit by the coffee shop, and he would be watching from afar, making sure she was okay. He could just watch her. The thought pleased him a little.

They were approaching Gallows Corner and the traffic slowed. The change in speed and sound was enough to drag Harvey once more from his thoughts.

"Turn left here," he said to the man.

They pulled onto a side road lined with tall trees. The houses were the basic council houses of working class, good people.

"Are you really going to do it?" asked the driver, staring at him in the mirror. "Are you really going to take him out?"

"I thought you didn't know anything."

"I heard a little."

Harvey didn't reply.

Harvey spoke of his exploits to two men and two men alone. John and Julios. Others knew of course. There was Sergio, John's right-hand man. And Donny, John's son. But the only people who really knew what Harvey was capable of were John and Julios.

He turned away and stared through the window.

"Look, mate," the man continued, as he pulled the car to the side of the quiet road and stopped, "we're in this together. I need to know."

Harvey said nothing. He gauged the distance to the flats where the target lived to be just under a mile. The guess was from memory as he hadn't had time to carry out his planning. But the guess would have to suffice.

"What's his name? Is it anyone famous?"

Outside, the world was a blur, and Harvey tried his best to tune the driver out.

"You've got a lot to learn, mate," the man said, with a hint of aggression in his tone. It was enough to get Harvey's attention. He met the man's stare in the mirror, a sign that he should watch his words. "We're in this together. We're all taking risks. We need to stick up for each other." He turned in his seat to look at Harvey. "Who do you think is going to back you up? You need friends in this game. You don't know what he's capable of. That's all I'm saying."

Harvey said nothing.

The man tutted.

"You won't last a day. And that pretty little bitch of yours—" Before he could finish his sentence, Harvey had his knife at the man's throat, and with his free hand, Harvey took hold of the man's hair.

"You talk too much," said Harvey. "You do your job. I'll do mine. Keep quiet, and you might live to see tomorrow."

His neck tensed against the blade.

The two scenarios Harvey considered ran through his mind. Kill him and take on Blue Eyes at the old hall, or do the job, play the game, and suffer the consequences.

But a third option presented itself. As the first trickle of blood teased from beneath Harvey's blade, he checked his surroundings for witnesses.

The road was clear of traffic. But on the footpath ahead of them, something caught Harvey's eye. A man was running their way. He was mid-fifties. He wore a green jacket with smart trousers and shoes, and his face was a picture of terror. He looked over his shoulder as he ran, then drew closer, and Harvey was sure.

SEVENTEEN

The phone in Norris' hallway was dead. Debruin rattled the cut-off button in anger, then dropped the handset. He pulled the door closed behind him, walked past the decrepit lift, and ran down the five flights of concrete stairs. He hadn't had to run in years and the slippery soles of his shoes made the job even harder.

He burst through the main doors into the car park and searched for Norris. But he found no sign of him. The group of teenagers that had been throwing bottles onto Norris' balcony were loitering at the entrance to the flats, doing their best to appear hard and threatening to passers-by. But their adolescence was clear. Debruin had seen groups like them a hundred times over. Their escapades would grow more and more serious. One, if not more of them, would go to prison. That was when the good kids made their escape and the bad kids got worse.

"Where did he go?" called Debruin. He walked towards them, and one of them looked his way, muttering something too quiet for Debruin to hear. "Tall man in a green jacket. He ran past here a few minutes ago."

"We don't know what you're talking about, mate," the largest of the group replied.

Debruin pulled his ID wallet from inside his jacket.

"Which way did he run?"

There were five of them in total. Five spotty faces steeled at the sight of his ID, and ten eyebrows raised in surprise.

"I ain't talking to a copper," the largest one said.

"Why don't you chase him?" said another. "Go on, give us a laugh, you fat bastard."

The largest of them laughed, and the others joined in.

He'd get nowhere with them. He ran the thirty metres to his car to the pleasure of the boys, who called out abuse. Their laughter was loud and clear, sharp like knives.

He hoped that one day one of them would have the smile wiped off his face when he found himself up against real criminals with time on their hands to teach him a lesson.

He climbed into his car, started the engine, and began to pull away. But something was wrong. The car was sluggish. It was then he realised the front of the car was low. He opened the door and leaned out to find the front right tyre was flat.

"Damn it," he said, and the boys' laughter grew. Even from afar, he could hear the malice and contempt in their voices.

He climbed out of the car, opened the boot, and began looking for the jack. But time was not on his side. He gave up the attempt, slammed the boot, locked the car, and despite the boys' show of mock applause, he ran in the direction he thought Norris would have taken.

He crossed the main road after waiting for a gap in the traffic and settled into a steady jog somewhere between running and walking. He turned off the main road and into a side street. The road was long and straight, and ahead of him, a tiny dot was moving with urgency.

Norris.

Debruin increased his pace.

He passed a bus stop, and for a fraction of a moment, he considered his fortune if a bus should arrive at that very moment. He glanced over his shoulder but found no such luck. A few metres on from the bus stop was a public phone box. Keeping sight of Norris, he opened the door, lifted the handset, and dropped a pound coin into the slot. He dialled from memory and waited for the call to be answered, while watching Norris grow smaller and smaller and closer to the end of the road.

"DI Hawes," came the response, when the call was answered, and Debruin imagined him with his legs crossed, still arranging the operation that was to take place that evening.

"Hawes, he's gone. I need uniforms."

"Sir?"

In Debruin's mind, Hawes sat up straight and was finding a clean space on his notepad to make notes.

"Norris did a runner. Long Acre Road. Green Barbour jacket, black trousers, and shoes. He's mid-fifties and balding. Get uniforms on it and come and find me."

"Yes, sir," said Hawes, wasting no time with further questions. Hawes was good like that. He was efficient and could read the tone in Debruin's voice well.

"Oh, and Hawes," said Debruin, with one eye on the escaping Norris.

"Sir?"

"Bring a jack, will you?"

He replaced the handset, checked the path was clear, and resumed his run, hoping to see the flash of police cars that would be appearing any minute. He guessed the time it would take for Hawes to get the message to the desk. Forty seconds. It would be another twenty to thirty seconds for the radio call to go out. The one thing in Debruin's favour was that police were kept busy in the area. There would be four to five units patrolling at any given time, more in the evening. He expected to see the first police car in under two minutes.

The distance between himself and Norris he calculated to be two to three minutes, given that they hadn't left the flat at the same time and Debruin had wasted at least a minute and a half with the teenagers and the car, and then the call.

He picked up the pace, finding a rhythm to his breathing when, at the end of the road, Norris turned a corner and disappeared from sight. Still at least two minutes behind, Debruin ran harder, as hard as he dared with his slippery soles.

He reached the corner, breathless and sweaty, but certain he had closed the distance, only to see a car door slam and a dark blue saloon wheel-spin away from the kerbside.

EIGHTEEN

"Drive," said Harvey, with one hand on Norris' head, keeping him low and out of sight. He checked behind for witnesses and found only a man in a short jacket looking after them, bemused and breathless, but not a threat.

The driver slowed at the end of the road, indicated left, and waited for a gap in the traffic. Three cars passed, and a fourth indicated. It was a police car, and a second was stopped one hundred yards further up the road.

"Hold still," said the driver.

His face was calm, and he tapped the wheel, as any driver might, to the rhythm of a song in his mind. The rear windows were tinted but not blacked out. Harvey held Norris down low, half in the foot well behind the passenger seat and half on the rear seat. To the onlooker, Harvey would have been a dark shape, his features barely visible. But his body language would have been easy to read. He sat upright, and looked ahead, and the police car stopped beside them at the junction.

The driver lowered the window.

"Officer," he said, in a causal greeting. One word from

Norris and the game would be over. Harvey forced his face into the seat to muffle any cries for help.

"We're looking for a man in his mid-fifties wearing a green jacket. He might be running."

"Is he dangerous?" said the driver, with a concerned look on his face.

"To himself," said the officer.

"I haven't seen anyone, but if I do, I'll call 999."

The officer nodded to the back of the car.

"Who's in the back?"

"Private hire," said the driver, and he lowered Harvey's window halfway. "He's my fare."

It was law for all private hire vehicles to display a yellow circular tag in the windscreen, but parked side by side, the officer wouldn't have seen it even if there had been one.

The officer searched past Harvey and saw nobody beside him. Norris struggled against the force of Harvey's arm, and it was all Harvey could do to turn his attention to the driver, as a paying customer might do. It was in that short period that Harvey found the driver's rear-view mirror and searched behind them. The man that had looked at them, bemused and breathless, was running towards them, and he was running fast.

"I'm running late," said Harvey, loud enough for the officer to hear.

The driver nodded to the officers, raised the rear window, and pulled away slowly, passing the second police car at a crawl.

It was only when they had turned onto the main road that the driver put his foot down, and Harvey released Norris.

"We need to get off the main road," said Harvey to the driver. "We were seen."

"Who are you?" said Norris from his position behind the passenger seat. He backed away as far as he could.

Harvey ignored Norris and checked behind them for any sign of the police Volvo.

"You're him, aren't you?" said Norris. "You're the man they're looking for."

Harvey ignored him again, leaned forward, and got the driver's attention.

"Did you hear me? We need to get off the main roads."

It was while Harvey was distracted that a sudden rush of air and loud road noise filled the inside of the car. Norris had opened the door and the force of negative pressure had sucked the door open. He hung with his feet in the foot well and his hands on the handle. The road rushed below him at sixty miles per hour. The sudden chaos caused the driver to turn in his seat, and the car veered across the road to the tune of blaring horns.

Harvey wrenched the old man back inside the car and the door slammed.

"Get off the main road now," said Harvey to the driver, and he pulled his knife from his jacket. He held the tip of the blade beneath Norris' chin. "Try anything like that again, old man, and I'll *push* you out. The best you can pray for is a big lorry behind us to kill you outright."

Norris was visibly shaken. He sat upright in the seat, the remains of his hair wild with the force of the wind, and his hands shook.

Harvey checked behind again. There was a police car five hundred yards behind. The flashing blues in the car's grille were on and, one by one, the other cars were moving lanes to allow them through.

"I see them," said the driver, and he veered off to the far lane, ready to exit the main road. "Seat belts on."

He turned into a side street using second gear to slow. The rear end of the car slid out a little, but the driver powered through it, using the momentum to perform the turn. By the time the police turned in behind them, the Audi was in fourth gear and racing toward one hundred miles per hour passing parked cars by mere inches on either side.

Norris pulled his seat belt across his chest, but his hands were trembling so hard he was struggling to find the catch.

The driver braked hard at the end of the road, found second gear, and, with the aid of the handbrake, slewed the car into the adjoining road. The police sirens were now blaring, and in front, the road was clear. The driver pushed the car hard. The full torque of the Audi forced Harvey and Norris into their seats. Ahead of them was a small roundabout. Harvey knew it well. Turning left would take them back to the A12, a highway into London. Straight on would take them deep into the back roads of Romford. A right turn would lead them on to the countryside and the hall. They were just two hundred yards from the roundabout when another police car entered the junction from the left. The police driver stopped the car on the roundabout, blocking their path, but the Audi driver, silent and skilled, forced the handbrake up, nudged the wheel right, and performed a controlled slide into the right-hand turn. There were now two police cars behind them, and Harvey knew from experience that there would be more ahead. The driver was good. He was accurate and made decisions in split seconds. But the police had the advantage of numbers and radios.

They roared through an area called Collier Row, a place Harvey knew well. With just one more crossroads ahead of them before they reached the winding country lanes where the Audi could outrun the police cars, the worst imaginable happened. Three more police cars blocked the junction. Other road users were urged to one side by officers in bright yellow jackets and all eyes turned on them as the driver forced the car as fast as it would go.

"What's he doing?" said Norris when he realised the driver wasn't going to stop.

"Hold on tight," said Harvey, as he pulled his own belt across his chest and braced for impact. The seconds passed in silence, as if Harvey's mind had blocked out the chaos and the noise. Two of the police cars had formed a V-shape in the middle of the junction, parked at forty-five degrees to block all four lanes. The driver's shoulders raised, and Harvey imagined him taking one final deep breath for courage. He aimed the Audi at the centre of the V. There was a space, but at well over one hundred miles per hour, the room for error was minute.

The passenger door mirror was torn off and cracked the rear window as it flew past. Harvey turned in his seat to see the amazed policemen staring after them. The two chasing police cars slowed for the gap, leaving the driver time to hit the country lanes with enough speed to put some distance between them.

They took the long, sweeping bends at speeds that even Harvey would have only taken on his bike. The trees rushed past and expensive houses were a blur of colour. The driver showed no sign of easing off.

He was extremely good, and Harvey found himself acknowledging his skill. But a driver as skilled as the man in the front couldn't have foreseen the young deer that stepped into the road sniffing the air at the end of one long, sweeping bend.

It was the first time the driver's decision had been a wrong one. He swerved. The front wheel caught the curb, and the Audi entered a spin. It left the road and disappeared into the forest at ninety miles per hour.

NINETEEN

Hawes stopped at the roadside long enough for Debruin to climb into the passenger seat, then pulled away again. A single police car was waiting at the top of the road, and a yellow jacket was standing at the roadside, monitoring the few cars that passed and waving them on when they slowed to see what was going on.

Debruin flashed his ID, and the officer waved them through. The radio that had been fixed to the centre console in Hawes' Ford was a riot of crackled messages, and in the sky a few miles away, a helicopter circled.

"I don't know how he's doing it," said Debruin, breaking the silence. His disheartened tone roused the anger inside of him. Self-pity had never been his style, but the frustration was getting the better of him. Soon it would cloud his thoughts. He needed clarity. He needed to be up there, in the chopper, getting a new perspective.

Hawes said nothing. He drove in silence, navigating the back streets like the rock solid professional he was. Debruin switched off the radio, ignoring Hawes' look of protest.

"I saw him get into a car. I saw the car speed off." He rested his head on the head rest and closed his eyes. "They even stopped to talk to the uniforms at the top of the road."

"Did he climb in, or was he grabbed?"

Debruin's thoughts were a jumble of confusion. He remembered the flat tyre. He remembered talking to the teenagers. And he remembered running after Norris. But then, the only memory he could recall was the door being slammed and the car speeding off.

"I don't know," he said. "I was right behind him, Hawes. A few hundred yards at most."

"So, what are our options here? The way I see it, he was either recognised and grabbed, or he somehow got a message to somebody."

"He has no friends. I saw the way the man is living. He has nobody to help him. It has to be an abduction."

"You think it's our guy? The killer?" asked Hawes.

"I don't know yet. The MO is wrong. The time of day is wrong. Our man doesn't work during the day. He prefers the shadows. He's ashamed of what he does but can't help himself. He doesn't abduct his victims. He strikes when they are in the right place. He's too professional. Too perfect. A street abduction is too risky."

Hawes gave him a moment to ponder the possibilities.

"Where are we going anyway?" said Debruin.

"Uniforms set up a roadblock in Collier Row. That was the last time anyone saw the Audi."

The word roadblock invoked a glimmer of hope. Debruin stared at Hawes, waiting for him to embellish the response. But when Hawes gave him a sideways glance, his face remained impassive with little sign of hope.

"Did they stop him?"

"He drove through it."

Debruin slammed his hand on the dashboard.

"From what I heard on the radio, there were two police cars on a crossroads. They tried to block his escape. It's not their fault, sir."

"Was there a pursuit?"

"Both cars gave chase, sir. He's gone."

Debruin popped open the glove box and rummaged through the booklets. He searched the door pocket but found it empty.

"A map. Do you have a map? I need a map."

Hawes passed him an Ordnance Survey map from the driver's door. "They were on Havering Road, and as far as I can tell, they went straight on towards Bower Park, sir."

"So, they either got away or they holed up in one of the houses. That's a long road and they are big houses."

"That's why I called the chopper in, sir," said Hawes, and Debruin stopped searching the map.

"That was you, was it?"

"Yes, sir. I've also arranged for the road to be closed off at both ends, from Havering-Atte-Bower to Collier Row."

"Good, so if Norris is there, we'll find him. We find him, and we find our man."

"Do you want uniforms to knock on doors?" said Hawes, and he reached for the radio.

"No," said Debruin, and he watched Hawes retract his hand. "No. If this is our man, this could be the breakthrough we need."

"Can I say something, sir?"

"Of course."

"Sir, if it really is our man, and he's holed up in one of the houses with Norris, there's a good chance Norris is dead already. Sending uniforms door knocking might be enough to keep Norris alive."

Debruin pondered the idea but said nothing.

"Sir?" said Hawes, then continued voicing his thoughts. "Sir, if he kills Norris, Hargreaves will have you. It'll be hard to prove your innocence. It'll be the third time the killer strikes and the third time you let him—"

"Let him what, Hawes?" said Debruin, knowing what he was going to say. "Slip through my fingers?"

"Sir, I didn't mean—"

"I know what you meant. You think I'm guilty."

"No, sir, I—"

"You believe Hargreaves."

"Sir, no."

Debruin stared out of his window, choosing not to voice his full opinion. He knew how it all looked. He knew that if Hawes believed Hargreaves, then the rest of his colleagues would all feel the same. He let the silence carry them, until he felt the car slow for the crossroads.

Two officers closed the gap as Hawes eased the car through the roadblock. Debruin flashed his ID, which after being scrutinised by a yellow jacket, wasn't enough to have them waved through. The car came to a stop and Debruin lowered his window.

"Detective Inspector Debruin?" asked the officer, confirming the name he had read on the ID.

Debruin nodded. The delay teased at his impatience. "What is it?"

"We were told you wouldn't be far away. I just thought you should know, sir," said the officer, and he pointed at the circling helicopter. "The chopper pilot has reported smoke from the forest. He thinks it might be the same car that came through here ten minutes ago. A dark blue Audi."

"Is there anyone at the scene?" asked Debruin.

"I've got two units there," said the officer. "No survivors."

TWENTY

The stillness and silence were marred only by a ringing in Harvey's ears. An incessant whine that neither dipped nor rose in pitch but seemed to swell with his pulse as it raced through the large bump on his forehead. A trickle of blood ran the length of his nose, then dripped onto his hand.

To his side, Norris was sitting upright with his head hanging forward. His seatbelt had held him in place, but the window beside him had shattered.

There seemed to be a ring of blurred vision surrounding a tiny area of focus, and if Harvey stared in one place for too long, it felt as if two hands were crushing his eyeballs.

He blinked away the pain and felt for the seat in front of him to regain some kind of balance, and with his free hand, he unclipped his seatbelt. It was then that the acrid smoke watered his eyes, and a stinging heat found his legs.

The smell of petrol was strong and sweet, and brought with it a light-headed sensation and the desire to close his eyes.

He groped for the door handle, seeking fresh air, and his eyes focused enough for him to pull the lever. But nothing happened.

And the incessant whine continued to sing that single-note melody.

Every instinct he had was screaming at him to get out. To move away from the growing heat, but his body seemed to move in slow motion and his mind seemed to take time to decipher the few things his eyes focused on and merge them with memories, as if they were telling a story.

The speeding car.

Norris beside him, motionless.

The great hall with its walls of climbing ivy.

The driver's confidence.

The spray of fine, red mist.

The spin. The world had passed by in a dizzying blur.

Blue Eyes and his arrogance.

Alice in a cage.

"Alice."

His voice surprised him. It was barely a whisper, yet audible above the high-pitched whine.

He spoke again.

"Alice."

And as if in response, the pool of petrol that had drugged his already dazed mind took flame. Through the shattered windscreen, a bright orange haze roared up high, consuming the front of the car.

And the whining stopped.

His eyes focused on the driver's ruined body. The man's arm was twisted through the steering wheel and bent back on itself. His legs were either pulled to one side, out of Harvey's sight, or they had been ripped off entirely. Harvey couldn't be sure.

Nausea worked its way up Harvey's throat, its rising heat and bile threatening to spew out at the sight. The air was thin. There was almost nothing left to breathe but the toxic fumes.

He pulled at the door handle once more and leaned against

it. But nothing moved. He barged with his shoulder, but the door refused to move. In desperation, he leaned across Norris' unconscious body and tried his side, finding relief when the door gave with ease, and fresh, cool air touched his face. Norris' body felt soft and weak as he climbed across him. Harvey's hands found the forest floor, and his body followed in an unceremonious heap. Then instinct told him to roll, to escape. He rolled until the heat no longer teased at the cuts and abrasions on his legs, then he dragged himself to a tree.

The ringing in his ears had all but dissipated, and the only sound was the hungry flames searching for fuel and reaching for air. Harvey rolled onto his side. The Audi had crashed sideways into a tree. The driver hadn't stood a chance, as the front end had been torn from the rear. The car had stilled in such a way that Harvey could interpret the scene with ease. The large bump and wound on the right side of his head must have been from smashing against the glass on impact, and his door had jammed as the tree had crushed the car's frame. Norris had been mostly unscathed save for his head rolling around like a wrecking ball.

But the driver's body was mangled.

The plastic dashboard gave off thick, black smoke and the front of the car was filling, like a fog from hell. There were just moments before the entire car was engulfed in flames. Harvey rolled onto his front and dragged himself further away, burying his elbows into the soft ground and finding purchase on the wild grasses that littered the forest floor.

It was morbid curiosity that caused him to stop a few metres on. He turned to watch the flames devour the car, thinking only of how he would get back to Alice. How he would report that Blue Eyes' request had been fulfilled. But hope that he didn't have to give an account of how Norris had died.

The raging fire burned with fury. The dashboard spat

molten plastic that hissed with every drop and the flames licked at the interior roof lining.

And still Norris was motionless.

The thump of a helicopter broke the sound of the fire's audible consumption, like the beating heart of something wild, free and unseen.

He could run. He *should* run. He needed to get away. The canopy of trees above was thick enough to conceal him. Nobody need know he had been there. The reports would say two men died in a car crash. There would be no mention of a third. Norris would be identified, and Blue Eyes would free Alice. He would have to. Harvey would not play his games anymore.

He scrambled to his feet, using the tree for balance, and the sudden urgency kicked his heart into a new gear. A warm injection of adrenalin found his fingertips and, for the first time since the car had left the tarmac, Harvey felt alive.

Until a single cough came from within the raging fire.

Harvey stopped, his body poised to run, his eyes focused on the trees ahead, and his ears attuned to the approaching helicopter. And in his mind, he saw only Alice.

"Help," said the voice.

It was followed by a sickly cough, fluid and guttural. And then panic. Harvey turned to find Norris beating at the burning seat in front of him. He started to scream. It was the scream of a man whose every waking fear was alive in glorious and savage brutality. Through the trees one hundred metres away, a car cruised by, then slowed.

Norris screamed louder, unable to move. The shock of the crash had stunned his body, and the fear that coursed through him pinned him to his seat.

The car on the road stopped. A single flash of blue light found its way through the dense trees.

Harvey had to move.

Above the trees, the helicopter was circling. The thick canopy blocked his view but there was no mistaking the thundering rotor blades as they thumped the air.

Norris held out a hand. His face was twisted away from the heat, but his eyes were wide with terror. "Help me," he called, as the first officer made his way into the forest.

The instinct to run was strong. But the police would save Norris. Blue Eyes would find out, and Alice would suffer.

Harvey cursed.

Using the car as cover, he dragged himself closer to the heat.

"Hurry," called Norris, as the seat before him took flame.

Thick smoke now billowed from inside the car and his face was ghostly as he peered out, groping blindly for help.

Harvey lay close to the ground. He saw the officer's heavy boots running. Eighty metres.

He reached up and found Norris' hand. For a second, there was gratitude at the human touch. There was hope in the way he squeezed weakly at Harvey's fingers. But Harvey reached for his wrist. He tugged at the old man, pulling him from the car. Norris seemed unable to move his legs. The upper half of his body emerged, and with his free arm, Harvey reached up and clamped his hand over the man's mouth. He pulled him close until they were face to face, and Harvey whispered, "Say a word, and I'll leave you to burn."

Norris' eyes were wide with terror and shock. His trembling body was cold, despite the ferocious fire from which Harvey had pulled him. The officer's boots were just fifty metres away, kicking through thick brush to reach the inferno.

Harvey worked his right arm around Norris, cradling him beneath his feeble arms. He climbed to one knee, braced, and keeping the car between them and the approaching policemen, he dragged Norris away.

He dragged Norris through a bed of nearby nettles and into

a wall of thorns and thicket, where the tendrils of life climbed high in a perpetual battle for light.

They crashed through the wall of thorns, and Harvey fixed the hole they had made to conceal their route. Ahead of them was a shallow drop into thick forest. Behind them, the shouts of police and flashing blues. And above them, the thundering helicopter drowned out the fury of the fire.

As the officers surrounded the car, searching the blaze for life, Harvey turned, reached for Norris, and heaved. Together, they tumbled down the shallow bank, out of sight, and out of options.

TWENTY-ONE

Firefighters were quick to react. They arrived just as Hawes was parking behind the two police cars that had been first to the scene. The crew jumped from the cab of the engine and two of the men scrambled into the forest with fire extinguishers, leaving four more behind to prepare the hoses.

Debruin and Hawes followed the firemen, keen not to get in the way. The blaze was visible through the trees, and thick smoke filled the canopy above them. They found the police officers a few metres from the burning wreck, shielding their faces, covering their mouths with their sleeves, and inching closer to reach the man behind the wheel.

"Get back," called the first of the firemen, taking control as he opened up the fire extinguisher through the shattered driver-side window. The flames abated a little, but not nearly enough for any man to get closer. Behind Debruin, two more firemen crashed through the trees carrying a rolled-up hose, and another followed.

Seeing the firemen in action, Debruin stepped forward to the police officers, grabbed the largest of them by the shoulder, and coaxed them back out of the way. Their faces had been blackened by the acrid smoke and their eyes shone like white diamonds in the walls of a dark cave. The smallest of them dry heaved and coughed. Debruin nodded for Hawes to help.

"Get them to the roadside, ready for the ambulance," he said. "There's nobody alive in there."

Hawes did as Debruin requested. He was halfway to the car with an arm around one of the policemen, when he glanced over his shoulder at the smouldering ruin of the Audi, and for a second, Debruin thought he saw something in his expression; it was doubt. He glanced across at Debruin for the tiniest of moments but couldn't meet his stare.

"Get back, sir," said one of the firemen, a large man with broad shoulders and a baritone voice that carried over the crackles of the flames and shouts of chaos. He urged Debruin to step backwards, leading him to a spot thirty metres from the blaze. And as if he expected Debruin to get closer, he stayed there, as the huge diesel pumps fired up, the hoses filled, and the remaining firemen braced for the powerful spray.

At first, the fierce jet of water only served to anger the fire. Flames reached up into the treetops in a huge cloud of hissing steam, like the agonised throes of a wounded beast. The fire fought back, searching for air and fuel as far as it could reach. But the firemen were skilled. They tamed the tenacious and hungry flames as they licked the forest limbs, burned the barks of trees, and sucked the stale air into the raging inferno. Another hose was reeled in. The ground was a fog of thick smoke and steam. Only the hardy shapes of the courageous men and the tall, sturdy trees were visible through the cloud. They encircled the Audi, bringing the blaze under control with astute professionalism.

From the roadside, Hawes pushed through the trees, holding branches back for two men to follow. They carried a stretcher and wore the bright green coveralls of ambulance men. They waited beside Debruin, watching the men at work.

Nobody said a word.

Debruin wondered if, by some chance, any of the men at the scene knew who the driver was. He considered if, by some chance, they knew that the charred and twisted remains belonged to a serial killer so cruel and cunning, his murders would make their blood run cold.

He doubted it.

And as the firemen used the jaws of life to tear the car door off, and the driver's stiffened limbs were untangled from the wreck, he considered what those hands had been capable of.

The killer was by far the deadliest man Debruin had ever pursued. He would have liked to stare into his eyes, across the cold, hard interview room desk. He would have liked the chance to learn about why he did what he did, and even more so, how he had stayed one step ahead.

His body was still smoking when they laid him on the gurney. A fireman spat at the stench, holding back the vomit that Debruin knew to be rising in his throat. The ambulance men carried the body away from the car and set it down a few feet from Debruin. He had expected to see an expression of agony etched onto the man's shriveled face. But there was none. The skin on his face had been burned away, and all that remained were black layers of muscle and bone like a grotesque, deformed piece of art. The man's mouth was open, but not wide like he had been screaming. In fact, the more Debruin studied the features, the more he appeared to be sleeping. The skin on the man's chest and arms had melted away to the bone, charred matte black but with a shiny texture where the sinew remained. The bones on the man's left arm were smooth, but the right arm had what appeared to be a deformity, like a growth. It almost looked like a weld on the bone. His arms had been wrapped around the wheel, taking the full force of the fire. But he hadn't felt a thing.

"The crash killed him," he said out loud.

"Probably," said one of the ambulance men, surprising Debruin with his response.

"He didn't even suffer."

"Dead on impact, I imagine," the ambulance man concurred, visibly disturbed at why Debruin would have wanted him to suffer.

"And the other one?" he asked, looking between them and the still smoking car.

They looked at each other, confused. It was the older of the two that replied. He had a thick Yorkshire accent, reminding Debruin of an actor in a comedy show that his wife watched after she had put Grace to bed.

"There's nothing left in there, sir."

"What do you mean?" said Debruin, and he left them, approaching the car with his hand over his mouth to suppress the sickening stench. Two firemen were working on the car, but the smoke was clearing. Debruin stood between them as they leaned in, using foam extinguishers to keep the small and stubborn flames from growing larger. One of them saw him and called out to a colleague.

"Jackson, I asked you to keep the area clear."

"I'm a detective," said Debruin, and he fumbled for his ID.

"You should know better then. Can you get back? The fuel tank is still full. The bloody thing could go up any minute."

But the man's words fell on deaf ears. The rear seat was empty. The foot wells were clear. He ran around to the far side. There was no sign of Norris.

"Sir, I'm going to have to ask you to–"

"Open the boot," said Debruin, not letting the man finish what he had to say.

"What?"

"The boot. Open it," Debruin positioned himself to see the contents. He looked up at the bemused fireman. "There's a man inside."

"Jackson, irons. Now," he called, and a young fireman came to the man's side. The older man issued a command that even Debruin followed. "Stand back."

The fireman jammed the shorter end of the crowbar into the panel gap, located the lock, then heaved. The boot lid opened with ease to reveal an immaculate space that even the raging fire had yet to consume.

It was empty.

The fireman gave Debruin a confused and bitter look, then turned to his colleagues and tossed the iron to the ground. "Clear the area. I want thirty metres." He left the boot lid open and resumed suppressing the smaller, stubborn flames. He stopped before bending into the car and he pointed a gloved index finger at Debruin. "And get him out of here."

The younger fireman offered Debruin a sorrowful expression. He raised his hand as if to coax him away, but Debruin brushed him off and stepped away. It didn't make sense. Unless Norris had been dropped off somewhere. Or had escaped.

He strode over to the paramedics, who had seen the entire episode.

"Do we have an ID?" he asked.

As if expecting the question, the older of the two produced a leather wallet. It was charred and stiff from the flames but opened easily and the driver's license was melted at the edges, but mostly intact.

"Hawes?" he called out, waving the wallet, and his dubious colleague made his way towards them.

"Positive ID, sir?"

"Trevor Banks," said Debruin, and he tossed the wallet at

him. "I'll travel with the body to the mortuary and I'll do some digging on the deceased. In the meantime, get on your radio. I want you to get a perimeter set up."

"Sir?" said Hawes, confused.

"Norris isn't in here. Which means he's out there somewhere. Clear it with DSI Barnes, and get traffic involved, and dogs too." Debruin stepped up to the top of the low rise. The ground dipped in front of him in a shallow bank, and a wall of trees hid anything and everything from view. "He's out there somewhere," he said. "He's out there, and I want him found."

TWENTY-TWO

Forest brush tore at Harvey's face. But the air was cool and fresh. Every lungful cleaned his airways, and every step away from the melee of emergency services led Harvey and Norris closer to safety. They were a kilometre from the crash site when Harvey spotted a thicket of heavy brush at the edge of the forest. Beyond the bushes were open fields. Tall, bright yellow rape danced in the breeze, and the border of wildflowers gave a balance of colour to the scene, which at any other time might have been glorious.

But right there and then, Harvey had other things on his mind.

He threw Norris down into the copse, checked behind them to make sure they hadn't been followed, and surveyed the open land.

Norris rolled, groaned, and turned to face Harvey, wide-eyed with fear. He backed away, pulling at grass roots for purchase. He watched Harvey from the ground, his face bloodied and bruised from the crash, then he tended his swollen ankle, raising his trouser leg to inspect the damage.

On the far side of the field, a distance of five hundred

metres, a small lane ran left to right. The rooftop of a small passing car was just visible above the hedgerow. Harvey traced the lane and the hedgerow to the corner of the field, where a small barn had been erected. Between the forest and the field was a drainage ditch. The water was dark and murky with reeds growing along the steep, six-foot bank.

"Can you walk?" asked Harvey.

"Who are you?" said Norris, ignoring Harvey's question.

Harvey didn't reply. His keen hearing had tuned into the forest, and every so often, he thought he heard a man's voice from the crash site carried by the breeze.

"We need to get across the field. Can you walk?"

He eyed Harvey with suspicion, then muttered, "With help."

Harvey closed the distance between them, and Norris braced to back away, until Harvey held out his hand.

"You're him, aren't you?" said Norris. "You're the killer the detective was on about."

Harvey retracted his hand, then locked stares with Norris.

"You've got two options. You can come with me or I can cut your throat right here. I don't mind which, just make a decision, or I'll do it for you."

Norris gave a laugh, yet his expression remained tortured. He glanced back in the direction they had come, as if he was contemplating what lay in store for him.

"Don't you see, you fool?" he said, and turned to face Harvey. "I'm dead already. One way or another, I'm dead. You might as well just kill me here."

Harvey pulled his knife from his jacket and took two steps towards Norris. He stood over him, his fingers falling into the familiar grooves on the hand-carved, wooden grip.

With his free hand, he reached down and gripped Norris by the scruff of his shirt. The old man steeled himself, preparing for the pain that was sure to follow. The blade teased at Norris' throat.

It was the bark of a dog that halted the action. Norris' eyes followed the sound, then returned to Harvey, almost pleading for him to go through with it.

"Do it," he hissed, but his lower lip trembled as he sucked in a breath.

Another dog barked, closer than before.

Harvey pulled him to his feet and shoved Norris through the brush. He stumbled and slipped, then rolled down into the ditch below. Harvey followed close behind and clamped his hand on Norris' mouth before he could cry out. He pulled Norris to his feet and helped him wade through the thigh-deep water. Thick mud sucked at Harvey's boots and, to Norris' credit, he offered little in the way of complaint. They emerged from the ditch one hundred metres away. Harvey pulled the old man out and together they crawled to the tall rape.

He checked behind them. The dogs were loud now, closer than before. They would find the copse and the dogs would lead them to the ditch, but then they would lose the scent. Before Norris could complain, Harvey had whipped Norris' shoe off. He stood, adopted a wide stance, and threw the boot in the opposite direction to throw the dogs off. He chanced a look around them, seeing the landscape above the crop. He saw the old barn five hundred metres away and with a little coaxing, together they crawled. When Norris faltered, tired and in pain, Harvey helped him along. A few times, they disturbed nesting lapwings. It was only then that Harvey stopped. He waited a full minute, listening to see if their pursuers had spotted the frightened birds, then moved on.

By the time they reached the far edge of the field, Norris was broken. He could barely drag his aged body another metre.

The helicopter that had hovered above the crash site passed

over them. But Harvey stilled. He used the crop as cover and watched them continue their search elsewhere.

"Wait here," said Harvey.

It was clear by the look on Norris' face that he had neither the strength nor gumption to run.

The barn was a fifty metre dash across open ground. The country lane that Harvey had spotted was close by, shielded only by an untamed hedgerow, and the helicopter had passed overhead. Dogs barked at the edge of the forest. It was now or never.

Keeping to a crouch, Harvey pushed himself up, and ran to the barn. He stopped behind the cover of an old oil drum to check behind him. Norris was peering out of the tall crop after him. There was activity at the edge of the forest, but nobody had ventured into the field, and the helicopter was searching an area to the north of the forest. Harvey prepared to make the final dash. He spied the open barn door and had taken just two steps when, above the hedgerow, the shiny roof of a black van flashed in the sunlight.

He stumbled, but stayed upright, and emerged from his crouch, sprinting to the barn.

The van's engine slowed, then stopped.

Harvey drew his knife and lay flat against the old, wooden wall.

He glanced inside the barn. It was empty save for hay bales and a corroded digger attachment. There were no hand tools, or anything Harvey could use as a weapon. But the place was dry and secure. It would serve its purpose.

The van door opened and was closed with care not to make a noise.

Harvey neither saw nor heard sign of anybody. With just the barn between him and the van, the driver, one of Blue Eyes' men, could come from any direction. Harvey made his way clockwise around the barn, knife in hand ready to defend himself.

He edged along the barn wall towards the lane, taking care not to make a noise. He reached the corner of the building and saw the shiny, black Mercedes in all its glory. It was the correct van, of that Harvey was sure.

An image of Alice trussed with ropes sprang to mind, and his fingers tightened on the knife.

He doubled back, edging his way to the front of the barn. The helicopter was still far away and there was no movement at the edge of the forest.

But the spot where he had left Norris was empty.

Harvey took a step forward, checking the horizon. Nothing moved.

He stepped in front of the open barn door, and all hopes of rescuing Alice faded away. One of Blue Eyes' men stood tall and proud, and on his knees before him, looking guilty as sin, was Samuel Norris.

TWENTY-THREE

The mortuary at Queen's Hospital in nearby Romford was a modern facility. The walls were immaculate. The floor was so clean it shone, reflecting the bright, fluorescent tubes. The benches and examination tables were polished stainless steel and the pathologist greeted them with the manners of a man who spent most of his day with the deceased.

The ambulance men needed no direction. They wheeled the gurney into the premises and together they manoeuvred the remains of Trevor Banks onto the examination table. The pathologist, who they referred to as Churchill behind his back, was unsmiling, cold, and had an accusing stare. The nickname, Debruin deduced, was due to the man's size, grim expression, and his uncanny resemblance to Britain's best-loved Prime Minister. In Debruin's mind, all he needed to do was replace the white smock with a three-piece suit and swap his pen for a fat cigar, and the transformation would have been complete.

The paramedics asked the pathologist for a signature, which he provided without question, and the oldest of the two ambulance men nodded a good luck to Debruin. He waited beside the stainless steel table, readying himself for the sight.

"We'll need a positive ID," said Debruin. "If there's anything we can save. Prints, teeth, hair."

"Chance will be a fine thing," said Churchill. "Teeth maybe, but prints and hair? Nothing but dust and the wind, I'm afraid."

"You haven't even opened the body bag."

"I've been doing this job for forty years, detective..." He waited for Debruin to complete the sentence.

"Debruin. Detective Inspector Mark Debruin."

"Well, Mark," Churchill continued, as he searched for the zipper on the bag. "I can tell you now that the only way you'll positively ID this body will be from the teeth."

He pulled open the bag, and the smell hit Debruin in the eyes and mouth; it was a double shot of foulness that he wasn't prepared for.

In the forest, Banks' body had been swathed in shadow, and the burning car had added a familiarity to the stench of death – burned plastics, material, and oil. But in the clinical facilities of the mortuary, there was no escaping the smell once Churchill had opened the bag.

Debruin offered a mumbled excuse and made his way towards the double doors on the far side of the room, much to Churchill's obvious amusement.

He savoured the fresh air, saw a nearby hand-washing basin, and spat. He rinsed his mouth with fresh water and washed his hands. It was while he was drying his hands with a paper towel that he saw the pay phone that had been fixed to the wall at the end of the corridor. Two nurses moved from room to room, oblivious to Debruin. It was only when he had moved to the pay phone that they even acknowledged his presence with a polite, "Good afternoon."

He dialled a number from memory, then, when prompted, he dialled the extension. The call was answered before the third ring.

"Hello," she said.

"Charlotte, it's Mark." He used first names with the civilian support staff. They responded better when spoken to as a human.

"Oh, hi. I have the information you asked me–"

"Not now. I'll come and see you. I need you to look up a name for me."

"Okay," she said, and Debruin imagined her preparing a space in her notepad.

"Trevor Banks," said Debruin. "Male. Caucasian. Driver's license has his date of birth as June the sixth, sixty-eight."

"Okay," she said again, and he imagined her bubble writing with the little circles above the i's. "Anything in particular?"

"Anything you can. Address. Spouse. Children."

"I'll do my best, Mark."

"I know you will," said Debruin. "Thanks, Charlotte. Call me back on this number."

He was about to hang up when he thought of something.

"Oh, Charlotte?" he said.

"Yes. Still here," she said, preoccupied with noting down the number on the caller ID readout.

"I need to identify his body."

She was silent for a moment, and Debruin was unsure if he'd struck on the part of the job she didn't enjoy, or if she was just penning more bubbles.

"Leave it with me," she said, offering no clue as to which it had been.

He replaced the handset and stared at the double doors at the end of the corridor. He'd seen bodies before. It was part of the job. Only a handful had been warm and soft. Those were the saddest to deal with. Most had been cold and hard, almost inhuman. There had also been the time a dog walker had stumbled across human bones in a field. But the charred remains of Trevor Banks trumped them all in terms of the sickness he felt.

Debruin had witnessed his victims' bodies. He had seen the terrible things the man had done.

The clinical walls and floors with sparse furniture offered Debruin a rare opportunity to think with clarity. A clutter-free thought process, whereby he could piece elements together.

He leaned against the wall beside the phone and pulled out his notepad. He tapped his pen on the spine as he tried to break the pieces down in his mind.

He began with a single word, scribbled at the top of the page.

Leak.

Debruin was the prime suspect for being the leak. He wasn't. He knew he wasn't. Until that morning, he hadn't even been aware there was a leak. Somebody was informing a gang of criminals of police operations. But why?

It had to be someone in touch with the guy Carver had sent in undercover. He wrote a name to one side of the page.

DS Butler.

He rested his head against the wall and let the bright lights clear his mind. Someone was feeding Butler information. It had to be someone involved in Debruin's case. Nobody else had known about the Hammersley sting. Nobody else had known about Slater, the killer's previous victim. Nobody except Hawes. And only two people had known he was going to see Norris.

"Damn it," he whispered, not enjoying one of the two options as he scrawled the name.

Hawes.

A pang of disappointment curled its bony fingers around Debruin's stomach.

And then a thought struck him. The killer was dead, and Norris was missing. The killer's death meant that Debruin's involvement in Carver's case was over. And if his involvement in the case was over, he had no way of proving himself innocent.

How had the killer known Norris was going to be on that street at that time?

He considered the events of the day from Hargreaves' perspective. The sly, cunning, and intuitive mind of a man who enjoyed watching others suffer for his own benefit would manipulate the facts to suit his theory. The evidence was far from irrefutable, but even so, it swayed in Hargreaves' favour. Debruin had visited Norris and had let Norris escape, which in turn had led to the killer being in the right place at the right time. Again.

The coincidence was uncanny. The evidence was stacking against him. Somebody was leaking information.

But he wasn't the leak. The real leak had to have something to gain.

Hawes.

He had never mentioned needing money, and as far as Debruin knew, the man had no problems. But Hawes had known who Carver was. During the debrief, he had said he had worked in the same station as him.

Was Hawes setting Debruin up? He thought of everything Hawes had told him. During the car ride earlier, he had suggested the entire department doubted Debruin's ethics.

The telephone startled him. There was something eerie about a pay phone ringing. Something sinister. He collected the handset and waited for her to speak.

"Sir?" she said.

"Charlotte, what did you find?"

The sound of papers being turned was loud and clear in the lull.

"Trevor Banks. Nineteen Carlisle Way, Romford."

"I know the road," said Debruin, and he waited for more information, keen to build on the picture he was forming.

"He's not married, but the electoral register shows a Joanna Ford living at the same address. Possibly a girlfriend. No kids."

"Okay, thanks," he said. "Did you find anything else?"

He was respectful of the young girl's emotions and avoided dipping his toe into a conversation that would force him to mention the manner in which the man had died, and the state of his remains.

"Banks was a delivery driver. A white van man."

A self-employed delivery driver fitted the killer's profile. He would have the freedom to hunt his victims.

"He did a three-year sentence in Her Majesty's Prison Belmarsh for assisting an armed robbery. He was released five years ago in ninety-six."

An armed robbery didn't really fit the profile, other than to highlight the man's willingness to go against the law. But Belmarsh was where Carver had said that Ebenezer Bloom, the only man in contact with Spider, had served. White was reading her printed report. Debruin waited for her to finish.

"He received a three-month extension to his sentence following an affray with another inmate."

"So, he's a fighter, is he? A brawler with a temper." He was speaking out loud and silenced, remembering that White was a researcher, not somebody to bounce his ideas off. But in light of Hawes' actions, she was the only one he could verbalise his thoughts to.

"During which," she continued, "Banks suffered a broken arm."

"A broken arm?" said Debruin, his eyebrows raised in hope.

"Two clean breaks to the humerus," she finished.

Debruin remembered the deformity on the dead man's arm.

"That's a positive ID on the body. I'll pay the girlfriend a visit," he said with a sigh. "I'll break the news and see what I can find."

White said nothing. She waited for Debruin to issue another request.

"Regarding what we spoke about earlier," said Debruin, "I know you have people beside you so don't mention any names. I don't want anyone to know about this. Not yet anyway. Just give me yes or no answers."

"Okay," she said, with a little hesitation in her voice.

"Debt?" he said.

"A little."

"Above average?"

"No."

"Thank you, Charlotte."

"Sir?" she said, as Debruin was about to hang up, and he realised she had called him sir. She had called him sir at the beginning of the conversation too. Something wasn't right. Somebody was listening to what she was saying.

"Yes?"

"I'm not sure if I should say anything," she said, her voice quieter than it had been.

"If you're in doubt, then you probably shouldn't. That's sound advice there, Charlotte."

She was silent for a moment, as if considering if she should reveal what she had to say.

"How about I say it for you?" he said. "Is it Hargreaves?"

"Yes."

"Is he in Barnes' office?"

"Yes."

"Are they looking for me?"

She said nothing. To confirm it would implicate her. So, Debruin verbalised his worst nightmare.

"Hargreaves has convinced Barnes that I'm the leak on the back of what happened today, and I'm going to be charged."

Again, she said nothing, but her silence said everything that needed to be said.

"Have they scrambled TSG to bring me in?"

"Yes."

By scrambling TSG, he could assume that Barnes and Carver considered him a risk of flight, or worse. As far as they were concerned, he was involved with dangerous men. They would be taking no chances.

"Take care, Charlotte."

He replaced the phone, but clung to it for a few seconds, staring at the notepad in his hand.

Hawes.

The skin on his tired face tightened and his throat was as dry as a desert. He didn't need to go back inside the mortuary. He had seen the damage to the man's arm. It was the break that White had mentioned. It was all the positive ID Debruin needed, and he was loathe to go back and talk to Churchill.

A sign on the ceiling directed people to the mortuary one way, and in the opposite direction, the sign directed people to outpatient services. Debruin pushed the doors towards the outpatient services and was immediately met by a hive of activity. Rubber-soled nurses moved in silence, and when they spoke, the language was short and concise. Nobody paid Debruin any notice. He followed the signs to the fire exit, leading him around a corner and into the main hospital reception.

It was there that he realised the consequences of the day amounted to nothing. It was there he realised that something far more serious than losing his job was about to change his life.

"Julie?" he called.

TWENTY-FOUR

"It looks to me like you're trying to escape," said the man.

He was over six feet by at least two inches. His shoulders were broad, and his body had the shape of a man who took care of himself. He wore a full beard that he trimmed to a neat fur, and his dark eyes glistened in the dark of the barn.

"He gave you an order," he said, and he nudged Norris forward with his knee to reveal a steel-wire garrotte around the older man's throat.

"I don't take orders," said Harvey.

"He gave you a job to do, and you haven't done it."

The man's voice was angry, almost emotional.

"So, you do it then. It looks like you're halfway there already."

"It has to be you," he said. "I can't."

"So, if you can't do it, let him go."

The man sighed. His body tensed, but his voice lost its strength.

"He has to die. It can't be me."

"And you're here because?"

Harvey left the question hanging. The man's agitation was

growing. He would make a mistake soon, and Harvey would tear him apart.

"I'm here because he sent me."

"Who did?"

"You know who."

"Blue Eyes?"

He nodded. "You have to do it. You have to do what he says."

"And if I don't?"

The man's hands were trembling. He rubbed his forehead with the tips of his fingers in frustration.

"You have to," he said. "You have to do what he says."

Norris stared at the floor in despondence. The steel garrotte created a fold in his neck, but he seemed oblivious to the discomfort.

Harvey took a step inside the barn.

"There are police everywhere. How did you get through?"

The man manoeuvred Norris between Harvey and himself. A human barrier.

"Just do what he asked so we can get out of here."

"How did you find us?" asked Harvey, ignoring the man's pleas. He wanted the agitation to grow, to consume him.

"The car. It has a tracker." The man refused to stare Harvey in the eye. He focused on Norris, who said nothing and waited for death to arrive by anybody's hand.

"*Had* a tracker," Harvey corrected him.

The man with the garrotte stared, his eyes widening as a realisation dawned on him.

"Where's Banks?"

Harvey shrugged. "Who's Banks?"

"Banks," said the man. "What have you done with him?"

It was clear there was an affinity between the man and the driver of the Audi. Something shared. A friendship, or something stronger.

"I burned him alive."

"You fool," said the man, and his body snapped rigid. The garrotte tightened, and with his knee pressed against Norris' back, he pulled tight. "You. You don't know what you've done."

Harvey took another step forward.

"Tighter," he whispered, enjoying the sight of the man's frustration growing. "They're probably pulling his burned body from the car right now. I imagine they'll have to snap his charred bones to get him out."

"Stop."

"The smell must be horrendous."

"No."

"Have you ever smelled burning flesh?"

He took another step.

"No more. Don't come any closer."

"Or what? You'll kill him?" said Harvey. "Be my guest."

"You don't understand."

There were tears in the man's eyes. He was close to breaking.

"It's sickly," said Harvey. "The smell of burnt flesh."

"Stop."

"It stays in the back of your throat. No matter how much you spit, you can't get rid of it."

"No more," he screamed, and a tear broke free from the man's eye.

Harvey smiled.

"Who is *he*? Who's running it?"

"He'll destroy us all."

"A name."

The man's demeanour stiffened. A bitterness spread across his features, tightening, hardening, and twisting, as if he was speaking of the devil himself.

"Spider."

"Last name?"

"I don't know." The words were carried on a breath from the pit of the man's gut. "Nobody knows. Nobody has even seen him."

"So, who is Blue Eyes? The old man?"

"He's nothing. He's a puppet. Like me."

"And is Spider expecting you to return to him with news of Norris?"

He nodded.

"And what happens if you don't?"

Again, those wild eyes widened, then narrowed to reveal the man's inner strength. He let go of the garrotte and pushed Norris to one side, then adopted a wide stance, with his arms up and ready to take Harvey on.

"I will. One way or another."

Harvey remained relaxed. He turned to his left, and began to pace a few steps, enticing the man to make a move.

The lure worked. The man ran at him, issuing a low growl as he rushed forward, preparing to shoulder Harvey to the ground.

But Harvey was ready. He sidestepped and used the man's momentum to send him crashing into the wall.

"You're a joke," said Harvey, as the man scrambled to his feet. "You're weak."

The man tried again, but instead of trying to force Harvey down, he came at him with his guard up in the stance of a boxer. He threw two punches. One left, followed by a right hook, hoping to catch Harvey on the duck.

But the ruse was transparent. Harvey let the first left jab find its mark, and as the right hook arced around, Harvey twisted his arm, turned the man around, and launched him into the hay bales. He stumbled and fell, and while he was climbing to his feet, Harvey took two steps forward and hit him hard, once, a clean punch that bloodied the man's nose.

He fell back against the hay, his arms stretched out for purchase, then he backed himself into a corner, eyeing Harvey as he closed in.

In an instant, Harvey had the man by his throat with his left hand. With his right, he drew his knife, and as he dragged the man to his feet, coaxed by the tip of his blade, Harvey leaned in and stared the man in the eye.

"You're going down. You're all going down."

"He'll kill her," said the man. His spittle rested in his beard, and the whites of his eyes were criss-crossed with tiny, red arteries. "Your girl. He'll do it."

"Is that right?"

"Yes. He'll make her suffer. I've seen it before."

"Not for another eight hours," said Harvey. "eight hours to kill you and everyone who works for him. I like my chances."

"No. You don't have eight hours. He's expecting me back. He'll know something has happened. He'll be watching. He can track the van and the car. He'll know I found you. If you kill me, he'll hurt her."

"How long do I have?"

"I don't know. He'll be watching the van. He might even send others."

"I'll kill them too."

"You don't understand. You don't know what he's like."

"So, tell me."

He broke. The frustration. The weakness. The humiliation. It all combined to reduce the man to an emotional mess. The bearded man fell limp in Harvey's grip, forcing Harvey to squeeze harder and tighter, until he could feel the blood flowing through the man's neck and his racing pulse as it beat like a drum.

Harvey pressed the tip of the knife into his throat.

"You have five seconds to tell me what I'm up against."

"No, you don't understand."

"Five."

"All you have to do is kill him," he cried. "You can stop it."

"Four."

"He's a monster. Just kill him. Not me."

"Three."

"You're making a mistake."

"Two."

Harvey braced himself, ready to slice across the man's windpipe. The wooden grip sat in his hand as natural as could be.

"He'll kill us all."

"One."

"Stop," cried Norris, speaking for the first time. His voice carried with it an authority that surprised Harvey. There was more to the man than his weak and fumbling demeanour portrayed. "You have to stop. He's as innocent as you."

"How would you know?" asked Harvey.

There was a silence, and Harvey's patience was at breaking point.

"Because I was like him once," he said. "I worked for Spider."

TWENTY-FIVE

"What are you doing here?" said Julie. She turned away from the doctors to face him, and in that instant, he saw something he hadn't seen since the day they were married. In those wide, scared eyes was a beauty so natural and pure. For years, it had been hidden by the ups and downs of Debruin being married to the force. The sleepless nights worrying, the long and drawn-out cases, and the lies she had endured, when her husband had tried to hide the grim truth of society from her.

But right there, in that very instant, she was as beautiful as the day they had met.

He didn't answer. He pulled her close and held her, resting his lips on the top of her head and holding her tight, the way she liked to be held.

"Where is she?" he whispered, more to the doctors than to Julie. "I want to see her."

The first doctor, a mature lady wearing thick-rimmed glasses, a loose, light blue blouse, and dark trousers gave a discreet nod to her younger colleague. The younger lady, who wore a nurses' uniform with plain white sneakers, stepped up to the mark.

"Follow me," she said, somehow managing to convey authority and empathy into those two words.

Julie peered up at Debruin from within his embrace but could not hold his gaze.

"I don't know if I can," she said, and she buried her face in Debruin's chest.

"You can wait in my office," said the doctor. "I'll bring you a cup of tea and when your husband joins us, we can discuss the options."

"Does that sound like a plan?" said Debruin, offering his wife a weak smile.

She nodded, then turned to follow the nurse and the doctor, reaching behind for Debruin's hand. The corridors were as clean and clinical as the mortuary had been, and the nurses and staff moved in silent grace.

But the scenery proved less of a distraction than the mortuary had. He stopped at the doorway to the nurse's office, kissed Julie on the cheek, and gave her a loving squeeze.

"No matter what happens," he whispered, "she'll be okay. I promise."

She pulled away, unable to hear him offer weak promises, and the nurse led him along the corridor. He tried to keep track of the signs and the left and right turns, but in the end, he could do little but follow her through the maze. He was so lost in the swirl of possibilities but when she eventually stopped beside the door to the paediatric ward, so small and pretty, her eyes told him all he needed to know.

What he would see inside the room would not be easy to deal with.

He inhaled through his nose and braced himself.

In his career, he had witnessed more gruesome sights than most people ever have to see in their lifetimes. From road traffic accidents, knife fights, and even a gunshot wound once that had torn a man's arm off. Only that morning, he had watched as paramedics had pulled a man's burnt body from a car fire. The flesh had been melted away to the bone, and it was, in Debruin's opinion, perhaps the most hideous and pitiful sight he had ever seen.

But when he stepped inside the little private room and saw his little angel on the bed, everything else fell away into the shadows. He knew then that he would never, ever forget the sight. She was unconscious, but stable. Tubes ran from her nose, her arm, and from beneath the sheets into a multitude of devices. The light was low and the blind was drawn, and somehow, despite the activity outside, the room was still and quiet.

"Would you like a few minutes?" the nurse asked.

"Thank you."

She left the room, and the only noise was the sound of the machines keeping Grace alive. The suck and blow of the ventilator. The beeps of the heart monitor. It was a tragic sight that tore Debruin's heart.

There was a chair in the corner, but he didn't use it. He dropped to his knees beside the bed and for the first time in as long as he could remember, he came the closest he had ever come to praying.

It wasn't really a prayer. He wouldn't have known how to pray, or what to say. But he had to say something. He had to ask somebody for help, and he had to say something out loud, something for Grace to hear in her subconscious. Something to keep her fighting, until he could work out a plan.

He was conscious of movement in the corridor outside. People passed by the window of her small room, but Debruin kept his head down. It was his time with his little girl.

"I don't know if you can hear me," he said, and a tear formed in the corner of his eye. He blinked it away. He had to be strong for his little girl. He wondered if he should look up to the heavens, or if he could be heard regardless. "I don't even know if what I have to say will make sense. But I have to say it. I haven't been an honest man. I've lied, I've cheated, and I've climbed on the backs of others when I should have helped them along. I know that now. Sometimes a man needs to experience the rough to learn where he went wrong. That was me. I was one of those men and I'm not afraid to admit it. But I'm also not afraid to help others. I do a good job. It hasn't all been bad. I hope you see that. I hope you can see that although I might have strayed, my wife, she hasn't. She's a saint. In all my short life, I have never met anybody as kind and generous as her. She doesn't deserve this. And my little girl, she doesn't deserve this either. I don't know if she's in pain. I don't know what's going on inside her body. I don't understand it. I tried, but I just can't see how a beautiful, innocent girl like her can be made to suffer, and I know in your heart, you feel the same. Whatever it is that's doing this, give it to me. Give her a chance at life. That's all I ask."

He'd said all he had to say to whoever or whatever was listening, and he felt no better for it. He remained on his knees and opened his eyes to look at his little girl.

"Grace," he said, "I'm talking to you now. I need you to listen to me, your father. Just this once, I need you to hear my voice. I can hear yours. I can hear what you said this morning, and yesterday, and all the days. I can hear it all, but by God I'd do anything to hear you again."

He dropped his head onto the bed. He tried to fight the tears, but they came so fast and so hot, they burned.

He sobbed out loud, stared up at the ceiling, then cleared his throat. A deep breath calmed him for a few seconds, but the wave of emotions was riding high. He dizzied and lowered his face to the soft sheet.

"For Mummy, Grace. Hang in there for Mummy. She needs you."

He rested his chin on his hands and stared up at her.

"Do you remember what I said this morning? Do you remember what I said, Grace? I'm going to work it out. I'll find a way to get you fixed. I promise I will. You just hang in there, okay?"

He reached out to touch her hand. Her skin was warm and soft. Her hands were delicate. He had always marvelled at how delicate she had been.

"Such a beautiful girl," he said. "Daddy will get you fixed."

He lingered for a few moments and thought of Julie. He didn't know what he would say to her. He'd think of something. He just needed to buy some time.

He stood, gave his daughter one last look, and wondered if it would be the last time he saw her alive. With that thought, he gave her a gentle kiss on the forehead. He wiped his eyes and cleared his throat again, then turned to find Julie in the doorway.

"Did you hear that?" he asked eventually.

She nodded.

"Everything?"

"Enough."

TWENTY-SIX

Outside, the world was still. The helicopter was nowhere to be seen, the smoke from the fire no longer rose from the treetops, and there were no police hunting the edge of the forest.

"It's quiet," said Harvey, moving toward the door.

"Not for long," said the man with the beard.

"Tell me everything."

Norris, with his renewed strength, seemed taller. He paced the room, not with agitation, but to think. It reminded Harvey of his foster father, John Cartwright. He would pace with his hands behind his back, mulling over a problem to the slow but sure rhythm that the heels of his shoes made on the wooden floor.

"If I tell you, there's no turning back," said Norris. "I don't know who you are, but I can guess why Spider wanted you."

Harvey didn't reply.

"Is it really you? The man from the papers? The killer?"

Harvey didn't reply. He wouldn't let Norris deviate. There wasn't time.

There was pity in Norris' eyes. He stopped pacing and stared at Harvey as a peer, unafraid.

"Who is it?" asked Norris. "Who does he have?"

Harvey said nothing.

"He has somebody. Somebody close to you. Somebody innocent, is my guess. Your mother perhaps?" He paced a few steps. "No. No, you're motherless. A man like you has no mother. He has no real family. A sister? Or maybe a girl? Somebody special nonetheless."

"Be careful, Norris."

"Do you want to hear the truth?"

"Just tell me."

"In my own time. He has somebody close to your heart. You're not married. A man like you can't love. But you might try. You might tease yourself into thinking you can love. But you can't. What's her name?"

"It doesn't matter what her name is," said Harvey, revealing all he was prepared to reveal.

"Ah, she sounds sweet." Norris stopped again and thrust his hands into the pockets of his Barbour jacket. His back straightened and his shoulders seemed to rise as he inhaled. "You've condemned her. The poor girl. You might think she cares for you, but after this, if she survives, she'll never see you again. One of you will die, of that I'm sure."

"Just tell me what's happening, Norris."

"I am. You see, I'm helping you to understand what drives our friend here to do what he does, and what drove poor old Banks to do what he did."

He wasn't making sense. Harvey digested the information, picking at the pieces of the puzzle as Norris spoke.

"Do you understand?" said Norris.

Harvey stared past Norris to the bearded man, who still leaned against the hay bale, his face a picture of misery.

"He has someone of yours too?" said Harvey, incredulous at what he was hearing. "You're being forced to do this too?"

"They all are," said Norris, and the bearded man averted his moist eyes to blink away his tears. "It's the perfect set-up, for Spider at least. Nobody knows who he is. Everyone who works for him does so because of his power. With every person he recruits, his strength grows stronger and stronger. He has drivers, such as Banks, computer nerds, security experts, ex-military men, bankers. The list goes on. He can call on them at any time. He watches everything they do. No mistakes."

"Giggs," said Harvey, remembering the execution he'd seen that morning.

"Giggs?" Norris cocked his head to one side. "Russell Giggs is a journalist. He's the one who has the right stories printed in the paper at the right time. He's part of the web. Spider is a cunning man. He knows how to manipulate the world to suit his needs. Giggs' job is to create distractions, create hype, open spaces for the Spider to grow his web."

"Was," said Harvey, and Norris' eyes saddened.

"The explosion," he said. "It shone the light in the wrong places. I thought that when I read the story. He's dead, isn't he? He must have made a grave mistake."

Harvey didn't reply.

"And his wife too, I imagine. Sad news. You see, Spider likes to display his power to newbies, like you. It's how he maintains control. How he ensures that his victims follow the rules."

"And Blue Eyes?" said Harvey, searching for the final piece of the puzzle.

"Ebenezer Bloom. Convict through and through. He's spent more time inside than out, and as far as I know, he was the second of Spider's recruits. He's institutionalised now, though. Part of the furniture. He's the only conduit to Spider. You break Bloom, and you catch the Spider."

"So, he knows who Spider is?"

"Don't get ahead of yourself. He knows as much as anybody

else. The only difference is that Bloom can communicate with him."

It didn't make sense. How could somebody communicate with another person and never have met them? As if Norris had read Harvey's mind, he spoke, with a hint of admiration.

"SMS messages."

"The police can trace them though?"

"The police can trace them if they know the number. Otherwise it's all guesswork. He used pagers in my day," said Norris. "But I guess the times have moved on."

"So, Spider gives the orders via SMS–"

"And Bloom makes sure they are carried out."

"And anyone who fails or makes a mistake–"

"Is killed. Along with their wives, girlfriends, sons, daughters. Whoever."

"And if Bloom fails?"

"He suffers the same fate, although I don't know if he's even married."

"And Banks?"

"He was a driver," said the bearded man, speaking for the first time since Harvey had broken him. "It's all he knew. He was sent to prison for armed robbery. He was the driver. Bloom recruited him there. In Belmarsh."

"And his family? Did he have somebody?"

"If they aren't dead already, they will be soon enough."

"Why?" said Harvey.

"It's the ultimate motivation. Making a mistake and being killed is one thing, but if that means your loved one will be killed too, you'll not make that mistake so readily."

"And the rest of the team will see it if you do," said Harvey, as the cogs of the sick plan fell into place. Except one very important cog. "Why me?"

Norris smiled at the question, although the sincerity of the smile was compromised as he searched Harvey's eyes.

"You're a stone cold killer. Think about it. Forgive me if I'm wrong, I'm piecing this together as much as you are. You're a serial killer. You target sex offenders. Am I right?"

Harvey didn't reply.

"Well, let's assume you are," said Norris, seeing Harvey's reluctance to incriminate himself. "Your last three kills have been in the newspapers. I've been following with interest. And a healthy amount of fear," he added, and his throat rose and fell as he swallowed that fear. "Do you think it's a coincidence that your case has been publicised?"

Harvey said nothing. He digested the information as fast as it came.

"Do you think that maybe someone had something to do with your story?"

Norris raised his eyebrows, and his lower lip protruded, as if to gesture at a truth that Harvey had never considered.

"As a result, the police force, our boys in blue, have been forced to act. They've been hunting you down, while Spider has been feeding you with new victims. Slater and Hammersley. He's been learning who you are."

"Giggs?" said Harvey.

"You're cottoning on," said Norris. "Giggs makes sure the papers reveal the release of known sex offenders, and if he doesn't, his wife dies. Spider knows that you'll go in for the kill, and he lines up the police to come very close to catching you. Close enough for you to see how powerful he is. He has eyes everywhere."

"How does he line up the police?" said Harvey, finding a flaw in Norris' theory.

"All he needs is a policeman in his pocket," said Norris. "A man with a beautiful wife, and a family to protect. A man like DS Butler here."

The bearded man stepped out of the shadows, and Harvey pictured him in uniform.

"I imagine DS Butler here has someone on the inside. The two of them exchange information to suit Spider's plans. He's one step ahead of you. He's one step ahead of you all."

Butler offered no contest.

"And you?" said Harvey, bringing the incredible story back to Norris. "You said you worked for him. Why would he want a–"

"Sex offender?" Norris finished for him. And for the first time, Norris bore an expression of shame. "I worked for him. Do you remember how I told you that Bloom was the second man to be recruited?"

"You were the first?" said Harvey, incredulous at the thought.

"I was. I did something that men like Butler here can only dream of."

"You escaped."

"Not without casualty," said Norris. "For me to escape, I had to lose everything I had. My daughter, my life, my pride." He paused, his mouth open, ready to reveal what Harvey was already beginning to understand. "My freedom."

There was no need to interrupt. Norris' eyes were keen and narrowed. He was remembering a time. The full truth was coming and somehow Harvey knew it would be shocking.

"You didn't think I really did all those terrible things, did you?" he asked.

TWENTY-SEVEN

There's only so many times a man can tell himself to be strong. Be strong for your dying child. Be strong for your heartbroken wife. Be strong for your own pride; don't let them see you upset. But by the time Debruin had taken a seat in the doctor's office, his wife's face, the doctor's calm and professional tone, and the wall of books on the shelf behind her began to swirl in a dizzying haze.

The words they said, his wife and the doctor, amounted to nothing but a low hum. Only the very centre of his vision was in focus, and even that was like an abstract painting. He stared so hard at the doctor's lips that they became animated, like a cartoon. His peripheral was blurred, and it seemed as if all his visual sense was able to do was focus on those two puffy lips. He stared so hard that he saw beyond the flesh and forest of fine down on her top lip. Beyond that, her skin was pale and taut. It was like he was seeing every hair follicle, and the texture of her skin was leather, as if he was peering at it through a magnifying glass.

"Mr Debruin?" she said, and for an embarrassing moment, he recognised the shape of the words and her tone. She had said them before, and she said them again. "Mr Debruin, are you okay?"

"Yes," he said, blinking his way back to reality. "Yes."

"Mark, do you need a drink of water?" said Julie.

"Yes," he said, with nothing else to add.

She pulled a clear bottle from her handbag and passed it to him. She always carried water, and for years, Mark had wondered why. Surely she could wait until she got home. But he was grateful that she had it now.

"Did you hear what Doctor Lansdowne said?" asked Julie.

"Yes. No. Not all of it. I'm sorry. I've had rather a strange day."

"That's okay," the doctor began. "I was just trying to prepare you both. Grace has a serious condition. Treatment could take some time."

To her credit, Julie was holding it together. It was right then that Debruin should have been the strong one. It was her that should have been upset, and he should have been her rock.

"Is that it?" he asked.

The doctor was not impressed at his response. The pinks of her eyes shone from within deep sockets.

"I'm sorry. I mean, is that all I missed?"

"How long did you think you were gone for?" said Julie.

"I need some air. Do we have a diagnosis, doctor? Do we actually know what's wrong with her?"

It was then that the doctor referred to the blue file on her desk. It was a move that both Debruin and his wife had seen dozens of times in the past six months.

"As I understand it, Grace has been suffering for the past six months?" said the doctor, confirming what she was reading.

"Doctor?" said Debruin, and she peered up from the file. "Please close the file for a moment. I want to ask you a question."

She did so, but it was with reluctance. She gestured for Debruin to continue.

"We've seen specialists, doctors, nurses, and we've even done our own research. We know what's in that file better than you. It's all we've thought about for the past six months. You seem honest, and I don't mean to patronise you. I just mean, judging by what you've seen so far, not in the notes," he added, holding his hand out to stop her referring back to them, "what does your gut tell you?"

"I'm a doctor. We work with facts, Mr Debruin."

"I know. I'm a detective. I work with facts all day long. A gut feeling doesn't hold up in court. But sometimes I have to work with my gut to find the facts."

"Mr Debruin—"

"A hint. You must have an idea. You must have a hunch of what it is that's killing our daughter. I'm not going to hold you to it."

"I can't—"

"But you do have one?"

She said nothing.

"Sometimes, I have to do things I shouldn't," he said. "I have to work around the rules. Sometimes morality and the rules aren't parallel lines. The rules go one way and morals go the other. Sometimes I have to lean toward the morals. I have to find the loose thread. Only once I have the loose thread can I start pulling to find the answer." He leaned forward on the desk, and her pupils dilated when he met them. "Tell me, Doctor Lansdowne, is there a loose thread we can pull on? My daughter is dying in there."

She considered what he had said and glanced at the door. It was clear she was uncomfortable, but she empathised. She wore a wedding ring and an eternity ring. There was a good chance she was a mother.

"Stem cell," she said. There it was, out. "I'm pushing for tests."

"We've waited for tests for six months."

"Not these ones. I've only seen a case like this once before. She's pale, weak, and the seizures pose a risk."

"How long?"

"For the tests?"

"Does she have?"

"I don't know. Look, I've said too much already. You wanted a thread to pull at. That's it. That's what I'm pushing for. But I have to tell you, if the tests come back positive, finding a donor will be a challenge."

"Can we go private?" he asked.

"Mark, we can't afford—"

"Can we?" he said to the doctor. "Will it help?"

"Honestly, with a case like this, if it was my child, I'd feel the same. But the reality is that we'll still need a donor. A private hospital would use the same donor resources."

"Stem cell. What is that? What does it mean?"

"Bone marrow. If I'm right, she has something called aplastic anaemia. Her body isn't producing enough blood cells to sustain her. She'll need a bone marrow transplant. But we *have* to wait for the test results. It's just a theory. You understand that, right?"

"A theory we haven't heard of until now. Why is it hard to find a donor?"

"Any haematological transplant is dangerous. Finding a match would pose a serious challenge."

"But not finding one would be an even greater risk?"

"Of course," she said.

"How about me? Am I a match?" said Julie.

"I'm afraid not, Mrs Debruin. We check blood relatives first."

"But I am, aren't I?" said Debruin. "Take what you need to take. Save her, Doctor Lansdowne."

"Mr Debruin, I'm sorry, it doesn't work like that. We'd be negligent if we tried. Look, let's wait for the results."

"What do I need to do?" he asked.

"As the donor, you would need to undergo five days of treatment prior to the surgery. We'd need to raise your blood levels through a course of injections."

"So, let's do it," said Debruin.

"Let's wait for the tests," said the doctor. "I'll expedite them, if it makes you feel better, then arrange for time off work. But until I see those test results, we can't do a thing."

"What would you do if it was your daughter?"

"I'd be in the same position as you. I'd have to wait for the results."

"Right now, what would you do if you were me?"

There was a compassion in her eyes, and honesty in her tone.

"I'd make the arrangements to have time off. But I don't think you can, can you?"

Debruin said nothing.

"You were in the papers a few days ago. I read the article. You're leading the investigation for that man. You need a clear and positive mind. You can't do this with something like that hanging over your head. It's a risky procedure."

Debruin's interrogation was wearing the doctor down. Beside him, Julie was close to breaking from both the emotion and the embarrassment. But Debruin wasn't giving in. It wasn't in his nature. For every problem, there was an answer.

"Look," said the doctor, keeping her voice low and adopting a tone that conveyed that the conversation was coming to an end, "there are organisations that will take the search for a donor international. If we can't find a UK-based donor, then our options are to wait or to go international. But it's expensive. It's not an option available to most people and unfortunately the

NHS just can't fund that level of donor search. If you choose to go that route, we'll work with the organisation, of course."

"I'll do it," he said. "If I'm a match, then I'll do it."

"Arrangements would need to be made should the results come back positive. Can you give up five days?"

"Anything," he said. "I'll do anything for her."

But then he saw something that brought him back to reality with a hard slap across his face.

And it stung.

A white, unmarked van stopped in the car park outside the doctor's office window. The side door slid open and four men stepped out. Four uniformed men, each of them armed. The passenger door opened, and a familiar figure stepped out.

Spencer.

Each of the men surveyed the car park and surrounding areas, while Spencer spoke on his radio. Then he nodded to someone out of sight.

DSI Barnes walked from behind the van with confidence. Debruin had seen the expression on his face before. It was an expression of disappointment, of reluctant duty, and of consequence.

He disappeared from view, heading for the reception doors.

Debruin recalled the conversation with White, and what she had said about Hargreaves in Barnes' office. The warning he had received. They were there to bring him in.

"Mark?"

Julie's voice was weak and troubled. She needed him. They needed each other. And Grace needed them both.

"I'll work it out," he said to her, then turned to the doctor as he stood from his chair, staring at Barnes through the window. "Get the tests done. I'll be back. Whatever it takes."

"Mark, what's wrong? Where are you going?" said Julie.

He made his way to the door, and the doctor glanced

through the window, seeing what Debruin had seen but not making the same connection.

"Stay with her, Julie. Stay with Grace," he said. "I just need time. A day."

And with that, he slipped through the door.

TWENTY-EIGHT

"Do you want out?" said Harvey, and he waited for Butler to acknowledge his question.

The bearded man seemed despondent. He shrugged and his voice was that of a man on a downward trajectory.

"Of course," he said. "But it's impossible. I've tried. I even spoke to a colleague once to see if he would help."

"What happened?" asked Harvey, knowing the answer already.

"He didn't even make it home."

"I need to know everything," said Harvey, and he caught Norris' stare. "From the start."

"That's a long story," Norris began.

"Good. You can tell me in the van."

Both men looked up and waited for Harvey to explain.

"Let's go," he said. "If they are going for Banks' family, we need to stop them there."

"Do you know where Banks lives?"

"No, but Butler does," said Harvey. "He's the policeman, remember?"

They stared at Butler, who looked as if he was about to protest, then relented. "I know where he lives."

But that wasn't enough to satiate Norris' arguments. "If Spider hunts you down, he'll hunt us down too."

"You're forgetting something. He's already hunting you down. That's why he sent me. By my count, we have under eight hours. We're going to stop him."

"How?" said Norris, his voice empty of hope.

"We take them down, one at a time."

"'Take them down? This isn't a game. We don't even know who they are, or where they are."

"I know where one of them will be," said Harvey, as he peered from the doorway across the empty field. The coast was clear. If they were going to move, now was the time.

"Banks," said Norris, seeing through Harvey's plan.

"It's my fault Banks is dead. If you're right, then his house is where Spider's men will be heading. I just hope we're not too late."

"What about your friend?"

Harvey was half out of the door. He stopped to consider Alice for a moment and looked back at Norris. "Make no mistake. Everything I'm about to do is to save her. I don't care about you. I don't care about the others. All I want to do is get her to safety. But I can't let innocent people die. So, let's move. Butler, you drive. Norris, I need to know everything."

With Butler at the wheel, Harvey ushered Norris into the back of the van, then followed. He sat in the spot where Alice had been lying in the photograph. Norris sat on the carpeted wheel arch, oblivious to the significance of the space Harvey had chosen to occupy.

The van moved off, and Norris' face conveyed his discomfort.

"I'm waiting," said Harvey. "Tell me everything."

The back of the van was dark, like a room lit by moonlight alone. Norris' features were outlined against the tinted rear window. His face was downcast, and his eyes were moist. He sucked in a breath, considering where to begin.

"My wife died eight years ago," he said. "Her name was Fiona, and she was the purest thing I ever knew. She never told a single lie, never cheated anyone. She was an angel. My daughter was old enough that she didn't need me for much, except money. Fatherhood didn't come naturally to me, but I loved her all the same. I had help, of course, a maid to keep the house clean, and kitchen staff. At that time, I ran a bank in London. It was a small bank with very specific criteria. We wouldn't take anybody off the street and give them a bank account. High net worth individuals. Aristocrats, Arabs, Chinese. We were secure. When my daughter grew up, I sent her to the finest school, gave her a good start in life, you know, despite the setback of losing her mother halfway through her education. Back then, I thought money was the only thing that mattered. I know different now. But never did I just hand my daughter cash. She had to know the value of it. She had to work for it. That was Fiona's wish. She didn't want our child to grow spoilt. So, I set her up with an education hoping that one day she would make her own money. I think she resented us for that decision. There was always a divide between us. If I had the chance, I'd do it all so differently."

"Keep to the story," said Harvey.

"This is the story, young man, and if you want to hear the end, you'll have to hear the beginning first."

His tone was indignant. There was no longer any fear in his voice. He spoke with the confidence of wealth and power, as if his story had resurrected his former self.

"One day, I was at my desk. It was a particularly busy time. The First Gulf War had ended, and money was being buried here, there, and everywhere. London was being snapped up by Arabs looking to get their money out of the Middle East. The same happened in New York and other European cities. We were doing well. I was opening my mail. I always began my day with the mail. It was before emails. These days, I suppose they have computers to do all that. But back then, things were different. Simpler. The only thing we used computers for was to move money."

"Get to the point."

"I opened a letter and found a photo of my daughter. She was bound, gagged, and half naked in what looked like a dungeon."

The van slowed and Harvey peered into the cab through the windscreen.

"We're being stopped," said Butler from the front. "Police checkpoint. They must be looking for you."

Harvey drew his knife.

"You're not going to try anything stupid, Butler, are you?"

The van stopped, and a policeman's boots crunched on the gravel outside, then came to a stop as Butler lowered his window.

"DS Butler," he said, and flashed his ID wallet. "Any sign of them yet?"

"Them?" said the officer.

Harvey fingered the wooden grip of his knife, listening for Butler's betrayal and keeping his eye on the sliding door beside him.

Butler was fast to respond, a welcome trait for any undercover officer.

"Him. Norris. Have you seen anything?"

"You're the first to come through. We've only been here ten minutes."

"Okay, keep your wits about you. He's a cunning old bastard

from what I've heard."

"Will do, sir."

The van pulled away, and Harvey slotted his knife back into its sheath.

"They think you're dead," said Butler to Harvey.

"They think Banks was the killer," Norris added, with a glint in his eye.

"Which means Spider's men won't be the only ones paying his wife a visit."

Butler stopped at a junction. The ticking of the indicator was loud. He turned in his seat and leaned into the back to catch Harvey's attention.

"We're two miles away," he said. "Are you sure you want to do this?"

"Let's get close. I don't really want to leave Banks' family in the hands of the police," he said. "They wouldn't stand a chance."

The dig was below the belt, but the fact that Butler offered no argument strengthened Harvey's opinion of Spider's capabilities. The van moved on, and Harvey settled in for Norris to continue.

"You were saying something about a photo of your daughter," Harvey said, drawing Norris' attention back to the story. "I'm guessing there was a message included."

Norris sighed, as if he was reluctant to relive the horrors of his past. But if Harvey was to trust the man that, only a few hours before, he was planning on killing, then he needed to know the truth, or at least hear what he had to say.

"Written on the back. I had to meet him somewhere, but he didn't show. I was going to go to the police, but I found an old cassette in my pocket."

"A music cassette?"

"Yes. He must have slipped it in there somehow."

"And it was him? He recorded a message?"

"Of sorts. His voice was disguised. I think he'd used one of those machines to hide his real voice."

"Why?" asked Harvey. "Why would he hide his voice?"

"The same reason that you haven't confirmed that you're the killer. You don't want to incriminate yourself. A tape with his voice on could be used as evidence."

"And what did he say?"

"It was a long message. Detailed to the finest point. He knew my business inside out. He knew how to work the computer system we had, and he gave me strict instructions."

"To do what?"

"To steal. To slice off a small percentage of accounts. A few hundred thousand here, a few hundred thousand there."

"Isn't it traceable?"

"No. Well, maybe now it is, but this was five years ago. Nineteen ninety-six. We specialised in off-shore accounts. British Virgin Islands. Isle of Man. Switzerland."

"So, you made him rich enough to start the whole thing."

Norris nodded.

"What was I supposed to do? He had my little girl. He even sent a clipping of her hair in the post."

"But you got her back?" said Harvey.

The van ground to a halt.

Norris shook his head.

"I never saw her again."

Harvey said nothing, preferring to let Norris' face do the talking in those few moments of silence. He was genuine. At least from what Harvey could tell, he was telling the truth.

"It went on like that for a while. I was close to having a heart attack every time I walked through the doors of my office. I expected the police to be waiting for me."

"But they never were? He was too smart."

"Yes," said Norris. "I was shaving less than half of one percent off eight-figure accounts and moving it to accounts that, in reality, didn't actually exist. Ghost accounts."

The question was on the tip of Harvey's tongue. Butler was listening to them in silence and Norris was lost in a world of his own misery telling a story he'd probably been trying to forget for half a decade.

"Then one day, I refused to steal any more. I hatched a plan." He paused to muse, and in the half-light, Harvey thought he caught a wry grin forming on the man's withered face. "I called a man I knew, who knew a man, who knew another man. I arranged myself a passport and driving license in another name, a new name, somebody that nobody had ever heard of. I even used my connections to set up a high street bank account."

"Why would you do that?"

The question fell on deaf ears. Norris was coming to the climax of his untold story, and he was savouring every juicy detail of his ingenuity.

"My problem was that no matter where I ran, Spider would find me. It had been a year since he had first blackmailed me. In that time, I had seen and heard things I will never ever repeat. Needless to say that there were others that came after me. Ebenezer Bloom was one, but there were others. They tried to run, but Spider had become so powerful. With the money I had stolen, he had eyes everywhere. Running was impossible. Hiding was out of the question. The only thing I could even consider was suicide."

He raised his head and stared across the empty space at Harvey.

"So, I did," he said, with that same wry smile. "The man I used to be ceased to exist."

"And the man you became?" asked Harvey.

"Ah," Norris began again. This time, his voice was lower and filled with shame. It was like he was two people. Each of his namesakes had a persona and a tone of voice to suit. "He's nothing but a dirty old man."

"You're not making sense," said Butler, joining the story for the first time.

"You're in the force. You must have first hand knowledge of the penal system."

Butler nodded his agreement and hummed a low confirmation.

"If the old me was to hide in prison, Spider would have me sniffed out in a heartbeat. I wouldn't have lasted a week."

"But the new you," Harvey began, "Samuel Norris, would be an unknown."

"Exactly," said Norris. "And tell me, I'm sure you both know the answer to this one, what types of criminals are segregated from the other prisoners?"

"Sex offenders," said Butler. "Sex offenders and paedophiles."

"Paedophilia was a little too far for my taste," said Norris. "It just so happened that Barking police were hunting down a sex offender. A mature man by all accounts and I fit the bill. So, I moved house, I played the game, and would you believe it, they caught me."

"The only way to get away from Spider was to become a sex offender?" said Harvey.

"I didn't become one. I simply confessed to the charges."

"What about your daughter?"

Norris quietened at the mention of her. He gathered his thoughts and spoke quietly.

"It was the hardest thing I ever did."

"You abandoned her?"

"You have to understand, by that time I hadn't seen her for months. They kept her locked away in an old warehouse that

Spider used. I asked to see her. But there was another challenge. Another task that he wanted me to do. I even broke into his little dungeon once, where he liked to keep her. She was nowhere to be seen. These things can drive a man to craziness."

"They killed her?"

Norris ignored the question. He was in full flow, relaying memories he'd rather forget.

"I thought that by the time I was released, Spider would have been caught. The police were closing in. I thought he would be out of my life, and that I could let Samuel Norris die to resurrect my former self. You know, one of those men who turns up after being missing for years."

"So, you're innocent?" said Butler.

"As the day I was born," he breathed, dragging his innocence from the pit of his gut.

"And you can't resurrect the old you until Spider is out of the picture?"

"More importantly, I can't shed this despicable life of Samuel Norris until I find my daughter's body and bury her with her mother."

"How did your wife die?" asked Harvey, a little ashamed to be asking the question.

Norris' watery eyes found Harvey's in the dark interior of the van.

"She couldn't cope with the divide between us and our daughter. It was like we'd lost her at that point. She wouldn't talk to us. We rarely saw her, and to top it off, my wife blamed me. Have you ever lost somebody so close to you that it feels like you lost a limb?"

Harvey nodded. He understood. "How?"

"I found her in a crumpled heap on the ground." He looked up at Harvey, and his eyes narrowed with the memory. "She threw herself from our bedroom balcony."

TWENTY-NINE

Julie called after him as he closed the door, and he hated every part of his being for leaving her to deal with Grace's illness alone. But there was no time to dwell on her. If he was going to save Grace, he needed to prove his innocence. The facts were simple. If he entered into the long and drawn out process of defending himself in the interview room, he would be there for days.

And Grace just didn't have days.

He ran to the reception, burst through the doors, and slid to a halt. Barnes was approaching the entrance, followed by two armed officers. The door to the mortuary was directly opposite where Debruin was standing. Perhaps if it had been Barnes on his own, he might have stayed and argued his case. But the two armed men were not escorting Barnes for company.

He ran on. He crashed through the doors to the mortuary corridor, and slid around the corner on the polished floor. The soles of his shoes found no grip whatsoever, and a startled nurse stopped in her tracks, forcing Debruin to barge past her. He made it round the next corner and was just through the next set of doors when the nurse called out to someone, who Debruin presumed to be Barnes and his armed friends.

A few seconds later, he fell through the doors to the mortuary in time to see Churchill talking to two uniforms. The grumpy old man raised his hand and pointed a finger, and the two uniforms prepared to give chase.

Without thinking, Debruin slammed the button on the wall to lower the huge shutters. He hurled a trolley containing a tray of standard operating tools their way, which they stumbled around. Debruin ran for the closing shutters thirty feet away. The steel doors rattled and the motor whined, and there was just six feet left for him to escape through.

But his jacket snagged on a shelving unit. The uniforms were charging at him. He considered ripping the jacket off and escaping.

Five feet.

The doors behind him crashed open. It would be Barnes' men. He didn't even have to turn and look. He fumbled with his jacket and just as the uniforms closed in, it came free from the unit. He ducked from their reaching hands, shouldered one of them out of the way, and ran for the shutters.

"Armed police," somebody called from behind him, and he stopped.

Three feet.

"Stay where you are," another called.

Two feet. It was now or never.

"Detective Inspector Debruin," the armed officer said, as he began to recite his arrest.

Debruin dropped to his knees, rolled, and was lying on the hard concrete outside before he'd even considered the consequences.

Bodies slammed into the shutter on the other side, and one man even hit or kicked it repeatedly out of frustration. Debruin

wondered if it had been Barnes, disappointed and angered by
Debruin's disobedience.

But he didn't know what was at stake. Nobody did.

He rolled to his feet, straightened, smoothed his jacket, and
searched the forecourt. The entrance to the mortuary was a
walled enclosure with an open electronic, sliding steel gate. The
walls were at least ten-feet high, and just three vehicles occupied the spaces: a new, blue BMW, an average looking Ford, and
a panel van decorated with the words *Private Ambulance*.
There was a refrigeration unit on the roof, designed, Debruin
presumed, to keep the bodies it transported cool.

A morbid thought occurred to him, that he could hide in the
rear of the van. But he needed to get away. He needed to put
distance between himself and Barnes. A buzzer sounded, an
orange warning light flashed atop the gate pillar, and the
twenty-foot-long barrier topped with razor wire began to roll
into its closed position.

Debruin ran. With just a few feet to go, he glanced back at
the shutters. They were opening. Twelve legs and feet each
waited with anticipation to give chase.

He slipped through the gate just as it closed. The road was
clear to his left and right. If he ran left, he would reach the main
ring road around Romford. Right would lead him into a small
park, and into a residential area beyond.

He turned right and he ran. He was breathless in moments,
and eased off after one hundred yards, remembering that he not
only needed to prove his innocence to undergo the transplant,
but he needed to survive too.

At the entrance of a small park, there was a kissing gate,
designed to prevent motorcycles from destroying the area. One
hundred yards away, Debruin jogged, keeping his breathing
regular and paying close attention to the irregularities of his
heart, his circulation, and the discomfort of pins and needles in

his feet. With just one side street to cross before he reached the gate, he slowed to a fast walk, loosening his collar to let the fresh air cool his sweaty skin. He stepped into the road, thinking only of two things: Grace's recovery and how happy Julie would be if their little girl could lead a normal life, and Barnes' face when he realised Debruin was innocent.

There was no room to think of anything else. His family and his job were everything, in that order. So, when van tyres screeched on the tarmac to his right, the sound barely registered in his mind.

Until it was too late.

The van struck him mid-stride. He rolled onto the steep bonnet, hit his head on the windscreen, then lurched forward, landing in a heap on the ground. Dazed and confused, all thoughts of Grace and innocence abandoned his senses, and self preservation kicked in. He scrambled onto his front, finding his right leg in agony. But he could move his feet and toes, and as far as he could tell, he had suffered no broken bones. It was his head that betrayed the rest of his aching body. He climbed to all fours, but his head swirled and dizzied. The tarmac below him was a succession of clarity and blurred vision, as if a cameraman was rotating the focus of a lens.

Then a hard kick found his ribs, and he dropped to the ground once more, the sharp stones digging into his face.

"Don't move, Debruin," said a familiar voice, and he knew the game was up.

"You've got it wrong, Spencer," he said, but speaking only served to antagonise his ribs. He curled into a ball, cradling the spot that Spencer's boot had bruised. But Spencer wasn't a man with a gentle touch. Using the sole of his boot, he rolled Debruin onto his back and looked down at him with bitterness written in the creases of his face.

"Detective Inspector Mark Debruin," he began, and for the second time that day, a colleague began to read him his rights.

It was over, he thought. All he prayed for was that Barnes would allow him to undergo the treatment. A few days was all he needed. Spencer's voice hummed just as the doctor's had and his face was framed in blue sky.

"Have you anything to say?" said Spencer, finishing his speech.

"It wasn't me, Spencer," he whispered, but his voice was so low that he barely heard it himself.

"Did you say something?"

He inhaled to speak but the movement of his chest aggravated his ribs. He tried to move his legs, but Spencer's boot had pinned him down.

"Sorry," he said, and again, his voice was inaudible.

Spencer leaned over him, his face twisted as he tried to comprehend what Debruin was saying.

"I'm sorry," he said, suffering the pain a little for Spencer to hear the words.

"Sorry? For what? For being the leak? For nearly killing my men?"

"No," breathed Debruin. "For this."

Spencer's eyes widened when he realised Debruin was reaching for his belt. But even the lithe and agile Sergeant Spencer wasn't fast enough to react to the barbed prongs of the tazer.

THIRTY

The news was clear. The man that Harvey had listed as a sex offender had proclaimed his innocence. But that wasn't new. Nearly every man that, over the course of his life, Harvey had hunted, watched, stalked, preyed on, and eventually destroyed had proclaimed his innocence. But one thing was for certain; every one of them was bottom-feeding filth that had destroyed lives with their perversions. Even if the penal system had deemed them suitable for society, Harvey hadn't. He'd looked every one of them in the eye and seen the fear of guilt.

That was the decider for Harvey. Guilt is what steers justice. Some men live with guilt and welcome the justice that claims them. But an innocent man who endures guilt will fight.

Samuel Norris was a fighter.

"I don't know who you are," said Norris, "but I know enough about the men you hunt that I would never stand in your way. I'm guessing I'm not the first convicted sex offender to plead innocence to you."

Harvey didn't reply.

"I thought so," said Norris. "I hope I get the chance to prove my innocence."

"Butler, what does it look like out there?" said Harvey, ignoring Norris' statement but fixing him with his gaze.

"Quiet as a mouse," came the reply from up front. "Nothing has moved since we arrived."

"Norris, you'll stay here. Butler, you're with me."

"What?" Butler turned in his seat to face Harvey. "I can't be seen walking about with..." He paused, and his face reddened at Harvey's expression.

"You're the one with the police ID."

"What about me?" asked Norris. "You can't just leave me here in the van."

Harvey didn't reply. He stood, peered through the windscreen, and readied himself to get out.

"I'll run," said Norris. "You won't see me again."

"Hang on," said Harvey to Butler, then turned to face Norris. "You won't run. You have nowhere to go. Without me, you'll be Samuel Norris for the rest of your miserable life. You won't see your daughter, dead or alive, and you'll always be looking over your shoulder."

An expression of self-hatred formed on Norris' face.

"Besides," continued Harvey, "your worst fear is me. And I'm standing right in front of you. If I was going to kill you, you'd be dead already. The same goes for you, Butler. Let's make one thing clear. If we do this, if we shut Spider down, then we do it my way. Right now, I'm the one with the most at risk. So, when I say do something, you do it. Do I make myself clear?"

Norris digested the information and nodded slowly.

"Butler? You're still a copper. If we do this right, you might still have a job when all this is done."

"Might?" said Butler. "It would take some kind of miracle now."

Reading between the lines, Harvey assumed Butler was referring to him crossing the line of duty at some point. He was a stout man. He could take care of himself. If Harvey was to walk into a potential trap with anybody, Butler was as good a bet as any.

"Let's go," said Harvey, as he pulled open the side door and dropped to the ground. He closed the door before anybody could see Norris inside, and walked beside Butler to the door of the house. He spoke quietly, keeping his language concise. "You do the talking. All we need to know is if Spider's men have been here yet."

Butler knocked on the door and turned, as a police officer might, to scan the street behind him.

Harvey listened and waited for the door to open. He'd seen every car on the street. He had made a mental note of every conceivable spot that he might watch the property from if the roles were reversed.

Butler knocked again, harder this time. The door swung open and he gave Harvey a look of concern.

They were inside the house in moments. Harvey closed the door behind them, but the locking mechanism had been forced. The wood was splintered. He pulled a framed picture from the wall and leaned it against the door. Then he motioned with his finger to his lips for Butler to be silent. He closed his eyes and tuned into the house, listening for movement. The one minute rule had been instilled in his methods by his mentor, Julios. His foster father's bodyguard had taught him all he knew about stealth, defence, and attack. The one minute rule was a key component of his training. An impatient or poorly trained man would not stay still for much longer than thirty seconds. He would venture out of wherever he was hiding to investigate.

But no such man showed his face.

Harvey opened his eyes and found Butler looking at him with a quizzical expression on his face. The minute had passed. Not a sound had been made. He moved past Butler and, for the first time, took in his surroundings. The house was terraced. The hallway had a laminate floor, and the walls were painted white. The staircase was carpeted, leading up to a gloomy upstairs landing. There were two doors leading off the downstairs hallway. The first, which was closed, was on the right-hand side. Harvey presumed it to be the living room. The second was open and from where he stood, he could see straight through to the kitchen.

He nodded for Butler to go through to the kitchen, while he opened the living room door. He turned the handle, opened the door a fraction, then stepped back as he pushed it open. Nobody came for him. Nobody stepped into view. Nobody uttered a single word.

The living room was narrow but long, extending to the back of the house. It was far from lavish but was still a respectable working class home. There were photos of Banks on the wall with a pretty brunette. No children. The furnishings, nice TV, couch, and small dining table were the markings of the house of a young couple beginning their journey.

He stepped back into the hallway, meeting Butler as he emerged from the kitchen shaking his head. A few of the stairs creaked under Harvey's weight, even when he used the very edges. Instinct kicked in and he made a mental note of the steps of the offending stairs.

There were four doors off the upstairs landing. The bathroom was on his left. The door was open and the room was empty. The shower had been used and there was a small heap of women's clothing on the floor.

Three doors remained. Two large bedrooms and a small box room. Butler moved to the second of the larger bedrooms and waited for Harvey to give him the okay. Harvey, at the door of the first bedroom, listened for a moment, then signed. Three, two, one.

They both pushed open the doors and stepped back.

Nothing moved.

They each entered their respective rooms.

In the back bedroom, Harvey found a double bed and built-in wardrobes. The curtains were open and the bed was made. A soft toy had been placed in the centre of the bed. Aside from a laundry basket, it appeared as though the room was used as a guest room.

It was then that two sounds changed everything.

The first sound was Butler, cursing aloud.

"They got to her," he said, his voice low but loud enough for Harvey to hear.

A pang of guilt gripped Harvey's stomach.

The second sound came from downstairs. The front door opened, and the picture frame Harvey had set up fell onto the hard, laminate floor.

THIRTY-ONE

It was a stalemate. Whoever had placed the picture frame against the door knew Debruin had arrived. And he knew they were there.

Unsure of what to do, Debruin waited, listening for movement. He heard nothing. He glanced back through the front door into the street. There was nothing out of the ordinary. There were a few cars parked outside houses, as there were on any street. A black van was parked one hundred yards away at the end of the road, but it wasn't TSG. He would have recognised one of their vans in a heartbeat, as they were all nearly identical to the one that he'd stolen from Spencer.

Spencer would have raised the alarm by now. Even when Debruin had left him lying in the road and reversed away, the fearless sergeant had been getting to his feet. There would have been an all unit call to look out for the van.

But at the time, Debruin hadn't been able to run and his options had been few.

The door frame was splintered, but other than that, there was no sign of a struggle, at least not in the hallway.

He took a step, and the heel of his shoe clicked on the laminate floor. He cringed at the mistake, but heard no reaction from the living room, kitchen, or from upstairs. His upper leg still throbbed, and his breathing was shallow, each breath sending a dull ache through his chest.

Aware that his breathing was loud, he did his best to control his exhales, moving slowly to the door on the right of the hallway. The living room walls were adorned with pictures of Banks with a woman. The curtains and soft furnishings were the result of a female touch and there was a nail kit on a side table, just like the one Julie used every night in front of the TV. She'd sit there digging, poking, and prodding, then finish with a buff.

Debruin did little about his own nails except cut them when they were long. For years, he wished he lived alone. The joyless marriage had grown stale, and Grace's illness had driven them apart like a stone chisel finding a weakness in rock. But the meeting with the doctor earlier had altered that. The hug they shared had changed it. He couldn't imagine being without either of them. And he would do everything in his power to make sure they got through it.

Banks didn't live alone either. He imagined the man sneaking out in the evenings to carry out his crimes. He would have lied to his partner, telling her that he had a delivery or a pickup. He would also have a tool kit or a bag in which he kept the things he would need. He considered Banks keeping a keepsake of each of his kills, but that was a trait of sexual predators. The man who had been killing sex offenders was more of a vigilante. It was like he was above the law, sweeping up where the legal system failed. He would be proud of what he did but would share the kills with nobody. He would savour those moments.

The most Debruin could hope for would be newspaper cuttings. A scrapbook tucked away in the bedroom, maybe? He

stepped across the laminated wooden floor to the stairs, but the
stretch evoked a groan of pain. It was as if somebody had their
fist inside his ribcage. He controlled his breathing and moved up
the stairs, keeping to the edge of each step to quieten his
approach.

Halfway up, he stopped and scanned the upstairs landing.
There were four doors. One was a bathroom, plus three
bedrooms. Debruin guessed at two large rooms and a smaller
spare room which might have been used as an office or a store-
room. His own house was laid out in a similar fashion. The bathroom door was wide open, and the doors to the larger bedrooms
were ajar.

He heard no sound from any of the rooms and moved on
with caution. At the top of the stairs, he peered into the empty
bathroom. There was a small crack in the door hinge of the first
bedroom. He eyed the space inside but saw nothing. There was
something about the darkness of the front bedroom that was
screaming for him to enter. The door opened at his touch, and
he let it swing back until it hit a bedside table. He didn't need to
step inside the room. From where he stood, the bloodied legs of
a young female were splayed, motionless, and those parts that
were not covered in blood were deathly white.

The closed curtains blew in the breeze from the open
window. Debruin used his elbow to turn the light on so as not to
leave a fingerprint. The woman was in her thirties, judging by
her appearance. She was naked save for a towel that covered her
modesty, but it looked to have been placed on her post-mortem.

"Why would you cover her up?" he asked himself.

He was confident that he was alone. He was confident that
Banks had killed his wife or girlfriend before he had gone after
Norris. The bedside table closest to the door belonged to a man.
It held a thriller book, a lamp, and a man's watch, plus a small,
square box of tissues. Using a tissue he tugged from the box, he

opened the top drawer. There was nothing there of note, some more books, some spare change, and a photo of the girl in all her living glory. She had been beautiful. A brunette with a slim figure and kind eyes.

Debruin shuddered at what her partner had been capable of.

"At least you didn't have to learn about what he did," he said aloud.

He tossed the photo onto the bed beside the dead woman. It was her. Of that he was sure. But the contrast was exceptional. The same alluring features, the shape of her nose, the natural pout of her mouth. But the tone and sheen of her tanned skin and the joyous life in her eyes had been stripped away, leaving nothing but cold death.

"What a waste."

He searched the drawers below and found nothing of interest. No bag of tools, no rope, no gaffer tape, and most importantly, no weapon. He had used a knife on Slater and the time before. And no doubt, if he had had the chance, he would have used it on Hammersley too.

The wardrobe ran the length of the room. It had eight doors in total, with mirrors on the two central doors. He strode across the room and opened the first two. The clothing was sparse, and what hung inside was basic, save for an old suit that looked like it hadn't been worn for a while. He searched the bottom of the wardrobe, but all he found was shoes, boots, and old trainers. The next wardrobe was where Banks had stored bedsheets and blankets. Nothing of interest. He sidestepped a large patch of blood to the next set of doors, and as he opened them, he caught sight of a shadow moving on the landing. It was fleeting. A trick of the mind maybe?

Or not.

It had been real enough for him to abandon his search of the wardrobes and return to the doorway. He brushed past the bed, and the dead woman's hand touched his leg.

He stopped and collected her wrist in his hand, then moved it to her side, placing it naturally, the way she might have lain had she been alive and resting after a shower.

The wounds in her throat were deep, and blood had cascaded down her body. He could see it now; he could see the event take place. She had been standing before the mirror, drying herself. There was blood on the mirrored doors. He hadn't noticed it before. Somebody had come from behind, reached around her, and slit her throat.

Cold. Ruthless. They had to attack from behind. They didn't want to look at her face. They were ashamed. If they had wanted to savour the moment, they would have taken their time. She would have more wounds. But this was fast. Almost like a hit. Not the work of a man who butchered sex offenders. In fact, the MO was entirely different. The killer had taken his time. He had made his victims suffer an agonising death. He had stared them in the eye.

But the man who killed this girl was a coward. He had slit her throat, and even lowered her to the bed. Before he had left, he had even covered her modesty with a towel.

Her wrist had been cold, but her limbs were free. Debruin had felt the rage of rigor mortis before. It starts at the jaw and works its way down the body. He collected the photo and sat down in its place. His bruised leg was complaining at his posture as he leaned over her. The mattress sagged under his weight, but he did his best not to disturb the body. Blood had congealed in her neck wound. A pathologist would suggest that it was almost certainly the cause of death. Debruin guessed either blood loss through the wound, or a severed windpipe, in which case she would have suffocated on her own blood. There was no spray of blood at her mouth.

She had bled to death.

Using the tissue, he carefully touched the skin on her face. She was so pretty. As delicately as he could, he worked her jaw. The onset of rigor mortis had certainly begun, but it had yet to take hold.

She had only been dead for an hour or two at the most.

Banks was dead over an hour ago.

He didn't smile at his own assessment of the scene, despite being right about the killer's MO. The man who killed the sex offenders was a sadistic bastard who savoured every slice of skin and tortured scream, the way a child delights in a sweet dessert. But the man who killed the girl was a coward. It might have been his first time. The wound ran from her shoulder to her throat; the cut through her jugular had been fortunate. A practised hand would have found the fat artery with ease. The slice would have been shorter in length. A practiced hand would have cut her windpipe so she couldn't call out or scream.

He considered his assumptions, rolling the photo over and over in his hands.

But when he looked down at it, and flipped the photo over, he saw three words printed in black ink.

You cannot run.

He inhaled, as all his theories dissipated.

But his efforts to piece them back together again were shattered by the sound of broken glass underfoot. Somebody had stepped onto the picture frame.

THIRTY-TWO

Harvey hadn't seen the body in full, only her bloodied legs and painted toenails through the doorway as he crept down the stairs, seeking the few steps that didn't creak. Butler had been waiting for him after dropping from the first floor window.

"You could have run," said Harvey, as they reached the van.

Butler, with his hand on the driver's door handle, eyed him carefully.

"I probably should have too," he said.

That was all he said. That was the only real clue he gave that he wanted out of Spider's web, and he knew that the best chance of getting out was to work with Harvey.

"Who was that anyway?" said Harvey, as he pushed the sliding door closed. "He had police written all over his cheap suit."

"Never seen him before," said Butler.

Butler reversed the van away from the house, keeping the revs low and quiet.

"That was Detective Inspector Debruin," said Norris. "I watched him arrive, but I had no way of warning you."

Butler found the old man in the mirror, and Harvey, keen to

learn why Norris would know the detective's name, prompted the explanation with raised eyebrows.

"I was running from him when you..." He paused, searching for the right word, and the confidence to say it out loud. "When you kidnapped me. When you pulled me into the car."

Harvey thought back to when he'd seen Norris running. He had been afraid of something, looking back over his shoulder.

"Why were you running from the police?"

"He was setting me up, or at least trying to."

"Setting you up for what?"

Norris sighed, and seemed to retract into the lowlife persona that masked his true identity.

"He was setting me up for you. The predator. The man in the papers. The man who butchers convicted sex offenders."

Harvey didn't reply.

"He's an odd man," continued Norris, reflecting on the detective's mannerisms. "He came to my flat. It was like he had something to prove. He was trying to coerce me into being bait."

"To catch the killer?" said Harvey, choosing his language with care.

"Catching the killer seemed to mean more to him than just an arrest. He wants you off the streets."

Harvey didn't reply, seeing the verbal entrapment closing in.

"He's hungry for it," said Norris. "I don't know what it is, but he has a lot riding on catching you."

"Is he a problem?" Harvey called out to Butler.

Butler pulled the van into a queue of cars at a traffic light.

"Ordinarily, yes."

"But?"

"But he's alone. Did you see the van that was parked outside the house?" said Butler, then continued, not waiting for a reply. "That was a service van. TSG."

"What's TSG?" said Norris.

"Tactical Support Group. The heavies. If there's a raid, or a sting, they're the guys with the firepower."

"So?" said Harvey, not seeing where Butler was leading them.

"So why would a detective be driving a TSG van? Why would he enter a house alone? He didn't call out. He didn't make his presence known, not purposefully. Something isn't right about it. I need to make a phone call."

He pulled off the main road without waiting for Harvey's response and parked the van in a side street beside a row of shops. As he opened the door, Harvey called to him.

"Butler," he said, his tone flat and calm.

They exchanged stares through the seats of the van.

"I'm not running," he said, answering Harvey's unspoken question. "I'm in this and I want out."

He closed the door, leaving Harvey to consider the sincerity of what he had said.

"What did you find in there?" said Norris, his voice a whisper in the quiet of the cargo space.

Harvey said nothing at first. He leaned into the front of the van and watched Butler open a phone box and dial a number from memory.

"She was dead, wasn't she?" said Norris, as if the silence had to be filled by something. "How did they do it?"

Harvey didn't reply.

"Was her throat cut?"

"I didn't see," said Harvey, more to shut the man up than to engage in a conversation about the dead woman.

"That's how Bloom does it," he continued, speaking low. "He's a sick man. He likes to watch them bleed out. He cuts their throats, careful not to slice their windpipe. He goes for the jugular."

Harvey had slit enough throats to picture the death. He'd made enough men suffer in their final moments to know that forcing a man to bleed out was a sure way to prolong the death. Organs close down one by one, but the heart beats on, trying its damnedest to pump some blood through the body. And the victim would be conscious of the entire affair.

"It was him, wasn't it?" said Norris.

Butler had left the phone box and was on his way back to the van. He thrust his hands into his pockets and did a good job of looking like any other middle-aged man. He would have been a good undercover cop.

"You're wondering how we find them, aren't you?" said Norris, and his persistence was beginning to grate on Harvey's ability to focus. "You're wondering how on earth we stop them. Debruin is on our tail and Spider is one step ahead."

It was as if Norris was delighting in Spider's capabilities.

"You can't surprise him. He's anticipating every move you make," he said. His voice was a tease in the half-light, almost as if Norris was smiling as he spoke. "All you can do is play the game. You can take his pawns and you can go for his rook, Bloom. But when you take them, Spider will disappear. He wins. No check-mate. He vanishes from the board."

Butler climbed into the van, disturbing Norris' insight. He said nothing at first. He just sat with his hands on the steering wheel staring forward, his mouth ajar and his eyes narrowed.

"I know what his next move will be," said Norris, and he turned to Butler at the front of the van.

"Debruin is working alone," said Butler, relaying his news. "He's suspected of leaking information. He's on a mission to prove his innocence."

"And they gave him a van to get about?" said Harvey.

"He attacked a senior TSG officer and took off in his van."

"The web gets stickier," said Norris, marvelling at the news. "That's why Debruin was so keen to catch you. To prove he's not the leak."

Harvey didn't rise to the bait.

"Or is he?" he said to Butler.

"The leak? No."

He offered no more than that. It was Norris who summarised the state of play, rising once more to his former self.

"So, you're hunting the Spider. Debruin is hunting me. And the police are hunting Debruin."

"What do we do?" said Butler.

Harvey considered the options and the facts, musing on what a man like Spider might do.

"When Spider realises you haven't returned, he'll go after your family, Butler."

"Very good," said Norris, applauding Harvey's intuitiveness. "But what then? We can't just guess where he'll strike next. He'll be one step ahead of us all the time. No checkmate, remember?"

"That's what he wants. He's shutting it down. He hasn't lasted this long by taking risks," said Harvey, finally seeing the pieces come together. "If he shuts it down, he'll disappear."

"Only to begin again somewhere else," Norris finished.

Harvey stared at the man in the front of the van. He was a strong man, and Harvey admired his control over his emotions. But in his face, there was a worry that belied his silence.

"The logical step is to protect your wife," said Harvey.

Butler said nothing. He gripped the wheel of the van and stared dead ahead, rage building inside him in visible silence.

"But we can't do that."

The words deflated Butler, although Harvey was sure he knew it was coming.

"If Spider shuts it down, we'll never find him. He'll kill

whoever he can, and you two will spend the rest of your lives looking over your shoulder."

Norris nodded his agreement, as if his own life was testament to the truth.

"We need to break the chain. We need him to chase us. He's one step ahead of us because we only have one way to go. How many men does he have working for him?"

Butler didn't reply. He was staring forward, his mind clearly focused on what Spider might do to his wife.

"Butler?" said Harvey. "We need you focused. How many men does he have?"

"A dozen, maybe more."

"But how many actually matter? Banks is dead and Spider killed his wife for his failure. The only other people who are at risk to him are you, Bloom, and the leak."

"I don't see your point," said Butler.

"Bloom is only useful to him while he's in control. Bloom was in control because he had access to you, and he has access to your leak."

"So, we go after Bloom and let him kill my wife?" said Butler, appalled at the plan.

"We can either go after your wife—"

"Or go after the leak? No. I can't let him get to her."

"Not the leak. He's expecting us to go one of two ways. Your wife or the leak. He leverages people's emotions. That's all he has. Take the lever away, and he's nothing."

Butler wasn't buying into the idea. It was natural that he would want to protect his wife. "If Spider shuts the whole thing down, we lose him. He'll send Bloom after the leak, you, your wife, and..." Harvey couldn't bring himself to say her name, but Butler knew what he was going to say. "Do you trust me, Butler?"

It was a few long seconds of silence before Butler looked at him.

"Tell me who the leak is," said Harvey. "They're protecting somebody. We need to know who it is and get to them before Spider."

THIRTY-THREE

Debruin pocketed the photograph and edged to the open window. He pulled back the curtain and judged the height. Too far to drop with his leg which was bruised and aching from the collision with Spencer.

A stair creaked in the hallway.

He searched the room for a weapon. There was nothing to hand. There was nowhere for him to run. He was about to move across to stand behind the door when it opened with a small squeak.

Hawes was standing there.

"For God's sake, Hawes," he said. "You nearly gave me a heart attack."

But the expression on Hawes' face did not match the genuine relief on Debruin's.

"You've come to take me in, haven't you?" said Debruin, unable to hide the resent in his voice.

"It's for the best, sir. Barnes has everyone out hunting for you."

"How did you know to find me here?"

"A hunch," said Hawes, and he looked up from the woman's body on the bed to search Debruin's eyes.

"Not me, Hawes. She was like that when I found her," said Debruin, realising that he sounded like a guilty teenager standing beside a broken window. "You have to listen to me, Hawes. It's more complex than you might think."

"I looked up to you, sir," he said, and the disappointment was evident in the break in Hawes' voice.

"Don't believe what they say, Hawes. You can make your own mind up."

"We're just an extension of the law, you told me. It doesn't matter what we think, that's what you said."

"I didn't kill her."

"It doesn't matter. It's gone too far. Spencer is pressing charges, Barnes is climbing the walls, and Hargreaves has everything he needs to nail you down for corruption and perverting the cause of justice. You'll lose your job and your pension you'll spend the next five years inside. More, if that was you." He gestured at the girl's body with a flick of his head. "And you know what's really sad, sir?" he said. "You're still lying. You're still trying to manipulate me. You don't get it, do you? You're destroying lives, sir."

"You're wrong about me, Hawes."

"I hope I am, sir," he snapped. "I hope I'm wrong so much, but you've put me in a position where I have to choose between breaking the law and risking my own career or doing what you taught me to do. Forget my thoughts and feelings and carry out the law."

"Okay, okay–"

"No, sir. It's not okay. What the hell are you doing here with a body?"

"I told you, I found her like that. This was his house, Hawes. His girlfriend. He was in here. I've spent six months chasing this bastard and when I finally catch up with him, when I finally get the chance to prove myself, he dies, leaving me looking like I'm guilty as sin."

"How did you know he lived here?"

The suspicion in Hawes' voice was new. It was as if, instead of carrying out the law as Debruin had told him, he was beginning to believe Barnes and Hargreaves. He was losing his faith.

"His driving licence."

"But you didn't call Barnes. Where's the forensics? Where's the warrant?"

"There was someone here before me. I just missed them," said Debruin. He had to get his story out before he lost Hawes completely.

"You came to a suspect's house alone. A suspect that the entire department believes you've been aiding and abetting."

"The entire department?" said Debruin. "Are you included in that?"

Hawes was silent. He looked around the room, but there was nothing to see save for the corpse on the bed.

"I am, sir."

There it was.

"Are you taking me in?"

"I have to. You know I do."

Debruin held out his hands.

"Are you going to resist?" said Hawes.

"I couldn't outrun you if I tried."

"So, put them down. I'll call this in and get the place sealed up."

Debruin stepped past the body and Hawes left room for Debruin to walk in front. They descended the stairs and exited through the front door, then Hawes radioed through for the house to be secured.

A nearby unit arrived less than two minutes later. Hawes

briefed them and Debruin waited in the passenger seat. He was proud of the man. Debruin had seen him rise through the ranks. He wasn't a perfect detective, but neither was Debruin, or any of the countless others he'd met. Hawes spoke to the men with a confidence that he hadn't had when Debruin had first taken him under his wing.

Debruin wondered if the whole thing was a charade. His disappointment had seemed genuine. If Hawes truly was the leak, then he was hiding it well.

By the time Hawes had returned to the car, Debruin was on the fence. Hawes said little. He drove in near silence, speaking only once to tell the story of Spencer's rage at having his own tazer turned on him. But the effort at conversation was weak and did little other than to fix Debruin's uncertainty as to if Hawes really was the leak. The only thing he had to gain from divulging sensitive information to criminals was financial, and Hawes seemed perfectly comfortable. His salary was mid-range, not high but certainly not low. He drove a nice car, nicer than Debruin's, in fact, and White had said his debt was average.

They turned off the A13, just a mile from the station, and the proximity to the inevitable clenched its clawed hand around Debruin's gut. He was heading for a disaster. If he stepped foot inside that police station, he wouldn't be released until he was either found innocent or charged. For him to be found innocent would require the true leak to be found. And right there and then, the chances of that happening were slim to none.

"You know, it's funny," Debruin said, as he peered through the side window at the lights of the city in the distance. "I've done everything I could to bring this guy in. Pulled strings, lied, cheated, and damn it, people have even died. Twenty-four hours ago, we were planning Hammersley's sting. I really thought we'd nail him."

Hawes gave him a sideways glance.

"I mean it," said Debruin. "Twenty-four hours ago, we were arranging Spencer's team. Seven hours ago, we were being debriefed. And six hours ago, I found out I was the prime suspect in an internal investigation. How the bloody hell did it go so wrong?"

Hawes said nothing. He pulled onto the high street, driving slowly, as if he was giving Debruin time to say what he had to say. Perhaps even waiting for an apology or a confession.

"When we were at the crash site, in the forest, I gave it all some thought. I didn't stop thinking about it. I couldn't have, even if I had tried. Do you know what I thought, Hawes?"

Hawes didn't reply, but he glanced at Debruin to show interest.

"I thought to myself, who knew about each and every one of those men? Who knew as much about the killer as I did?"

He left a silence for Hawes to judge where the monologue was heading. They were just five hundred yards from the station, if Debruin was to act, he'd need to do it fast.

"Who else, apart from me, knew that I was going to Slater's flat to warn him? Who else knew about Hammersley? About Norris? Only one person, Hawes."

Hawes looked across at him, his mouth opening to argue his case, but he could find no words. Debruin seized his opportunity. He reached across, pulled hard on the steering wheel, and braced for impact. Hawes braked, but they were travelling too fast to stop in time. The car mounted the pavement and nosed into a side road before burying itself into the side of a row of shops. Hawes hit his head on the wheel and reeled. His nose was bloodied. In an instant, Debruin whipped off the handcuffs Hawes carried on his belt and slapped one end onto the steering wheel. He fixed the other end to Hawes' wrist, and opened his door.

"I'm sorry to do this to you, Hawes. It's not me. I'm not the leak."

Hawes frowned, still in shock from what had happened. He held the cuff of his shirt to his nose and glared at Debruin as he leaned into the car.

"I have to prove it's not me. You'll understand. When I prove it, you'll understand."

THIRTY-FOUR

"That was it," said Butler, as he pulled up outside a small row of terraced houses on a main road. "Back up the street fifty yards. Thirty-four. Black door."

"Are you sure it's the one?" said Harvey, leaning into the front to peer through the windscreen. It was a busy road, busy enough for two men to climb out of an unmarked van without drawing too much attention.

"Certain," said Butler, and his eyes conveyed his sincerity.

"Norris, you're with me," said Harvey. "Butler, you stay here. We might need to leave in a hurry."

"Me?" said Norris. "I can't go anywhere. I've only got one shoe."

Harvey didn't reply. He opened the side door, dropped to the ground, and waited. Norris huffed, but he got the message. He climbed out and stretched his back. He was a mess. What hair he had was windblown. His jacket was crumpled and creased from being in the back of the van. And on his shoeless foot, his sock was filthy.

"How do I look?" he asked, his tone contemptuous.

"Give me three blasts of the horn if trouble arrives," Harvey said to Butler, and slammed the door closed.

He strode along the pavement with Norris in tow and knocked on the front door of number thirty-four, then stepped back. It was early evening and still light, so the door opened without question, and Harvey was inside before the man could even think of what to say or try to stop him.

He took a swing at Harvey, which Harvey ducked. He grabbed the man's wrist, using the momentum from the punch and bent his hand back, twisting his arm behind him.

"Mr White?" he said.

The man resisted, but a little pressure on his wrist quelled his effort.

"Are you Mr White?"

Harvey pressed his face against the wall, and he responded with both fear and anger.

"Yes. Yes, that's me. What do you want?"

Norris peeked through the doorway, then closed the door, unsure of what to do next. Harvey led the man into the living room with gentle tweaks of his wrist.

"I can break your arm in one snap," he said. "Try to fight me and you'll lose. Try to run and you'll get hurt. If you listen to what I have to say, you'll realise I'm not here to hurt you. I'm here to help."

"Who are you?" said Mr White, and Harvey forced him over the back of the sofa.

"Did you hear what I said?"

The man said nothing. He was bent over, and he stared at the open door into the hallway.

"I said, did you hear what I said?" said Harvey, and he tweaked his wrist just enough to make sure the message hit home.

"Yes, yes, yes," said Mr White.

"Are you going to fight me?"

"No."

"Are you going to run?"

He shook his head.

"Are you going to listen to what I have to say?"

He nodded.

"I said, are you going to listen to me?" said Harvey, raising the aggression in his voice.

"Yes. Yes, I'll listen."

"Good," said Harvey. He released the man's wrist, pulled him upright, then shoved him away to put distance between them. A frightened man will try anything, and the last thing Harvey wanted was to hurt him.

Mr White straightened his shirt and smoothed his hair, but he kept his distance and eyed the pair of them.

"Mr White, you don't know me, and you never will. I have reason to believe that you're in danger and I want you to come with us. We won't hurt you. We want to keep you alive."

"Keep me alive?" he said. "You barge into my house, assault me, and then tell me you want to be friends? Clear off. Get out. I don't want your bloody help."

"I'm not leaving without you."

"I'm calling the police," he said, and he took two steps towards the house phone, which was on a glass-fronted wooden sideboard. The cabinet was filled with various bottles of alcohol. Before the man had even picked up the telephone, Harvey kicked through the glass, grabbed a heavy, green bottle, and smashed it down onto the handset.

Mr White stepped back again, and Harvey tossed the remains of the bottle to one side.

"I warned you once, Mr White. I rarely give a second warning."

"I don't understand. What is this all about?"

"Your wife," began Harvey. "Charlotte is in trouble. She's being blackmailed."

"Charlotte? Blackmailed? I don't understand. How do you know Charlotte?"

"We don't have time to explain."

"She works for the police. How can she be blackmailed?"

"She's being forced to do things she wouldn't normally do. I believe she's being forced to divulge information to criminals."

"She wouldn't do that. You're wrong. She loves her job." His voice was high. Fear and adrenaline were coursing through him. Harvey eased his voice to calm the man.

"Mr White, look, I promise you, we're here to help. You're in danger."

"Daddy?"

The three men froze. They turned to face the source of the voice and in the doorway, behind Norris, a little girl appeared, holding a soft toy.

"Sweetie, go to the kitchen. I'm talking to these men," said Mr White, and there was a parental strength to his voice. He eyed Harvey and Norris to make sure neither of the men touched her.

"You're shouting, Daddy. What's wrong?"

"Sweetie, just give me two minutes," said Mr White. Then he stared at Harvey. "These men are leaving now."

She looked up at Harvey, and with that curiosity that only children dare to display, she searched his expression, as if somehow she could read him.

"Norris," said Harvey, his eyes never leaving the child's, "take her to the van."

"No," said Mr White, and he lunged for her. But Harvey was expecting the move. He stepped forward, grabbed Mr White by the back of the neck and slammed him into the wall. "Norris, go now. Don't hurt her. Just take her."

"I can't do that," said Norris, his voice as high as Mr White's had been. "She's a kid, for crying out loud. I'm not...I can't."

With Mr White struggling beneath Harvey's firm grip, he gave Norris a choice.

"Get her out to the van and stay there. Or leave her here and she dies. What do you want on your conscience?"

"Norris?" said Mr White. "That's where I know you from. You were in the papers. You're the pervert." He kicked out into Harvey's shin. The kick smarted, and Harvey forced his knee up into the man's lower back.

"Now, Norris. Get her out."

"No," screamed Mr White. "Don't you dare touch her."

Norris collected the girl up, and the moment her feet left the floor, she screamed for her daddy. Harvey waited for the sound to fade. Tears fell from Mr White's eyes and rolled across his reddened face. "If you hurt her—"

"You need to listen to me, Mr White. I'm not here to hurt you. I'm not here to hurt your daughter. I'm here to keep you alive. The sooner you realise that the easier this will be."

With his face pressed against the wall, Mr White spoke through the side of his mouth, spitting with rage.

"You've got a funny way of showing it. Bring her back."

Harvey calmed his voice but retained the pressure on the man's back and arms.

"I'm going to let you go and we're going to walk out of here calmly. If you make a scene or try to run, what happens?"

"I get hurt."

"That's right."

"And my daughter?"

"I'm not going to touch her. Nobody is going to touch her."

Harvey waited a few seconds for him to calm.

"Are you ready?" he asked.

Mr White nodded, biting his bottom lip to withhold the emotion.

"Right," said Harvey, and he released his grip. "Where are your keys?"

"By the front door."

"Good. We're going to walk out of here. You're going to lock the front door, as if everything is normal. Then we're going to walk to the van, climb inside, and none of the neighbours will bat an eyelid. Is this understood?"

He nodded.

"Let's go."

Mr White did as he was told. Harvey waited on the pavement while he engaged the security locks. He stood as if he was a friend and they were all going out together, but in his peripheral, Harvey watched every car that passed by and spied every driver.

"What time does Charlotte finish?" he asked, when Mr White joined him and they were walking the fifty yards back to the van.

"She finishes soon."

"Good. We'll pick her up."

"If that man touches my daughter."

"He won't," said Harvey, shutting him down before his emotions ran wild. "Trust me on that."

"Trust you?" he muttered under his breath, seething at the position he was in.

Harvey slid the van door open and stepped back to let Mr White climb in first. The man peered inside, glanced at Butler, who averted his eyes, and looked around the van.

"Where is she?" he asked, and he stared at Harvey in disbelief. "Where's my daughter?"

THIRTY-FIVE

Debruin had never felt so alone. There had been times when he enjoyed the peace and quiet of solitude, when Julie had taken Grace to see her parents. He'd been alone then. He would watch TV in his boxer shorts and leave his used dishes on the coffee table. He could even have a nap without being woken to carry out some meaningless task.

At least he'd had choice then. He could have gone to the pub for a pint, or in a rare state of parental obligation, he might have joined his wife and daughter at his in-laws.

But on that street, on a cool evening with commuters passing by in waves and lines of cars waiting at the traffic lights, he knew what it was to be alone. He couldn't even go to the hospital. He couldn't go home. He couldn't call anyone. Everyone he knew either worked with him or was family. It was too risky to reach out, and time was not on his side.

He sat in a bus shelter, using members of the public as a shield. He scanned the passing cars for familiar faces in unmarked police vehicles, and mused on his predicament in solitude, shrinking into the collar of his jacket.

Norris was out there somewhere. Banks was dead. The only

way he could prove his innocence was to find Norris or wait until the true leak was found. If it was Hawes, then he had a window of opportunity. It would be a while until Hawes was freed from the car and alone to make a call.

But Hawes had seemed so genuine. Debruin hated himself for doing what he had done. But self-preservation was just that. Entering the station would close any doors of hope Debruin had. He'd make it up to Hawes if he could. If he proved to be as innocent as Debruin. But it was every man for himself right now.

The glass sides of the bus shelter had been scratched with keys. Apparently GH loved FR, and a crude smiley face substantiated the claim. On any other occasion, Debruin would have seethed at the vandalism, but he relished it in that moment, hoping the scratches would obscure his features from the other side.

Brakes squealed and a bus stopped beside him, hissing as the brake cylinder released the air. The doors opened and clunked against the interior of the bus. Passengers disembarked, while others queued to get on. His shield was leaving. He considered getting on the bus, but he had no cash in his pockets. He didn't even know how much a bus ride would be, let alone where the bus would take him. It had been years since he travelled by bus. The last time would have been when he was a teenager, sitting on the top deck at the back with his friends, making paper aeroplanes from the bus tickets and seeing how far they would fly through the open windows. People smoked on buses back then. The top deck had always been filled with a blue haze, and the smell seemed to stay on clothes for the rest of the day.

These days, buses had cameras, there was no conductor, and the driver was guarded by shatterproof glass or Perspex.

He wasn't sure why, but he recalled a time when he had

been on the bus to meet friends in Romford. It was the 252 bus, a number he would always remember, as it was the only bus that passed by the top of the street where he grew up. He would get the 252 everywhere. On this one occasion, a young mother had boarded the bus with her child. The child had some kind of disability. He remembered the pang of guilt he had felt when he imagined how hard life must have been for the mother. But he hadn't truly been able to empathise. He was still a child himself. But if somebody had told him that one day he'd have a child of his own who would have a life-threatening illness, he would have laughed in their face. He had been fiercely naive, as many youths seem to be.

The bus pulled away, leaving Debruin open to inspection from passing cars. He found himself staring across the street, his eyes unfocused and blank, lost in memory. He blinked and lowered his face into his collar again, but as he did, he spied somebody on the far side of the road. It was somebody he hadn't considered. A route to his freedom, perhaps?

He stood and, spying a break in the traffic, and ran across the road. The pavement was busy. Commuters had to step into the road as they passed a pub, due to the group of workmen who had stopped to wash the dust from their throats after a day of grafting. Debruin was just thirty yards behind the familiar bobbing head in front. He stepped into the road to pass the workmen and had to turn sideways between a couple, who both turned and scowled as he forced his way between them. He was against the flow of pedestrians, making progress where he could. But he became so infuriated by the effort, he stepped back into the road and ran to gain some distance. In the corner of his eye, he caught sight of the bright, Battenburg livery of a police car. He re-joined the pedestrian battle and increased his efforts, becoming ruthless in his attempt to make ground. And he was a metre behind his target when they crossed the entrance to an alleyway.

He grabbed hold of her jacket and wrenched her into the alleyway.

"Sir," she said, when he turned her around and planted her back against the wall.

A few passers-by stopped. One man called out to her to ask if she was okay and if she needed help. But a flash of Debruin's badge was enough to quell the man's bravado, and he re-joined the stream of commuters as fast as he had appeared.

"You need to tell me everything you know," said Debruin.

"I don't know anything, sir," said Charlotte. "What the hell's going on?"

"Don't give me that. It's you, isn't it? Of course it is."

"What is? Let me go," she said, and she tried to pull away from his grip.

"You're the leak," he said, and suddenly, it all made sense. She knew as much about the case as he did, and anything she didn't know she could have found on the computers.

She stopped her struggling but couldn't meet his eye.

"I'm right, aren't I?" he said, letting go of her arm. He kicked out at the wall beside her. "How could I have been so stupid? It was you. I was feeding you the information and you've been passing it on." He lowered his voice to a growl, feeling the anger boiling inside him like water, frothing and spitting. "Who?"

"I don't know."

"Charlotte, who is it? Whoever it is, I need to know."

"I don't know," she screamed, and a few passers-by at the top of the alley peered inside as they crossed its entrance. She softened. "You'll never understand."

"Try me."

"You don't know what they'll do," she said, and her voice was like that of a child, helpless and weak. "You don't know what they're capable of."

"I'm beginning to get an idea," said Debruin. "How long?"

She turned away to stare at the passing commuters.

"How long, Charlotte?"

She shrugged and wiped her eye. "Six months."

"Six months? What have you told them?"

"It started when the killer began. The vigilante. They wanted to know everything. Who he was targeting, how he was killing them, and..." She paused to breathe, closing her eyes to the truth.

"Where we thought he would strike next?"

She nodded.

"Jesus, Charlotte. Why? Why didn't you come to me? You could have come to any of us. You're one of us. We look after our own."

He considered how true that statement was, in light of what he was going through and what he had just done to Hawes.

"I'm sorry, I..." Her voice faltered, then broke into a whimper. She opened her bag and rummaged inside. A few moments passed as she sifted through the junk – tissues, makeup, a diary – and then she found what she was looking for. "I got this in the post," she said, and handed him a photograph. "There are more. It's not the first."

Debruin held the photo. It was a portrait shot, and judging by the slight lines around the edges, it looked as if it had once been framed.

He turned it over in his hands, knowing what would be there but praying that he was wrong.

You cannot run.

THIRTY-SIX

"You let that sick bastard run off with my daughter." Mr White squared up to Harvey until they were nose to nose. "Where's he gone? Where's he taken her?"

Where most men would have leaned or steeped away from the enraged father, Harvey didn't move an inch. "Get away from me," he snarled, then turned and shoved Mr White to one side. "Butler, where did he go?"

"I thought he was with you."

"He came out a few minutes before us. I told him to sit in the van and wait. He had a little girl with him."

Butler shook his head. "He didn't come this way."

"Who the hell are you people? You're not police. You don't work with Charlotte. Who are you?"

"Butler, show him your badge," said Harvey.

Butler did so, but Mr White was not convinced. He shook his head and backed away, and his voice broke, high and pained. "This is wrong. This is all wrong."

Before Harvey could react, Mr White turned and ran. He ran into the road heading in the opposite direction and car tyres screeched on tarmac, stopping just in time. With his hands on the bonnet of the car, he looked up at Harvey, shook his head one more time, then ran into the next road. Harvey was about to give chase, but he felt a strong hand on his shoulder.

"Leave him," said Butler, now out of the van and appraising the situation with a keen eye. "We need to move. We need to get to my family."

"Your family?" said Harvey, turning and brushing Butler's hand away. "There's a kid out there with a..." He lowered his voice, aware that what he was about to say didn't need to be broadcasted to the entire street. "There's a kid out there with a convicted sex offender."

"You heard what he said. He's innocent. He made it all up."

"Yeah, I've been giving that some serious thought. He lied about his name, who he is, and what he did. Even he doesn't know what's true and what's not. How can we take his word for it? For all we know, he actually did those things and we've let him run off with another kid. I can't let that go, Butler."

"Well, I can't stand around while my family is in danger. I helped you as far as I could help you."

"We can't just leave him, Butler."

"Watch me," he said, and he turned his back on Harvey, making his way to the driver's side of the van.

Harvey glanced back at where Mr White had run. There was no sign of him on the busy road. There was a row of local shops a few hundred yards away, and the street outside was filled with parked cars. A delivery driver slammed his side door shut and waved to the shop keeper. Harvey watched him climb into his van. He watched as the van indicated, waited for a break in the traffic, and then pulled out to reveal a police car parked in the road.

"Are you coming or not?" Butler called. The engine was running, and he was growing impatient.

Mr White was leaning on the driver's door. He stood up and

pointed in Harvey's direction just as the driver flicked on the blues and twos.

Harvey gave the area one last scan for Norris and made his way toward the van's open side door. But he was too late. Before he reached the van, Butler floored the accelerator, and Harvey was left standing in the street, alone and with the police car bearing down on him.

THIRTY-SEVEN

"Are you going to take me in?" asked Charlotte, wiping her eye with the sleeve of her jacket. She looked miserable, and for the first time, Debruin noticed how tired she looked. He hadn't ever really paid attention to her appearance. She had always been pleasant, smart, and professional, and he had always crouched beside her desk, which was never the most flattering angle to look at somebody from. But the bags beneath her eyes were dark and lined with creases in her skin. The eyelids sagged from lack of sleep and her shoulders hung like they were carrying a vast weight.

"Go," he said. "Go and be with your family. Take them somewhere safe. A hotel maybe? Pay cash. Leave no trail. Just get them away, Charlotte."

"And you?" she asked. "What will you do?"

"I have the full weight of the law hunting me down, Charlotte. Thirty minutes ago, I had two options to prove my innocence. Find the real leak or find Samuel Norris."

She stared at him, the whites of her eyes red with tiny arteries.

"Now, I only have one option," he said. "I need to find Samuel Norris, prove my innocence, and put a stop to all this."

She smiled her thanks, although it was weak.

"Go on," he said, and gestured for her to leave. "Before I change my mind."

She shouldered her bag and moved toward the entrance to the alleyway. But as she reached the top, Debruin called after her.

"Charlotte," he called, and she turned, her eyes hopeful. "Keep them safe and tell nobody about this."

She smiled; this time it was genuine. She turned away and, with her head low, she disappeared from view.

Debruin fingered the photograph, turning it in his hand.

You cannot run.

"Arrogance," he said, and tried to imagine a man writing those words. The carnage that whoever had written those words had created was beyond belief. He pushed himself off the wall, pulled the collar of his jacket up and shoved his hands into his pockets. Then he headed back up the alleyway to join the throng of people who marched past, eager to get home. He turned left, heading against the flow of people again. But this time, he was in less of a rush and found spaces to navigate a path. He was running the photographs through his mind, drawing conclusion upon conclusion, then blank after blank.

None of it made sense.

It still made no sense when Debruin came to a crossing. He joined a few other people as they waited for the lights to change, and for the little green man to sign it was safe to cross. He stood there among the commuters lost in his own world. There was an office worker in a cheap suit. The young woman beside him had a cigarette hanging from her mouth and was searching her bag for a lighter.

The sight of the people around him registered in some

subconscious level, but his concentration was focused on those three words.

You cannot run.

It just didn't make sense.

He barely registered the little green man making an appearance, and he paid even less attention to the car that had stopped to let them cross the road.

So, when Spencer tackled him to the ground, he was sucked from his thoughts in a heartbeat. He hit his head, but before he could even register the pain, Spencer had rolled him onto his front, twisted his arms behind his back, and cuffed him.

There were words, of that Debruin was sure. But they were jumbled and dreamlike. His head ached and he was sure he felt blood. There was a cool patch, but he couldn't tell if it was wet blood, or just a scrape from the concrete.

Another member of Spencer's team helped hoist Debruin to his feet, and they dragged him to the car. It was never an easy task to bundle a handcuffed person into the rear seat of a vehicle. Debruin had done his fair share. But when Debruin was in and upright, Spencer leaned into him, covering the open doorway with his mass.

"This is for earlier," he said, and he jabbed Debruin hard on the nose. The lights went bright. The taste of iron grew at the back of his mouth.

And then darkness.

He came around in a bright room. The light stung his eyes and woke the headache that had been developing even before Spencer had jabbed him. He raised his face from the table, feeling his skin peel from the stainless steel. His cuffs had been re-arranged, so that instead of his hands being behind his back, they were at his front, but the cuffs had been fastened to the steel eyelet to prevent prisoners from making a run for it, or attacking the interviewing officer.

"Wakey wakey, Detective Inspector Debruin," said a voice that was familiar, but which was as welcome as a dose of herpes. "Or should I say, soon to be Her Majesty's Prisoner Debruin?"

Hargreaves stared down at him, framed by the bright light above and smiling like all his dreams had come true. He leaned in close and whispered with evident glee, "I told you I'd get you, didn't I?" He flopped a heavy, blue file onto the table in front of Debruin. "Shall I run through the evidence against you?"

"Can I get some water?"

Hargreaves took his sweet time to stroll across the interview room floor. He opened the door and requested for the guard to fetch some water, then closed the door and leaned against the wall on the far side of the room.

"What you did to Hawes is the nail in the coffin," he said. "You just added about four more charges to your case."

"How is he?" asked Debruin. The fog was clearing, but the headache remained.

"He's okay. A patrol found him and picked him up. It could have been a lot worse."

"As long as he's okay."

"You ran, Detective Inspector Debruin."

The man's lust for announcing his full rank was wearing thin, prolonging the delivery of each sentence.

"I had to," said Debruin. "I'm innocent."

"So, prove it."

Debruin said nothing. He wanted to. He wanted to tell Hargreaves about Charlotte White. About the photo she carried in her bag. The photo in his pocket. But she needed time. She needed to get home and get her family to safety. If he mentioned her name, regardless of the truth, Hargreaves would have her picked up and that sweet, little girl in the photograph would suffer the same fate as Banks' girlfriend. Debruin could handle all the grilling Hargreaves had to offer if it meant that Charlotte White could get her family to safety.

"Without the killer to testify, and without Norris to back my statement up, I can't. More importantly, while I'm stuck in here, I can't do anything about it."

"Well, that's not likely to change anytime soon."

"Shouldn't you be recording this?" said Debruin, remembering the man's diligent verbal updates for the benefit of the recording during their previous meeting.

"Who is it you're leaking information to, Detective Inspector Debruin?"

Hargreaves paced the area close to the door. His hands were in his trouser pockets and he appeared confident that he would have his own way. That he would be right in his theory.

"I'm also pretty sure I'm entitled to call my lawyer."

"Why are you leaking information, Detective Inspector Debruin?"

"There should also be witnesses. None of this will stand up in court."

"When did you first make contact with the suspect, Detective Inspector Debruin?"

"I haven't been read my rights. This is unlawful detainment. That's a chargeable offence."

Hargreaves stilled. He stared at Debruin with all the malice he could muster. But the mental battle the two men were engaged in was broken by the door opening, and Debruin's heart sank a little, as Hawes stepped inside.

"The file you asked for," he said to Hargreaves, and offered him another blue folder, unable to look Debruin in the eye.

"Why don't you join us, Detective Sergeant Hawes? I was just about to learn why your colleague has been divulging sensitive information to known criminals, perverting the course of justice, and aiding and abetting criminal activity. You might want to hear this."

There seemed to be no limit to the man's condescending tone. Even Hawes, from the look on his face, seemed to be less than impressed. He took the seat opposite Debruin, but still averted his gaze, choosing instead to watch as Hargreaves resumed his pacing.

He stopped almost immediately and turned to face Debruin.

"We're waiting," he said.

For the first time, Hawes looked across at Debruin and met him eye to eye. He seemed to be making a decision. But there was nothing for Debruin to convey other than the shame for not trusting his colleague, and for what he had done. Hawes rested his elbows on the desk and linked his fingers. He said nothing. But his posture afforded Debruin a view of his watch. It was seven p.m. Charlotte would have had plenty of time to get home and get her family somewhere safe.

It was time to lay his cards on the table. He stared back at Hawes. Hargreaves didn't deserve his attention. It was Hawes who deserved to be told the truth. He'd worked just as hard as Debruin on the case and he'd suffered as a result.

"I know who the leak is," said Debruin. Hawes was unflinching. It was as if he half expected Debruin to accuse him. To point the finger of blame on his colleague as he had done in the car.

"Is this another wild accusation?" said Hargreaves.

"No," said Debruin, and he took a breath, hoping that Charlotte had managed to get herself and her family away. He couldn't wait any longer. If he didn't make the announcement, he knew he would be destined for the cells for a few more hours at least. And with every passing hour, his chances of proving himself innocent dwindled, and his chance of being there to help Grace faded.

"I found Banks' girlfriend dead in her home."

"That's still to be proved."

Debruin had addressed Hawes, but it was Hargreaves who spoke.

"There was somebody there when I arrived."

"Who?"

"I didn't see them."

"Ah."

"I heard them leave."

"That's not exactly a concrete statement, is it?"

"I searched the room before DS Hawes found me."

"Did you find the weapon?"

"No. I found a photo. It was of her. The girlfriend."

"I can't see where you're going with this, Detective Inspector Debruin."

He took another breath, closed his eyes, and put the pieces together in his mind. He opened his eyes and found Hawes again, and prepared to articulate everything he knew. If it failed to impress Hargreaves, he would be marched to a cell. And that would be that.

"DS Hawes and I have worked together on this case for six months. No other police officer knows as much about the killer as I do than DS Hawes. He knew about the lack of evidence. He knew about the targets. He knew about the sting operations."

"Detective Inspector Debruin, if this is a feeble attempt to incriminate your colleague, I would seriously consider what you're about to say."

"He knew everything. So, when I heard about the leak, and when I became the prime suspect, it was only natural that I should try to understand who the real leak was."

"Keep to the facts, Detective Inspector Debruin."

The interruption triggered Debruin's temper. The delivery of his account was paramount to Hawes believing what he had to say.

"You, Hargreaves, have been so fixated on finding me guilty that you've been blinkered from the truth. You can't see the wood for the trees. You can go around in circles all you like looking evidence to have me on a charge, but all you have is coincidence. In forty-seven hours, I'll be released."

"Or charged."

Debruin turned back to Hawes. He needed to convey his sincerity and if anyone was going to respect him enough to listen, it was him.

"The evidence was stacking up against Hawes. Yes, I left the room during the Hammersley sting, but that left Hawes free to communicate with the killer. A fact you seem to have over-looked. In fact, every piece of evidence you have against me applies to DS Hawes. I paid a visit to Norris to get him on board with the sting. DS Hawes would have had plenty of opportunity to feed the information to the suspect. Who else knew about that?"

"Spencer?" said Hawes.

Debruin shook his head. "Spencer might be a tough nut, but the evidence against you and I doesn't apply to him. There's no other police officer that knew as much about the case as you or I."

"So, you are pointing the finger of blame on your colleague?" said Hargreaves. "I thought you'd have a little more integrity than that."

"It wasn't until we were in the car leaving Banks' house that I began to question Hawes' involvement." Debruin made sure he held Hawes' attention before continuing. "DS Hawes is an outstanding detective. In the few years I've known him, he's been nothing but professional. He's loyal and has never once wavered from the law."

"You're buying time, Debruin. Don't play games."

"There was one other person, except DSI Barnes, that had access to the information we did."

Hawes cocked his head, and in true Hawes form, he made the connection.

"Charlotte White?"

"I found her when she left work today, a few minutes before Spencer tackled me to the ground."

"Who's Charlotte White?" asked Hargreaves.

"Civilian support," said Hawes, and he was beginning to fall in with Debruin's theory. "She worked with us in the background."

"Civilian support are not given sensitive case files."

"No, but she had access to them. She would have overheard information, been involved in meetings. She would have had enough information to pass on."

"Do you have proof of this, Detective Inspector Debruin?" Hargreaves spoke slowly. It was clear he hadn't bought a single word of it.

"Hawes?"

"Sir?"

He still called him 'sir'. There was a chance he had Hawes back on his side.

"Check my right-hand coat pocket," said Debruin, and made a point of pulling the cuffs against the eye bolt.

Hawes stood and walked around the table. He delved into Debruin's pocket and, for a moment, Debruin wondered if the photos had been removed. He hadn't been arrested, he hadn't been processed, so there was a chance he hadn't been searched.

Hawes produced two photos. He looked across to Hargreaves, who was intrigued but clearly annoyed at the slightest chance that Debruin might be telling the truth. He edged closer, his eyes never leaving the photos.

"The first one is Banks' girlfriend," said Debruin, leaving a pause for them to find nothing special about the photo. "The second is Charlotte White's daughter."

"So?" said Hargreaves, attempting to bring the tension down.

"Turn the photos over."

Hawes did so. He held a photo in each hand.

"You cannot run?" he said, his voice chilled at the words.

"When I found the photo of Banks' girlfriend, I wasn't sure what to make of it. But when I caught up with White, when she gave me the photo of her daughter and explained–"

"There's nothing to explain," said Hargreaves, ripping the photos from Hawes. "These are just photos. They aren't evidence."

"I believe the killer was being blackmailed," said Debruin, raising his voice to counter Hargreaves' outburst.

"Rubbish. Detective Inspector Debruin, you have the right to–"

"I believe Charlotte White was being blackmailed into feeding information to a criminal organisation," said Debruin, ensuring his voice overpowered Hargreaves'.

Hargreaves stopped. He took the few steps back to the table and picked up the file Hawes had walked in with.

"This," he began, "*this* is evidence. You supplied the information. You wasted police time." With each statement, he slapped the file on the desk in anger. "You aided and abetted a criminal, and it's you who will pay the price, Detective Inspector Debruin."

He slapped the file hard with the final statement and something fell from inside. It was a photo. But who the photo was of, Debruin couldn't tell.

"Where did that come from?" asked Hargreaves, his voice low and without anger.

"It fell out of the file," said Hawes. "This is the file from your desk. You asked me to bring it."

"That's my wife."

The three men each looked as horrified as each other. Hargreaves slid the photo to the edge of the table, as if he was frightened to pick it up. He flicked it over with his index finger, and there, in large, black capital letters, three words had been written.

You cannot run.

THIRTY-EIGHT

Harvey ran.

He ran in the direction Butler had left, with the police car fast approaching behind him, sirens blaring. He cut into a side road and heard the screech of tyres behind him as the police car followed suit. In seconds, they overtook him. The driver pulled a handbrake turn to block the way, but Harvey slid across the bonnet as the passenger door opened.

With one officer on foot and the other at the wheel, Harvey's options were running thin. He turned into another side road with the officer matching his every step. He slowed to take a corner, reached out to grab hold of a fence, and pulled himself into a dead stop. The officer shot past him, skidded on the gravel, then scrambled to his feet.

But he was too late. Harvey was on him in moments. He forced the man's head back to the ground, knelt on his back, and leaned to whisper in his ear.

"Don't do it," he said. "I don't want to have to hurt you."

Harvey tugged his knife free from the sheath inside his jacket. In two swipes, he cut through the officer's boot laces so he couldn't give chase . Then, just as the police car approached, its tyres crunching on the gravel, Harvey jumped up, leaving the scared policeman on the ground, and ran around the corner. He ran out of the alleyway and into a grim looking back street, then slowed to a walk to listen for footsteps behind him. There were rows of large industrial bins and cars parked beside what appeared to be the rear entrances to the row of shops where he had seen Mr White talking to the police. To his left was a dead end. To his right, the road led down the side of the shops. He glanced behind him, one last check that the officer he'd disabled wasn't running after him, then turned right and walked fast.

He turned the corner just as an unmarked police car skidded to a halt. Both doors were flung open. On the main road behind the car, another police vehicle lurched into action. Harvey turned and ran back the way he'd come. He ran past four of the shops' back doors, and with nowhere else to turn, he barged through the fifth door into the kitchen of a Chinese takeaway.

All hell broke loose. Two men in greasy, white aprons shouted in a language Harvey couldn't understand, the second of which raised a big knife and pushed his friend to one side. There were shouts from outside; the police were following on foot. Harvey launched a nearby bowl of rice, big enough to feed an army, at the man. Then he bolted through a pair of double doors on the other side of the kitchen. He found himself behind the counter, where a young Chinese girl screamed, and two customers stepped back in alarm. Whipping a towel from where it hung beside the doors, he tied the handles together as fast as he could. He vaulted the counter, the young girl screaming all the while, and peered through the glazed front door. Two police cars were idling, and Harvey imagined their radios buzzing with activity.

In the corner of the room, beside a long bench designed for waiting customers, was another door. It was wooden, painted white, stained with grease, and marked with a small sign that read Private. Harvey kicked it open just as two large policemen came crashing through the double doors. He was through the door and up a set of stairs before they had even moved the young Chinese girl out of their way. At the top of the stairs was a small, unkempt flat. Three black bin bags were on the floors, which instinctively, Harvey tossed back down the stairs to make the journey harder for his pursuers. At the end of the landing, a door was open, it revealed a large living room area with cheap furniture and children's toys all over the floor. Two of the other rooms were closed, but above him, a pull-down ladder had been fixed to the ceiling beside a trapdoor. He had just pulled the ladder down when an old lady emerged from a small kitchen screaming at him. The two policemen were thundering up the stairs, and their screaming radios added to the chaos.

He climbed the ladder two rungs at a time and shouldered the trapdoor open. Bright light filled the space, and the cool air found his sweat-soaked t-shirt. Harvey found himself on the roof, which was a large, flat area as long as the row of shops, with nothing but air conditioning units and old chimneys.

The ladder creaked below. The first policeman was climbing up after him. Using his heavy boots, Harvey stamped down on the ladder. The officer was just one rung away when, after four or five hard kicks, Harvey managed to break the fixings, and the ladder fell backward with the policeman still clinging to it. He slammed the trapdoor closed and searched for an exit. He was trapped, and judging by the activity below, he would be surrounded any minute. He ran to one end of the building and peered down. The unmarked car was still there with the doors wide open. He ran to the front and two officers saw him and pointed, the first of which spoke into his shoulder-mounted radio.

Harvey bolted to the far end. There was no ladder down.

The rooftop was a firetrap, fifty feet high with nothing to cushion his fall. The only element of the building he could use was an old pipe. It was painted a burgundy red and appeared to be made of cast iron. It was as old as the building, which was at least fifty years.

He had no other choice. Cautiously, Harvey swung his legs over the ledge and wedged his boot into the far side of the pipe. Then, he committed. He shifted his weight onto the pipe and grabbed it with both hands.

The trapdoor burst open just thirty feet away.

He dropped out of sight. Below him was a small alleyway, a little wider than a man's shoulders. Harvey found that by wedging his boot behind the pipe, he could support his weight, while he wedged the other boot further down. It was slow progress, but a mistake would be costly. When he was halfway down, he glanced left and right. He was about to drop the remaining twenty feet, when an officer ran around the corner from the front of the building. Harvey pulled himself closer to the building and stilled. He dared not chance another look in case the movement caught the policeman's eye. The man's radio crackled.

"Control, this is two-two-four. I'm at the east end of the building. No visual. Over."

The radio spat another garbled message. Men were calling out, shouting, and the controller, the only female officer's voice, was doing well to steer the units and stay calm.

The officer was directly below Harvey. His footsteps stopped and Harvey's boot slipped an inch, creating a small shower of dust from the brickwork. Harvey winced, but didn't move. All he could do was hold on, keep his legs tensed, and stare at the brickwork in front of him. The pipe was connected by a circular clip every eight feet. There was one directly in front of Harvey, and whether time had weakened it, or his weight had loosened it, either way, the screws were pulling from the wall.

He tried not to move, but he was sure the screws were further out each time he checked.

There was another burst of radio, and the officer's boots clicked in the alleyway, moving away. Harvey glanced down and saw the officer reach the end. He stopped to listen to the controller.

"Control, this is two-two-four. Area clear. Please advise," he said, and just as he disappeared around the corner, the pipe fixing gave way. The pipe moved away from the wall and Harvey's foot was no longer wedged. His feet kicked at the air, searching for something to hold onto. He looked up, just as the heads of two policemen peered down at him.

Harvey dropped the remaining twenty feet and rolled when he hit the ground.

He looked up to find at least six officers now peering down at him. Then the first returned to the alleyway, holding his shoulder radio to his mouth as he began to run. Harvey bolted from the alleyway with at least one officer in pursuit. Ahead of him was a busy crossroads, with a steady stream of traffic flowing left to right. Lorries, buses, vans, and cars, all moving at forty miles per hour.

But there was no letting up. Harvey ran on. He searched for an exit in every conceivable place, and once he glanced over his shoulder, he saw the officer, with all his cumbersome equipment, was at least one hundred yards behind.

Harvey approached the main road at speed, timing his run to coincide with a break in traffic between two buses. The buses sped up, and so Harvey increased his pace, psyching himself up as hard as he could. He burst through the space between the two vehicles, causing the driver of the second bus to slam on his brakes. There was a long screech of tyres, and the bus swerved.

A van coming in the opposite direction then swerved to avoid the bus, and ploughed into a parked car, and Harvey, just inches from the devastation, rolled out of the way.

The tyre squealing and screeching stopped. The sound of shattering glass ceased, and diesel engines shuddered to a stop. On the far side of the junction, the police officer stepped into view, his way blocked by the carnage. He spied Harvey, locking stares with him, but it was too late. Harvey slipped into a side street and disappeared into the maze of East London back streets.

THIRTY-NINE

Hawes' hand pinned Hargreaves' to the telephone on the steel-clad table.

"What are you doing?" said Hargreaves. "I need to call my wife."

"I can't let you do that," said Hawes, and Debruin sighed a breath of relief.

"Get off me," said Hargreaves, and he ripped his hand away from the telephone, making his way to the door. He tore it open, surprising the officer on guard.

"Jacob, stop him," said Hawes, and he followed Hargreaves toward the door. "He's about to interrupt an ongoing investigation. Don't let him out of your sight, and don't let him make any calls."

Debruin craned his neck, pulling on the cuffs as far as they would allow, to see what was happening. Hawes rushed back to him, retrieved his keys from his pocket, and held Debruin by the wrists, about to unlock the cuffs.

"I'm trusting you now, sir. Are you certain about this?"

"As certain as I can be," said Debruin. "It's the only theory we've had that fits."

Hawes nodded, eyeing Debruin, feeding the last glimmer of doubt in his mind.

He unlocked the cuffs and Debruin sat back, rubbing his wrists.

"Thank you," he said.

"No time for thanks, sir," said Hawes, and he arranged the three photographs in a row before opening the file. "If you're right, Banks was blackmailed into killing those men. He and his girlfriend are dead."

Hawes placed Banks' file beneath the photo of his girlfriend and moved to the next photo. He selected the second file and was about to summarise Debruin's theory when the door opened, and a bleak and upset Hargreaves stepped in. He eyed Debruin's free hands, the photos, and the files, and took the third seat at the table.

Both Debruin and Hawes were silent. Hargreaves looked as if he was about to burst into tears, but he held it back, choosing to speak only when the wave of emotion had passed.

"Are you sure about this?" he said, speaking directly to Debruin. But it was Hawes who answered.

"As sure as we can be," he said, as a homage to Debruin's earlier comment.

"I want somebody watching my house."

"Done," said Debruin, and he felt the man's gaze deepen as Debruin reached for the telephone.

"Sergeant Spencer, interview room two, please."

He replaced the handset and stared back at Hargreaves, who nodded his appreciation in a silent admission of thanks.

"Charlotte White," said Hawes, his voice loud and clear in the moment. It was good to see him in control. Perhaps a break like this was what the man had needed to shine. Instead of flying in the shadow of Debruin's wing. "Your theory says that she's been passing information to a criminal organisation. The same criminal organisation that blackmailed Banks into killing. Am I right?" he asked.

"Yes," said Debruin, keeping his answers concise to expedite some action.

"And now, Mrs Hargreaves," said Hawes, placing his hand where a file might have been.

"Sophie," said Hargreaves, and both Debruin and Hawes caught his voice breaking. He stared back at them, retaining whatever strength he had left. "Her name is Sophie."

"Sophie Hargreaves," said Hawes. "How is he doing this?"

"He has a network of people. Bankers, computer engineers, specialists of all kinds that he can call on," said Debruin. "He can achieve whatever he needs to achieve. He can recruit whomever he needs to recruit. He has a core of individuals who all work for him in fear."

"Including killers?" said Hargreaves.

"Including killers. Find the right weakness and push the right buttons. That's all he has to do."

The door opened, and Spencer walked in. He saw immediately Debruin's uncuffed wrists, and he glared at Hawes.

"There's no time to explain," said Hawes. "Get two men in an unmarked car to Hargreaves' address. No action needed. Just surveillance and reporting at the front and back of the house."

"What's the address?" said Spencer, refusing to look in Debruin's direction.

"Thirty-one Birch Road, Romford," said Hargreaves, without looking up at him.

"Anything else?"

"Be quick," said Debruin. "Be very quick."

Spencer left, and as his heavy boots faded in the hallway, more footsteps approached, running. A uniformed officer burst into the room. He was a young man. Debruin had seen him around but had never heard much about him.

"Sir," he said, breathless from the run, "we've had a call. I thought it might be relevant to you."

"Go on," said Debruin, standing from the table for the first time in what seemed like an eternity.

"Charlotte White, sir. She's civilian support."

"Yes, we know her."

"Her daughter has been abducted."

Hargreaves turned and Hawes stood up, knocking his chair over.

"When?"

"The report just came in. Her husband was there. He reported it."

"Did he see the man who took her?"

The young officer nodded.

"Yes, sir. Three men. He said one of them was the guy who just got released from prison. The old pervert. He said he had one shoe on."

"Norris," said Debruin. "And the other men?"

"One guy waited in their van, a black Mercedes Sprinter. He said he was a policeman."

"Butler," said Debruin.

"Who's Butler?" said Hawes.

"No time to explain," said Debruin, and returned his attention to the young, uniformed man. "What about the other one? You said there were three of them."

"Just some bloke in a leather jacket who roughed Charlotte's husband up. Some tough bloke."

"Is that all?"

"He said the man in the leather jacket is dangerous. Local units gave chase, sir. I heard it all over the radios. He sounds like a right lunatic, sir."

Debruin jumped into action. "Hawes, get hold of Spencer. I need two more of his men to meet me at DS Butler's house. You take whoever else he has and go after the daughter. Make sure Charlotte is okay."

"What about me?" said Hargreaves, keen not to be left sitting and waiting for news on his wife or the case.

Debruin placed his hand on his shoulder. He understood. He disliked the man, but if the shoe was on the other foot, there was no way Debruin would sit by idly.

"Are you up for his?" he said.

"Of course I am."

"You can come with me, Hargreaves."

FORTY

At the far end of the road, where Harvey found himself far enough away to walk, the tops of trees swayed against the London skyline. The sight marked a park which stretched on to the West, where the setting sun was casting its blanket of shadow.

It was a road that Harvey had never been down before, but he knew of it, and he knew of the park. Why he knew of the area was of little importance. For now, it was a refuge, a place to stop and gather his thoughts. A place to plan his next move, whichever shape that might take.

The Harvey Stone that ruled his heart had been thinking of little else than Alice for the entire gruelling day. But that other part of his mind, that tenacious, embittered, and ruthless being that lost his sister to the likes of Samuel Norris, was not one to be quietened with matters of the heart.

He was torn.

The park was broad and long with a footpath that snaked from where he was standing to a lake in the distance, and beyond. A narrow river cut the scene from right to left, feeding the lake with fresh water. At the far end of the lake, Harvey

imagined another river formed and meandered off to find the
Thames not far away. To his right, a mature forest offered sanctuary. It wasn't a dark, foreboding forest, such as Epping Forest,
where he ran most mornings. The trees were spread apart, and
the remaining sunlight cast an orange hue on the forest floor in
the few spaces between the long shadows of trees. It was a
haven for him, and he felt the difference in the atmosphere the
moment he stepped inside.

A squirrel froze, eyed him, then bolted to a nearby tree. The
leaves fluttered in the flurries of a late summer breeze. But there
was no other movement.

"Norris," he called, his keen eyes searching potential hiding
places for a man on the run. A man with only one shoe and the
fragile mind of a scared child in his arms. There were places
where local kids had been sitting. The further Harvey walked
through the forest, the more signs he saw. A small copse of
thorny bush had grown into a natural windbreak. There were
beer cans, cigarette packets, and the residues of cigarette papers.
On occasion, he found a wrap of tin foil, charred and discarded
as the owner had succumbed to the fumes of its contents and
settled against a tree to enjoy the ride.

The forest reminded Harvey of the orchard on his foster
father's estate. The light was similar, but in place of the beer
cans and drug paraphernalia, John's orchard bore fallen and
rotting fruit. As children, he and Hannah had played in the
orchard. They had climbed the trees, picked the apples and
pears, and they had even teased the fat, over-indulged wasps
that feasted on the fallen fruit, before running to the sanctuary
of the willow.

The willow was a lonely tree that seemed out of place in the
centre of John's wide lawn. It stood beside the stream that ran
from the very top of the three-hundred-acre estate, carved an arc
behind the house, and then disappeared behind the stables and

barn at the far end of John's land. The willow was a crossing
point. The stream, which during the summer was little more
than a trickle, and in the winter was a knee-high, raging torrent
two feet across, had been something far wilder in their minds.
Their imaginations had carved scenes from books that Hannah
had read and relayed to her younger brother. The stream was a
wild river that cut through the landscape; it was a port where
great ships docked; it was a sea where pirates, in the great
willow ship, walked the plank. It was the place where the char-
acters in their minds lived and died.

It had been the centre of their imaginary world. The
moment they stepped out of the great house each morning, they
had made for the willow. Most times, they had played there, or
just sat in its protective shade. Other times, they crossed the
stream and headed for the orchard. The crossing was made
possible by a large rock in the centre of the flow. As a boy,
Harvey, who had been younger than Hannah, struggled to leap
the narrow stretch of water, often falling in and soaking his
shoes. But the rock opened doors to him. It had been his access
to the world beyond the willow. They often mused on where the
rock came from. They knew every inch of John's estate and no
other rock like it existed in shape, size, or colour. It was just
another element in the magic world of make believe that he and
his sister had imagined.

Harvey reached the far end of the forest. Open grass
stretched before him toward the river he had seen. In the
distance were a few dog walkers, stretching their legs after a
day's work.

The sun would set soon. The shadows across the grass
seemed to stretch and fade. The river cut a dark line in the grass
three hundred yards ahead of him. Beyond that was an urban
blend of houses and what appeared to be an old factory, no
doubt situated there originally to spill its waste into the river.

From where he was standing, he had a clear view of the river. The path on which he had entered the park was adjoined to another that ran beside the lake. To the crossing point.

A crossing point.

The bridge was concealed by trees that reached high from the riverbank, and then hung their long limbs down to the water's edge.

Willows.

The footpath disappeared from view behind the dropping branches, and the shadow of the factory beyond the park shrouded the space in darkness. It was a sanctuary.

In that moment, Harvey had stepped from John's orchard and was looking down at the willow. It was the only place to cross the stream and the centre of their imaginary world.

Harvey strode across the grass, growing surer with each step. His walk became a jog that became a run, until he was just thirty metres away. The bridge was thirty-five feet long, four feet wide, and had a handrail on each side. It was wide enough for a pushchair or a bike, and in the sunlight, it would have been a place of beauty, where families might cast bread down to the swans and ducks below. But in the shadow of the great factory a hundred feet away, it was gloomy and foreboding.

Halfway across the bridge, a dark shape was still. It was a man, lost in his own world, his own imagination.

"Norris?"

The figure moved.

Harvey took a step forward.

"Norris?"

"Stay away."

It was him. His articulate voice pronounced even those two words with such clarity and annunciation that it could only have been him.

"Where is she, Norris?" Harvey moved forward.

"Don't come another step."

Harvey reached the end of the bridge, close enough to see Norris' features in the gloom. The water below was fast-running and deep. Its shimmering surface would soon turn inky black. There was no sign of movement down there, save for the ripples of the current.

"I said don't move," said Norris, and he reached behind him. He collected the girl in his arms and hoisted her above the water. "I will. You know I will."

The girl, who clawed at Norris' arms but failed, began to scream and cry, so that Harvey had to raise his voice to be heard.

"What have you done, Norris?"

"It's the only way," called Norris, pulling his face away from the girl's desperate fingers.

She began to wail. She screamed something unintelligible, its clarity lost to the tears and fright.

"What's the only way? How is this the answer?"

"It'll never stop. It'll never stop, and I'll always be running. I thought there was a chance. But all we've done is run. He's always one step ahead." His voice softened, losing its authoritative tone as if his hope had succumbed to the same fate as his mind. "I'll always be Samuel Norris. Richard Valentine is dead."

Harvey reeled at the mention of Norris' true identity. He stared at the old man, seeking some kind of familiarity in his features. But all he saw was a bitter old man, wretched and weak.

"Have you—"

"Touched her?" Norris finished. "Don't be disgusting. But they don't know that. All they know is that I'm a sick old man. They'll find me. They'll find her. And I'll go back to where I came from. The girl will be fine. I haven't touched a hair on her head. And I'll be safe. Safe from his reach."

"It doesn't have to be like this, Norris. Bring her back. Put her down."

Harvey stepped onto the bridge.

"You can't do anything. You can't help," said Norris, holding the girl as far away from Harvey as he could. Her feet kicked in the air, and her cries had turned to miserable whines.

"I can, and I will."

"What can you do?"

"I'm going to end this. It's gone too far." He took another step.

"You can't stop him. Nobody can."

Harvey closed the gap, moving slowly to avoid sudden movements.

"Get away," snapped Norris, and he edged back.

"Norris, listen to me. I can stop Spider. I know how to stop all of this. But I need your help and you need to put that child down."

FORTY-ONE

The space where Debruin usually parked his old car was empty. It was still outside Norris' flat with a punctured tyre. He imagined that the teenagers might have even torched it by now.

"I need a vehicle," said Debruin to the two TSG officers who followed, snapping the Velcro straps of their body armour in place as they walked.

Without hesitation, the first man tossed Debruin a set of keys. He caught them, hit the button on the fob, and the lights of a nearby Ford flashed. On the outside, the car was a standard Mondeo. But Debruin knew better. TSG were one of the best equipped units in the region. They trained hard, worked hard, and, as a reward, they were given the best that budgets could buy.

Hargreaves' door had barely closed when Debruin pulled away, letting the wheels spin on the tarmac. He half expected Hargreaves to tell him to stop and put his seat belt on, but he hoped they were past any nonsense of superiority. They were of equal rank, and out of the blue, Debruin had been given a rare second chance at proving himself. He couldn't let it go to waste.

They were tearing down the high street with the blue lights

in the grille flashing and the siren blaring. Traffic moved out of their way, and even buses made a path for them; it was a far cry from the battle Debruin had had while attempting to walk along the footpath.

"Detective Sergeant Butler," said Hargreaves, reading from the blue file on his lap. His mouth hung open as he read Carver's notes. "He's rogue? He should have been reported."

"He's been undercover for too long. He's in too deep."

"You knew about this?"

"Only since this morning. I got the rundown after our chat earlier," said Debruin, as he navigated the roundabout beneath the A406 North Circular Road. "I need the address. It should be on the back page."

Hargreaves read it out loud and had the sense to pass the details over the radio to the TSG officers who were tailing them in the car behind.

"Two minutes out," said Debruin, and he glanced in his mirror. The TSG officer in the passenger seat was preparing. His name was Connor. Debruin had worked with him on a few cases. Short of being fortuned with Spencer's fast thinking and no-nonsense approach, Connor was a safe pair of hands.

"Are there any other secrets you might want to let me in on?" said Hargreaves.

"Secrets? No," said Debruin, and he couldn't help but smile at the turned tables. "Except that I'm innocent, and that one day in the not too distant future, I might let you buy me a beer by way of an apology."

He reached for the radio, hit the push-to-talk button, and looked at the two men in the car behind them.

"One minute out. Here's the plan. DS Butler has been working undercover. We don't know who's watching his house and we don't know if he's rogue. Forget the politeness, forget protocol, and forget the doorbell. I want that front door taken care of and the house secure. He could have a hostage, in which case we secure the premises and call it in."

"Roger," came the reply. Connor was a man of few words.

"Here it is," said Hargreaves. Grosvenor Road. He held onto the door as Debruin took the bend as fast as he dared.

One thing struck Debruin the moment he turned the corner. A black Mercedes Sprinter was parked at the end of the road. Sprinters were a common enough van, but not in black. And in that neck of the woods, any van owner would have parked the van as close to their house as they could. Car crime was rife, and smashed windows were more often than not the result of kids looking for a quick win by way of a bag to steal, or a wallet.

Debruin slammed on the brakes, and the car skidded to a halt. The better trained TSG driver had managed to stop far more efficiently, and Connor was out before Debruin. He ran to the front door, put his back against the wall, and readied himself. The driver, a tall, dark-skinned man, was close behind him with a ram in his hands. Without breaking stride, the driver swung the heavy ram back with both hands and lunged forward. The door, as Debruin had hoped, was torn off the hinges.

Connor was inside in under two seconds, clambering over the door. The only protocol they had kept to was the warning of the armed police, which was paramount should shots be fired. The TSG driver stood to one side to let Debruin through. He climbed over the door and was a few metres from Connor when Butler reached out from the living room, grabbed Connor's weapon, and pulled him back. By the time Debruin had reached the living room door, Butler held Connor with his arm twisted up behind his back and the muzzle of the weapon pressed into the back of his head.

"Stay where you are," called Butler.

"I'm Detective Inspector Mark Debruin. I'm investigating a

missing child and you, Detective Sergeant Butler, are one of the
men last seen with her." He kept his voice calm and clear, and
stepped into the room, holding his hand out to Hargreaves and
the TSG driver behind. He spoke to the TSG driver. "Lower
your weapon."

"On the ground," shouted Butler. "Put the gun down and lay
on the ground. Hands behind your head."

"I'm not going to be putting my hands anywhere except
inside my pockets," said Debruin. "And I certainly am not going
to be lying on the ground."

From his pocket, he retrieved his wallet. He let it fall open
for Butler to see the ID.

"How about we put that gun down?"

"I don't believe you. How do I know you're real?"

"You've been working undercover too long, Butler. You
report into DI Frank Carver. How would I know that?"

"That doesn't prove anything," said Butler, and he pulled
Connor back, putting distance between them and Debruin.

"Okay, okay," said Debruin. "I'm going to reach into my
pocket one more time." He held his hands out in a gesture of
peace and slowly reached into his right-hand pocket. He
produced three photographs, then held them out to show that he
wasn't holding a weapon.

As Butler eyed them, his eyes widened a little.

"This one," said Debruin, holding out the first of the
photographs, "is this man's wife." He pointed to Hargreaves,
who bit his lower lip but said nothing. Debruin selected the
second photograph. "This is Emily Bull. She was Trevor Banks'
girlfriend. She was killed earlier today."

Butler edged back as if the sight of the photographs was too
much to bear.

"And this one," said Debruin, holding the last of the three
photographs out for Butler to see, "is Rosie White. She's the

daughter of Charlotte White. I believe you know who Charlotte White is, don't you?"

He turned the final photo over to reveal the writing on the rear.

"She's in danger, Butler. Where is she?"

Connor struggled against Butler's hold, but the rogue officer tightened his grip.

"Easy, Connor," said Debruin. "Nobody is going to get hurt. All we want is to find Rosie. We know you were recruited. We know that none of this is your fault. Let's keep it that way."

It took several seconds for Butler to relent. He shoved Connor toward Debruin, who caught him and stopped him from stumbling, by which time Butler had opened the magazine of the weapon, released the slide, and let the pieces fall to the floor in a heap.

"I'm not a bad man," he said, his voice dejected.

"Nobody said you are."

"I don't have her. It wasn't meant to be like this."

"What wasn't? Talk to me, Butler. Talk to me, my friend, because right now we have a missing child, and you are the closest thing we have to a suspect. Let us help you."

"The old man has him. Norris. They were only meant to keep her safe. But he ran off with her and left us."

"Us? Who else was there?"

"I don't know his name. He was recruited, like me."

"Recruited? What for?"

Butler looked confused, as if the answer was obvious.

"He's a killer. He's been killing all those men."

The news came at Debruin like a sledgehammer. His heart skipped a beat, and for a moment, he was breathless.

"Banks wasn't the killer?"

"Banks?" said Butler. "Banks was a driver, and he was damn good as well."

Debruin turned to Hargreaves, who was one step behind in piecing the puzzle together.

"The killer is still out there."

"And so is Samuel Norris," said Butler. He held out his hand, looking beyond Debruin into the next room. A woman who, Debruin presumed, was Butler's wife, stepped cautiously toward her husband. She reached for him and he pulled her into a hug, keeping her safe. "Like I said. I'm not a bad man, DI Debruin."

"No. No, you're not."

A silence followed, as Debruin sought the next move. But just when he thought the tangled web of thoughts was too far gone to decipher, Connor's radio burst into life with Spencer's short, concise messages. "Control, this is echo-four. We've found Samuel Norris. He has the child. She's alive. We have him in our sights. Are we clear to take him down?"

PART THREE

FORTY-TWO

A pale orange glow on the horizon marked the sunset with water-colour strokes of mauve stratus that seemed to stretch across the sky and vanish into the gloom of the night.

The factory and houses on the far side of the river were nothing more than featureless patches of black where nothing seemed to exist. The river below them, as it hurried toward the lake, was the only source of movement.

"We need to move, Norris," said Harvey. "They'll be hunting you down. Bring the girl back. Put her down."

Norris was visibly tiring. The adrenaline that had fuelled his escape and given him the strength to hold the girl above the water was waning, and the old man's arms were drooping.

"I've been hunted since the day the newspapers showed my face and told the world who Samuel Norris is. I was hounded before the trial, I was hounded in prison, and I'm hounded now. Do you know what it's like to fear stepping out of your door?"

Harvey didn't reply. He watched the girl, readying himself for the moment Norris' strength gave up and she fell.

"Even in prison, it was the same. They time the meals and

the showers so that the likes of me, the sick and perverted, never have to cross paths with the likes of you."

"The likes of me?"

"Criminals. Killers. Men who go out of their way to disfigure or maim men like me." He spoke softly, but there was a bitter undertone. "There's a balance. To find the balance, you have to sacrifice everything. It's the prison guards mainly. You live by their rules, not the prison rules. Break one of their rules, and they'll arrange for the nastiest piece of work they can find to be out of their cell just when you go to shower. You can scream all you like. There's nobody to save you."

"Bring the girl back, Norris."

"Then, of course, there's mealtimes. You learn to eat fast, you learn to get back to your cell, and you learn not to make eye contact. It's not solitary confinement, but it is a solitary existence."

"You're innocent. You said so yourself. You don't have to go through that again."

"You were coming for me, weren't you?" said Norris, ignoring Harvey's reasoning. "You were coming for me tonight. What would you have done?"

Harvey didn't reply.

Norris sat the girl on the handrail. She wasn't safe, but at least her life no longer depended on the strength of the old man. All he had to do was let her go, and she would tumble backwards. As Norris spoke, Harvey made a plan. If she were to fall, he would dive into the water on the other side. The current was fast, it would drag her towards him.

"What did you do to those men? The less fortunate ones?"

Harvey said nothing.

"Oh, come on," Norris said, raising his voice. "We both know you killed them. We both know what you're capable of."

"So why do you need me to tell you?"

"I want to hear it from the horse's mouth. Tell me about Slater. I read all about him and what he did. I can only imagine what you did to him, like a scene from a film. One of those brutal thrillers where the victims scream and cry. How did it end for him?"

Over the years, Harvey had killed dozens of men. He could recall every detail of every kill. But often, the faces merged. Over time, the people he tortured, maimed, and forced to suffer were wiped from his memory and only the kill remained. But his recent kills were fresh. He rarely reflected on a kill. The kill only served to satiate the wild dreams he had. Slater was still fresh.

"It isn't like the films," said Harvey, and in that moment, he knew that Norris would never live to tell his story. "It doesn't happen like the way movies portray a murder."

"And Slater? Did he scream and cry?"

"He cried," said Harvey, remembering the childlike wails. "Most men do."

There was a sharp intake of breath from Norris, as Harvey conveyed his experience in a single sentence.

"Tell me how you do it. Tell me how you like to kill."

"I don't *like* to kill."

"So why do it?"

"I had a sister."

"Oh," said Norris, and he seemed to be getting pleasure from Harvey's confession. "Had?"

"She was raped. She killed herself."

"And you vowed to kill any man who did the same thing." Norris surmised. "You're a vigilante, doing what the police dare not to do."

"No. There's no vow. There's no vigilante. Only dreams. Dreams that torture me. I see her. I hear her laugh." He paused, having never divulged the information before. But there was no turning back. "It's the only way to stop the dreams."

"Until they return," finished Norris. "And you have to kill again."

"Bring her down, Norris. "You're not a killer."

"You didn't tell me what you did to poor old Slater."

"Do you really want to know?"

"I want to know what you would have done to me, given half a chance. How do you do it?"

"It depends," said Harvey. "It depends on the circumstance. It depends on what they did and where they are."

"And Slater? I'll not bring her down until you tell me."

"I hung him by his ankles. I bled him out."

"He died slowly?"

"Not slow enough," said Harvey. "But he was aware of every single second."

"And me? What would you have done to me?"

"Do you really want to know? I would have cut you open from your balls to your chest. I would have opened you up and you would have suffered every living moment of it."

Norris was silent. The girl had stopped struggling, and Harvey regretted saying those terrible words in front of her. But if it convinced Norris to bring her down, it was a small price to pay. She buried her head in her hands, and Norris, softening to the feeble cries, pulled her close to him.

"And now?" he asked, his voice cracking with fatigue and emotion. "What will you do now?"

"You're not a predator, Norris. You're harmless to anyone but yourself."

In the time it had taken for Harvey to break Norris down and bring the girl back to safety, the night had become dark and the river was nothing more than a ribbon of inky gloom several metres below them. The buildings behind were lost to the shadows and a faint glimmer of glass reflected the moonlight somewhere in the expanse of industrial structures.

But it was a faint glimmer of glass that hadn't been there before. It was a faint glimmer of glass that was joined by another.

And Harvey knew.

"Get down," he said.

Norris appeared confused. The two flashes of moonlight in the shadows behind them moved, then fixed, as if they locked onto the target. Harvey ran at Norris. He grabbed the girl from him before Norris could even offer resistance, and he pulled Norris to the ground as the first round ricocheted off the handrail and whistled through the air.

"They're shooting," said Norris, stunned, and frozen on his hands and knees.

"I can do this, Norris. I can beat Spider. But I need you. I can't do it without you."

A second round found the bridge floor just two inches from Norris' right hand, and Harvey realised they had missed before because he was holding the girl. They had waited for a clear shot.

The girl was screaming louder than before, and the two reflections adjusted to Norris' position.

"Are you with me, Norris?" said Harvey, shouting to be heard over the girl.

Norris appeared terrified. His eyes were wide, and he looked as if he might break down in tears any second.

"I'm with you," he said, glancing behind him.

"When I say run, you run as fast as you can," said Harvey, crawling with the girl to cover Norris. He stared up at the police snipers, hoping his defiant and embittered expression could be seen through their night vision scopes.

"Run," said Harvey.

FORTY-THREE

Debruin was breathless when he reached the bridge with Hargreaves in tow. He took Connor's radio, looked back at the old factory, and searched for Spencer in the dark.

"Is this it?" he asked over the radio. "Is this the bridge?"

"He was standing right where you are now. He was holding the child over the railing."

"Which way did he go?"

"They ran east. Back the way they came. They took the girl with them."

"They?" said Debruin, picturing the scene. He lowered the radio and peered over the railing at the black water below. "Are you telling me he wasn't alone?"

"It was just him and the girl at first. We couldn't get a clear shot. Another man joined him and talked him out of it. I've got a team heading them off."

"Talked him out of what, Spencer?"

"Killing the girl, sir."

Spencer's voice was cold and almost robotic over the radio. The man's ability to conceal any emotion was why he did what he did, and why he did it so well.

"Come down, Spencer," said Debruin, and he passed the radio back to Connor. If Spencer was watching through his NV scope, he would see the move and know the conversation was over.

A group of men emerged from the shadows walking directly toward the bridge. They were one hundred yards away when the shiny buttons on Barnes' tunic glimmered.

"Now what?" said Debruin, and he turned to face Hargreaves, who had been silent for too long. His face seemed to sag with worry. "We'll get to her."

His voice seemed to rouse Hargreaves from a daydream. He raised his eyebrows and nodded.

"I'm just a bit worried, Debruin. That's all."

"We've got two of Spencer's men keeping tabs on her. She's safe."

Hargreaves attempted a smile but failed.

"Debruin," called Barnes. He walked beside Carver, Hawes, and Spencer. "This is a bloody mess."

"Yes, gov. We're doing what we can."

"Well, do more. Hargreaves, I hear you received one of these photos."

"Yes, gov."

"Spencer assures me his best men are watching her. You have nothing to worry about."

Hargreaves' attempt at a smile improved with Barnes' reassuring words, although Barnes' voice was hardly a comfort.

"Debruin, give me an update on everything that has happened since you visited Norris. I want to know why you're not in an interview room awaiting a charge. I've had half a story from Hawes and half a story from Hargreaves. Maybe you can fill in the blanks."

A public reprimand was not the best way to convey a case update. But Debruin had seen Barnes in this type of mood before. It wasn't worth rubbing him up the wrong way. But it also wasn't worth wrapping anything in cotton wool. The man wanted facts. Concise facts.

"I went to Norris' flat. Norris ran. I chased him. The killer picked him up."

"You lost him?" Barnes summarised.

"I lost him, yes, gov."

"Go on."

"The car crashed near Havering-Atte-Bower earlier today. The driver, who we assumed to be the killer, was killed. Norris escaped. However, we now know that the driver was not the killer. The real killer escaped with Norris. The driver's name was Trevor Banks. I found his girlfriend at home with her throat slashed this afternoon."

"So, Banks and his girlfriend are dead, and Norris and the killer are still at large?" Barnes had a way of reiterating the negative facts, so that even as Debruin spoke, he understood Barnes' point of view.

Debruin inhaled, long and deep.

"Yes, gov. Banks wasn't a criminal. He was being blackmailed. As is the killer."

He waited for Barnes to digest the information.

"Go on," he said.

"When you came to the hospital to take me in, I had to run, gov. I worked out who the leak is, and I have a confession."

"Charlotte White?"

"Yes, gov."

"And let me guess, she's also being blackmailed?"

"Norris and the killer abducted Charlotte's daughter an hour ago."

"And Butler?" said Carver, the first input he had given since his arrival. He seemed perturbed at the progress Debruin had made in such a short period of time.

"Blackmailed. We've been to his house."

"Seems like an awful lot of blackmail, Debruin."

"It's not a criminal organisation. It's a single criminal with a hold over everyone he needs to do whatever he wants them to do."

"You're telling me that Butler has not gone rogue?" Carver's Scottish accent, which until now had been subtle and almost alluring, returned with an underlying aggression.

"DS Butler is a seriously disturbed individual. He doesn't know who to trust and all he wants to do is protect his wife. I recommend we offer him counselling."

"Counselling?" said Carver. "He's played us like fools."

"The man has clearly been through a lot. I've got a TSG officer at his home, just in case. But I believe he's as legitimate as you or I."

"Well that's just it, Debruin," said Barnes. "Your legitimacy is questionable. Either that or your competency. One of them is off. Why don't you tell me which one it is?"

"There's nothing wrong with this man's integrity," said a voice from behind them.

The party turned to find DS Butler emerging from the darkness. He appeared to have lost the weight that had been hanging from his shoulders. He walked with confidence and purpose.

"Butler?" said Carver. "You've got some nerve."

"Detective Inspector Carver," he said, by way of a greeting.

"What the hell do you think you're doing?"

He came to a stop beside the group, looked at each of them individually, then settled his determined gaze on Debruin.

"I want to help," he said.

"Over my dead body," Carver began, but Debruin overruled him, and to his surprise, even Barnes held out his hand to silence Carver.

"What do you have to offer? Are you up to it?"

"The TSG officer is looking after my wife. If I can help, I will."

"We seem to have two problems, Butler. We have a missing child, and we have a spider's web of blackmail," said Debruin.

"I might be able to help. Samuel Norris is not Samuel Norris."

Butler let the cryptic statement hang there for the men to ponder.

"Go on," said Barnes.

"I don't know his real name. He didn't say what it was."

"What *did* he tell you?"

"He told us that he was the first of Spider's recruits. He worked in banking. Spider took his daughter, and Norris had no way out. Things got so bad for him that the only way he could escape was to adopt a false identity and go into hiding."

"You're not saying–"

"Samuel Norris is innocent," he finished. "Yes. Where better to hide, with all the protection he needed, than in prison?"

"That's a terrible plan," said Carver. "Do you know how sex offenders are treated inside?"

"It's a brilliant plan," countered Debruin. "He would have been isolated. As long as he kept his nose clean, the guards would have kept him safe."

Butler nodded.

"He served his sentence without putting a foot wrong, during which time Norris hoped Spider would have been caught, and he could have resumed his true identity."

"That's why Norris confessed," said Debruin, piecing the information together. "That's why he had to convince the jury he was guilty. I've seen his file. There's almost no evidence at all. No DNA, no prints. Just a confession to a rape charge where the victim didn't see her attacker's face."

"So why has he taken the girl?" said Hawes. "It doesn't make sense if he's not guilty."

The circle of men silenced as each man searched for a conclusion. Hawes, Butler, Barnes, Carver, Spencer and Hargreaves. A fine team of minds and skill. But it was Debruin who was closest, and he voiced his opinion.

"He wants to go back inside," he said. "Spider is still active, and I've seen the way Norris lives. Prison would be safer for him. He can't resume his old life until Spider is out of the picture."

"This is all conjecture," said Barnes. "Why would anybody want to be put away, least of all for abduction as a crime?"

"With all due respect, sir, Spider is ruthless. He has eyes everywhere. He has a network of people working for him. Some of them active, like I was. Some of them sitting idle. But every one of them has something hanging over them, and if you choose to disobey him, the consequences are severe," said Butler.

"Are you telling us you have witnessed him murder?" said Carver.

"No. Spider doesn't murder anybody. Bloom does it for him."

"Ebenezer Bloom," said Carver.

"If anybody tries to run, he'll kill them and whoever they care about. If anyone tries to report it, they die. If they make a mistake, they die. The whole thing is built on fear, and Ebenezer is the executioner. Only one man has ever escaped."

"Samuel Norris," said Debruin. Then he remembered something Carver had said. "DI Carver, how long have you been trying to bring this down?"

"Years," he grumbled, as if the word came from the very pit of his stomach.

"You said you were close to stopping it once. You said you were close to nailing one of them, but they vanished."

Carver's mouth fell open, and the group waited for a name to follow.

"Richard Valentine," he whispered, and the pieces that had been jumbled in his mind since he began the case came together. "He didn't disappear. He was hiding in plain sight."

"What do we know about him?"

"He was a banker. Worked for some private bank in London."

"That's why he was recruited," said Butler. "Spider had him syphoning off cash from wealthy individuals' bank accounts to fund the start-up."

"He had a daughter," said Carver, and he waited for Butler to offer an insight.

But Butler simply shook his head, and the group silenced, imagining the girl's fate.

"It's time to put a stop to all this," said Butler, and he found Debruin's stare. "I know where to find him."

"Spencer, I need half of your team with Hawes. Find Richard Valentine. He can't have got far," said Debruin, forming a plan as he spoke. "I'll take the other half with Butler."

Spencer reached for his shoulder-mounted radio and prepared to rally his troops. But Barnes quashed the plan with a single statement.

"Stop," he said, shaking his head, and he eyed Debruin with contempt.

"Gov, I can do this. I need this chance."

He seemed to take an age to respond. He searched Debruin's eyes for the faintest sign of weakness.

"Spencer, get me an update from your team. Hawes, Butler, make a plan of attack. Debruin, walk with me," he said, and as the cogs began to turn, Debruin's heart sank.

They moved away from the crowd, over the bridge, and along the footpath. To their left was a dark patch of forest, and to their right, a footpath branched off to run alongside the lake.

"I saw Julie at the hospital," Barnes said. He walked with his hands in his pockets and seemed to study the ground beneath his feet. "I spoke to the doctor she was with. She seems competent. She said you're a spirited man. A good father." He stopped and glanced back at the bridge to make sure they were out of earshot. "Why didn't you tell me?"

Debruin sighed.

"It's my personal life, gov. This is my job. I can't let the two merge."

"That's admirable, but tell me, when you get home at night, do you switch off? Do you leave the case at work and think only of your family?"

"Of course not, gov."

"So, when you have a sick daughter that needs your care, do you switch that off while you're at work?"

"I try to."

"But you can't?"

Debruin nodded.

"I can't let you go after Spider, Debruin."

"Gov, I–"

"Your daughter needs you. The doctor was quite clear. The chances of finding a donor are slim. She said your wife can't do it, but you could."

"I need treatment, gov. I have to have a course of drugs to raise my red blood cell count."

"And what happens if you get injured going after Spider?"

Debruin said nothing.

"That's why you ran, wasn't it? You had to prove your innocence. If you were charged, you wouldn't be able to help your daughter. I agree with the doctor. You are a spirited man, Debruin. I didn't know you had it in you."

"She's my daughter. I'm the only chance she's got."

"That's why you're taking a back seat."

"Gov, no."

"I couldn't live with myself if something happened to you."

"I'll wear body armour."

"You'll do no such thing."

"Gov, I've come this far. Carver has been on this case for years and I've got further than him in a single day."

"By pure luck, ignorance, and not without casualties, I might add."

"Gov—"

"Bring me Richard Valentine and get that little girl back, Debruin. Leave Spider to Spencer and Hawes. That's my final word."

FORTY-FOUR

"What's your name?" said Harvey to the little girl he held in one arm.

Norris limped behind them, and Harvey kept a brisk pace, listening to the sirens in nearby neighbourhoods, and making his way through the network of back streets.

"Rosie," she mumbled. She buried her face into the crook of his neck. It was hot with tears.

"Well, Rosie, we're going to get you back to your mum. Just give me a little time to find her, okay?"

He felt her nod and she gripped his shirt collar with her little hand.

"Are you keeping up, Norris?"

Norris said nothing.

Harvey took a few more steps. He needed to push them harder. He needed Norris to walk fast or, better still, run. He turned to face him and waited for the old man to catch up.

Norris came to a stop a few metres from Harvey, keeping his distance.

"I wasn't going to hurt her," he said.

"You could have drowned her."

Norris shook his head. "No. I just—"

"Just what?"

"I can't see a way out."

"We take Spider down, whoever he is. It's the only way."

"He's too connected. He'll have people watching everything we do."

"If he had people watching everything we do, we wouldn't have made it this far," said Harvey. "He might have blackmailed men into working for him, but what he doesn't have is loyalty. It's falling apart. His empire is cracking. And those people that live in fear, those men and women who would do anything to get out, they'll see those cracks. He's lost Banks. He's lost Butler. And he's lost his leak," said Harvey, not wanting to mention the woman's name in front of her daughter.

"You still have to get past Bloom."

"I'll deal with Blue Eyes when I see him."

"And if you fail?"

"I won't fail," said Harvey. "*We* won't fail. There are too many lives at stake."

"And your girl? What do you think will happen to her if you launch a full scale attack?"

Harvey considered what he said. Norris was right. The only reason Harvey hadn't tried to take Spider down already was because Alice would be made to suffer. The two locked stares. The weak Norris that had taken the girl was at bay, and the man who had been in hiding for so long showed his face.

"When you did what you did, all those years ago, you did it knowing your daughter would suffer. It was the only way out."

Norris nodded.

"It's what I have to do," said Harvey. "There are too many lives at risk. It's bigger than I ever imagined. I have to go in and bring him down, and I have to do it fast. Before he kills her."

"Can you live with that?"

"I'll have to. The same way you did."

Beyond Norris' shoulder, a car passed by the top of the road. It drove slowly, then stopped and reversed.

"We need to go," said Harvey.

Norris looked over his shoulder, but Harvey pushed him forward. "No time to sightsee. Move," he said.

With only one shoe, Norris was making slow progress. The car behind them was just two hundred yards away, moving slowly. With the girl in his arm, Harvey couldn't run. They passed an old house. The windows were boarded up, and the front door was adorned with graffiti.

"In here," said Harvey.

He glanced back at the car. It was one hundred yards away, crawling between the parked cars. He kicked through the front door, stepped inside, and dragged Norris in after him.

The house was derelict. Nearly all the internal walls had either been knocked down or had fallen down. The ceiling had collapsed, exposing the floor above. Their entrance startled two pigeons. They took flight, their wings flapping noisily as they searched for an exit. Harvey pulled Norris in and pinned him against the wall beside the front door. He listened for the passing car.

But the car did not pass. It stopped, and the engine was cut.

Harvey peered through the open doorway. It was an unmarked vehicle, and the officers were armed.

"Have they seen us?" whispered Norris.

Harvey held the girl out for Norris to take.

"What are you doing?" asked Norris. "I don't want her."

"Take her," said Harvey, raising his voice as much as he dared. The policemen outside may not have heard Harvey, but his aggression was not lost on the girl. It started with a high-pitched wail that soon developed into a full blown breakdown. Harvey shoved the bewildered old man into the centre of the space. Norris turned to look for somewhere to hide with the screaming child in his arms.

But it was too late.

Two officers, both armed, stormed into the derelict house with their weapons aimed at Norris.

"Armed police. Put the girl down and get on your knees."

Norris froze.

Before the officer could repeat his warning and command, Harvey had one hand on his colleague's throat, and the other on the weapon. It took less than two seconds for Harvey to disarm the man and position him as a human shield.

"Put it down," said Harvey, his voice calm and clear. He aimed the weapon at the armed policeman. "I *will* shoot if I have to."

There were a few seconds of hesitation, which Harvey allowed, given the man's predicament. He made his weapon safe, ejected the magazine, and laid it on the ground, holding Harvey's stare all the while.

Harvey gestured at the man's side arm. "That as well." The officer laid down his second weapon. "Now move away," said Harvey. Then he turned to Norris. "Hand her over and pick up the weapons."

Norris did as Harvey instructed, then came to stand by his side. The man beneath Harvey's grip began to struggle. Without being asked, Norris removed the man's side arm. Then Harvey shoved the officer across the room toward his colleague and took one of the handguns from Norris.

"Get in the car," he said to Norris, and Norris bolted from the building. When Harvey had heard the car door shut, he addressed the two men, the handgun aimed at the first.

"Who's running the investigation?"

"Detective Inspector Debruin," said the first man.

Harvey pictured the man he had seen.

"Tall guy, long coat, hair too grey for his age?" asked Harvey.
"That's him."

"And who are you?"

"Casey."

"Get Debruin on the radio, Casey."

The man leaned into his shoulder.

"DI Debruin, this is echo-five, come back."

The three men waited a few seconds, and Casey repeated his message.

"DI Debruin, this is echo-five, come back."

"Debruin," came the crackled reply, slightly breathless.

Knowing that Harvey would not chance getting within arm's reach of him, Casey tore the battery cable from his radio. He unfastened it from his vest, and tossed it to Harvey, who caught it one handed, his aim never wavering.

"Is this DI Debruin?" said Harvey, keeping his eye on the two officers.

"Who is this?"

"I have two of your men and I've given them the girl. You can tell her parents she is safe and unharmed."

"Are you looking for a prize? You still abducted her. The jury won't be any more lenient with you."

"There won't be a jury."

Debruin offered no retort. He steered the conversation toward Harvey's kills.

"Talk to me about Hammersley."

Harvey didn't reply.

"Don't be shy. How about Jack Slater?"

Again, Harvey said nothing to incriminate himself.

"Where's Samuel Norris? Are you with him?"

"He's nearby. He was never going to hurt her."

"And what about you? What's your next move?"

Harvey said nothing.

"You're going after Spider, aren't you?" said Debruin. "You can't play the silent man with *me*. I know why you did what you did. It doesn't make it right, but I know why. Why don't we talk about it?"

"If you're buying time to trace my location, Debruin, you're already too late. Get the girl to her parents. Forget about me," said Harvey, as he backed toward the door.

"How can I forget about you? I don't even know who you are."

Harvey stopped at the door, disassembled the handgun, and let the pieces fall to the ground.

"I hope you never have to find out."

FORTY-FIVE

"Damn it." Debruin tossed the radio handset into the car and kicked the rear door. "It was him. I know it was him. He's going after Spider. I know he is."

"We've got Rosie back," said Hargreaves. "Come on. I'll drive."

"Have you any idea how long I've been hunting this guy?"

"I know," said Hargreaves, as he climbed into the driver's seat, leaving Debruin little option but to ride shotgun. "He's careful. But if you're right, he's about to do something reckless."

Hargreaves requested the address from Casey over the radio and waited for a response. His calm was doing little to ease Debruin's frustration.

"You haven't failed, if that's what you think," said Hargreaves, as he manoeuvred the car between the parked TSG vehicles. He put his foot down as soon as the address came through. It was a two-minute drive.

"I can get him, Hargreaves. I know I can. He was so close."

"You should know, I spoke to Barnes. He said not to let you out of my sight."

"I'm being mothered, am I?"

"You're lucky," said Hargreaves. "Two hours ago, you were up on a charge."

"What else did he tell you?"

"Nothing, just that we're to get Rosie back to her mum and leave Spider to Hawes and Spencer."

Debruin studied his profile, searching for a hint of deceit. He wondered if Barnes had told him about Grace. But Hargreaves' face offered no clue.

They pulled up at a derelict house. It was detached, which was fairly rare in the neighbourhood. The windows were boarded up, the front door was on the ground, and there was graffiti all over the exterior, even in places where there was no real means of a place to stand. He often wondered how the vandals managed to reach some places. The roof had more tiles missing than in place, and at the other end of the house was a chimney.

The two TSG officers were standing outside. Casey held Charlotte's little girl in his arms. She was asleep, maybe. Probably exhausted from the emotion. Casey walked her over to the car, opened the back door, and sat her in the rear seat. He strapped her in then walked around to Debruin's open window.

"She's okay, sir," said Casey. "A little shaken, but no real harm done as far as I can tell."

"You saw him?"

"The guy? Yeah."

"Tell me about him."

"Leave it, Debruin," said Hargreaves. "You're winding yourself up."

"I need to know. What does he look like?"

"Average height. Average build. In his twenties. Confident."

"No defining features?"

He shook his head. "It was dark. He's the type of man who

could blend into a crowd. Except he wears a leather motorcycle jacket."

"But no motorcycle?"

"He stole our car."

"Let's go," said Hargreaves, and he engaged first gear.

"One second," said Debruin. "If you saw him again..."

"The only thing I would recognise is his eyes, sir," said Casey. "They were cold. They were–"

"Come on," said Hargreaves. "Leave it for Hawes."

"Go on," said Debruin to Casey, in anticipation.

"He's ruthless. He's capable. I'm certain he's your man."

Debruin sighed. He had been sure of it himself. Knowing he had been so close stirred the thing inside him that hungered for the hunt.

They drove in silence. Rosie stirred once and whined. Debruin leaned into the back seat and held her hand. She was no older than Grace. Her little fingers clamped around his. They were cold and clammy. He pulled off his jacket and laid it over her, tucking it behind her back to keep her warm. Until then, she had been the victim of an abduction and nothing more. A piece in the melee of moving parts. There had been little time to feel for her, to empathise. But in the back seat of the car, swathed in shadow, so small and innocent, she could have been Grace. He knew how much she meant to Charlotte and her husband. He had an idea of what the girl's parents were going through. He could empathise with them and he could empathise with the girl. He held onto her hand for the remainder of the journey.

"I won't let you go," he whispered while she slept. "You're safe now."

Hargreaves glanced across when he spoke but said nothing.

Charlotte White's street was busy, but quiet. Flashing blue lights atop a police vehicle lit the houses, and neighbours gathered in respectful silence. Debruin removed the girl from the car, who was bundled in his jacket. Hargreaves held the garden gate open, and as Debruin carried her toward the front door, one of the neighbours gave a gentle clap. More joined in, each of them keen to demonstrate their approval. He turned at the front door to see them. He needed that. He was grateful for the gratitude. A tiny amount of his faith in humanity was restored. It was moments like this that reminded him of why he did his job. He couldn't prevent every murder, he couldn't catch every killer, and he couldn't stop a significant percentile of crimes at all. But when a young child is returned to her parents, and the community shows up in numbers, it means something. He wondered if the surgeon would feel something similar when he or she performed Grace's operation.

He couldn't offer the small gathering a smile. But he tried anyway.

He couldn't even say a few words of thanks to them. His throat was closed and thick with emotion. So, he nodded, and held the girl tight, then turned to find a female police officer at the front door. She held it open and Hargreaves waited for Debruin to lead the way.

Mr White was sitting on the couch in the living room with his face buried in his hands. Debruin unwrapped the girl from his jacket and stepped over to him, saying nothing. White saw his shoes, and slowly raised his head, his eyes widening as he registered what he was seeing.

"Oh my god," he said, jumping to his feet. "Oh my..."

Words failed him. Debruin held Rosie out for her father to take her, then stepped back to enjoy the sight. He felt Hargreaves settle beside him.

"Was she..." Mr White began, and Debruin shook his head.

"Not a hair on her head."

His relief was evident. He wiped away the tears and all the while, Rosie slept.

"Where's Charlotte?" said Debruin, slightly ashamed to break the moment.

Mr White looked confused. "She's with you, isn't she? I haven't been able to reach her."

"You haven't spoken to her?"

"She isn't picking up her desk phone. I figured she was working."

Debruin gave Hargreaves a sideways glance.

"Is she working late?" said Mr White, seeing the look between Debruin and Hargreaves.

"I don't know. I'm sure she's on her way home."

"She's usually home by now. When she didn't answer her phone, I figured she knew. I thought she hated me for letting it happen. Does she even know?"

The truth was that Debruin hadn't even considered Charlotte. The entire team had been so focused on finding Rosie.

"We'll find her," said Debruin. "I'm sure she's fine."

"They said we're in danger. The men who took Rosie said we had to get out."

His raised voice woke the sleeping child. She took a lungful of air and issued a high-pitched whine that deepened into a wail. Her face reddened, and she cried.

"Where is she?" said Mr White. "Find her, damn it. She's in danger."

Debruin gave the female officer a look and gestured for her to intervene. She walked over to Mr White and offered to take the child.

"No. Nobody's taking her from me. I want my wife. Find my wife. Rosie needs her mum."

"We'll find her, Mr White," said Debruin, urging Hargreaves

back through the door. He caught the officer's attention. "Stay here. Make him tea. Keep them safe."

She nodded but stood helplessly.

Debruin stopped at the door and turned back to Mr White. He was going to say something. There was so much he wanted to say, yet so much he couldn't reveal. They hurried to the car, ignoring the neighbours' enquiries as to whether the child was okay. Debruin climbed into the driver's seat, and Hargreaves settled into the passenger seat without argument. He handed Debruin the keys.

"Where are we going? Do we try the train station?"

"No," said Debruin. "She's not there. She's not on a train. If you want to get out, then do so now. I can't guarantee your safety."

"What are you talking about? You're not–"

"There's only one place she could be, Hargreaves."

"You heard what Barnes said."

"I can't stand by and watch anyone else die," said Debruin. "Are you with me?"

FORTY-SIX

The police Ford was faster than it looked. It took just a few minutes for Harvey to navigate his way to the A406 North Circular. From there, he floored the accelerator, ignoring the flashes of speed cameras. He settled into the ride, manoeuvring between slower cars. He glanced at the clock, then once at Norris.

Norris said nothing. Harvey couldn't tell if it was from fear of where they were heading, or fear of the speed at which Harvey was driving. But he didn't slow. He took the Epping turn off on the M25 with the tyres at their limit, coaxing the vehicle around the sweeping bends, using the gearbox to slow the car. It wasn't until they were approaching Epping town centre that Harvey eased off, and Norris spoke.

"You have a death wish, my friend."

Again, Harvey was unsure if Norris was referring to their destination or the speed of his driving. He presumed the latter, but the former still applied.

"Says the man who just abducted a child in the hope of spending the rest his life behind bars," said Harvey, without looking his way.

"A life behind bars is still a life."

"Not from where I'm sitting."

"Do you have a plan at least? Because you know, I'm not in any condition to storm a building and fight my way out. Even if I had both shoes."

There was a humour in his voice, at least Harvey thought so. But his expression was grave, and there was a sheen to his skin in the light of oncoming cars.

"What are you worried about?" asked Harvey. "Not dying, surely?"

Norris stared out of the side window, tracking a woman with her daughter as they crossed the street.

"Of all the things I am, of all the things I've done, and lied about, there is one thing that has got me through life. Without it, I would have crumbled in that cell years ago."

Harvey didn't reply.

"My memory, dear boy. I can remember the look on my daughter's face twenty years ago when we bought her first horse. I can remember the sound of her tortured screams when her mother died. And I can remember every inch of her perfect face as it was when she was born right up to the moment I left her to die."

Harvey said nothing. Norris was leading somewhere, and he would get there in his own time.

"I remember well when you first pulled me into that car, young man. I remember everything. I remember what you said in that barn when we met Mr Butler." He paused, as if he was giving Harvey time to think of what he had said. "Do you?"

Harvey could not relay the exact words he had spoken. His memory just didn't work that way.

"You told me that your friend deserves to live. You told me she's innocent."

Harvey remembered.

"The moment you step foot in that building, you'll condemn her. Do you know that?"

They passed through the town centre and into the country lanes just a mile from Dukes Hall, the old building where Blue Eyes had taken Harvey. Instead of putting his foot down, Harvey let the car cruise.

"What do I do? Leave her there? Wait for someone else to die? Or wait for him to come after me? He's running out of people. It won't be long before he gathers his strength and has a new wave."

"Fresh blood?"

"Something like that."

"I have to ask you something, and I want an honest answer. There's something we haven't discussed." Norris' tone had changed. Before, it had been casual, almost reminiscent. But now it was serious, like a judge condemning a man to life imprisonment, or worse.

Harvey said nothing. He turned into the narrow lane that led to Dukes Hall, stopped the car, and switched off the engine. He knew what Norris was going to say. It was the only topic that had yet to be raised during that strange and exhausting day.

Norris smiled a half-smile, but his eyes saddened.

"How long do I have?"

Harvey didn't reply.

"He gave you a time limit. Of that I'm sure." He looked across at Harvey. "It's what he does, you see? So, tell me, and I'll know if you're lying. How long do I have?"

The dashboard clock seemed to glow brighter.

Harvey took a breath.

"Less than thirty minutes."

"That's cutting it fine."

Harvey said nothing.

"I've done nearly everything you've told me to do today,"

Norris mused. "I've crawled through fields, stolen vehicles, and done things I could never have dreamed of. All without question."

Harvey offered him a sideways glance.

"Well," Norris added, "mostly without question. But the fact is that it's my turn to give you an order, and I won't hear a damn thing against it."

Harvey offered no argument. He knew what was coming.

"I want you to take me in there. And if there's a chance she can live, I want you to put this gun against my head. And when you finally see Spider, or Bloom, or whoever it is...Give that poor girl a chance." He fingered the sidearm Harvey had taken from Casey.

Harvey considered what he had said. He cleared his throat and checked his side mirror out of habit.

"Okay," he said.

Norris stilled.

"Okay?"

"Yeah. Okay. I'll do it. I'll put a gun to your head and march you in there. I'll force you to your knees and when, and only when, I have Spider's attention, I'll put you out of your misery."

Norris swallowed hard. His throat rose and fell, and his nostrils flared.

He nodded.

"Okay."

"Is that settled?" said Harvey, checking the clock.

Again, Norris nodded.

Harvey turned the key, checked his mirror, and pulled out onto the lane. He killed the lights and drove slowly. The huge, old hall was pitch dark against the night sky, and before long, it loomed above them. The scenarios that had played out in Harvey's mind involved him crashing through the great front doors in the stolen police vehicle. If Spider had men on the door, it would have been a fine way to gain entry and to make a point. But instead, he parked as if he were parking outside an expensive hotel.

But there was no valet parking. And there was no group of men on the door ready to fight. In fact, the only person Harvey could see was a woman. She stood at the foot of the few steps, gazing at them like she'd been drugged. Harvey climbed from the car and took a single step forward. She raised a handgun in the air, swaying on her feet as she took aim at Harvey.

"Put the gun down," said Harvey.

A wild shot ricocheted off the Ford.

Norris edged backward towards the rear of the car, but Harvey stayed put.

"You don't have to do this," he called out to the woman forty feet away. "Put the gun down."

He took a step forward. She re-aimed but was unable to keep the gun still. He took another step, his hands held up in a show of peace. "I'm not going to hurt you."

The gun quivered in her hands, and the closer Harvey stepped, the clearer the anguish on her face became. Her mouth was downturned, her frown formed deep lines across her brow, and her eyes were wide, streaming with tears.

"Leave," she said, doing her best to control Harvey. But her voice was more of a breath, and it lacked the punch it needed for such a command.

Harvey stopped.

"Charlotte?" he called, and she seemed to react to the name. "Charlotte White? I know who you are. Your daughter is safe."

The mention of her daughter heightened the woman's emotions. She was breathing hard. The gun shook in her trembling hands and her knees buckled and stiffened, as she sought control over her body.

"I'm going to reach into my jacket," said Harvey. "Don't shoot. I'm going to do it very slowly. I'm not going to hurt you."

Harvey had stopped just twenty feet away. A handgun at that range, in the hands of the untrained, was almost useless. The recoil would send the bullet high, and the weight of the weapon, after holding it for more than a minute, would make aiming impossible. An untrained person would almost certainly aim for the head, whereas trained marksmen aimed for the centre of mass. The chest, the largest part of the human body.

But there was always the chance of a lucky shot.

He reached into his jacket, keeping eye contact with her.

"Nice and slow," he said. "Nobody is going to get hurt." He pinched the grip of the officer's sidearm with his thumb and forefinger, and with his free hand, he opened his jacket wide for her to see. Slowly and carefully, he raised the gun into the air. The sight of it caused a stir. She seemed to shuffle, seeking a stronger stance from which to fire.

And a single gunshot rang out, its missile singing through the air somewhere far above Harvey's head.

He tossed the weapon to one side.

"There," he said. "I mean you no harm. We've come to take you away. Your daughter needs you. Rosie needs you."

The mention of Rosie's name was the straw that broke the camel's back.

She cried out loud, falling against the door frame.

"She's with the police, Charlotte. Nobody can hurt her. She's safe. Your husband too. They're both safe."

He took a few more steps, and she dropped the gun to her side, exhausted, defeated, and terrified. She glanced back into the building, her eyes darting from one side of the hall to the other, and just when Harvey was only a few feet from her, she straightened and raised the gun with renewed vigour.

But still, her emotions ran wild, and she was unable to hold the weapon steady.

"Don't," she whispered, and her entire body was shaking. "Don't come any closer."

"I'm not going to hurt you," said Harvey. His voice was soft yet retained the calm control he needed right then. He raised his hand toward the weapon. "Give me the gun, Charlotte. It's over. You can leave."

Keeping eye contact, he placed his hand on top of the gun, and closed his fingers around it, pushing it away to point harmlessly at the ground.

Norris' uneven footsteps were loud on the gravel behind him.

She looked past Harvey, and he saw the recognition in her eyes. He saw the fright take hold of her body, and she froze. Her eyes found Harvey's and her lips trembled.

"You're him."

Harvey didn't reply.

"You're him. I know who you are. You're the killer." She turned to Norris, who reached for her, his body language far gentler than Harvey's. "And you, you're the..."

"We've come to take you away, Charlotte," said Norris. "We've come to put a stop to all of this."

She was torn. Behind her, somewhere in the building, was the man who, Harvey guessed, had forced her to take them down. And before her stood two men who she knew to be dangerous.

Slowly, Norris came forward until he stood beside Harvey.

"It's over, Charlotte. You can go home," he said.

Her hand tensed on the weapon that both she and Harvey still held, and Norris embraced her in a moment of strength. Her body, stiff with fright and fear, seemed as if it might shatter like glass.

"Hush," said Norris, and he smoothed her hair from her brow, cradling her head into his shoulder. "Nobody is going to hurt you. Rosie is safe. She's with your husband and the police. You've nothing to fear."

He spoke with a tenderness that was far from Harvey's reach. It was a voice born of compassion, feelings, and fatherhood.

Her hand relaxed and fell from the gun, and all the strength in her was spent. She fell into Norris' arms and he took all of her weight.

Harvey watched as the man who had displayed such cowardice throughout the day led the woman to the Ford. He helped her into the driver's seat.

"Go," he said, before closing the car door. "Go and be with Rosie. She needs you."

From behind the well of the car, Charlotte looked small, almost childlike. She reversed away from Norris, turning to face the way they had come. She stared at Norris through the windscreen as if she doubted him, or even doubted everything she had heard. A brazen-faced Norris stared back at her, unmoving, even as she drove slowly away and the headlights grew smaller in the narrow lane.

Harvey said nothing, even when Norris tore his eyes from the rear lights of the car and turned to face him. But Norris must have read the question on Harvey's mind in the quizzical expression on his face. He strode toward him and climbed the few steps, resting his hand against the old stone of the building, as if marvelling at its age.

"There are some moments, my dear boy," he began, resuming the strength of the man he had once been, "that only a father can fully understand."

FORTY-SEVEN

It was fully dark by the time Debruin and Hargreaves pulled away from the Whites' house. Debruin kept to the speed limit, and Hargreaves was silent. There were a few times when Debruin thought he was going to voice his opinion on something, but he stayed silent. Not until they were driving through the village of Theydon Bois, just two miles from Epping, where Butler had said Spider had holed up in an old hall, did he finally talk.

"I'm not a vindictive man, Debruin," said Hargreaves casually, as if he was telling him his favourite colour or movie. "I just strive to do a good job."

Debruin said nothing. He focused on the winding lane named Piercing Hill, which, with its long, sweeping bends and steep inclines, required concentration.

"All the evidence pointed at you. If I hadn't followed up on the lead, I would have been called out as negligent. You understand that, don't you?"

"I do," said Debruin. "But to be honest, I was hoping we were past all that." He checked his rear-view mirror and glanced at Hargreaves. He wasn't a large man, slight in frame, well-groomed, well-mannered, and as result of his conscientious nature, he was well-positioned for the role he played.

"We are. I just want you to know I'm a good man. I get the impression most people think that I'll do anything to climb the ladder. I've come far in a short space of time. Through hard work, you understand. You deal with criminals. You must get a huge amount of satisfaction from putting somebody away."

Debruin said nothing.

"And when you do, you have the entire force behind you, patting you on the back. Do it well enough and you climb the ladder. That's the difference between what you do and what I do. For the most part, I'm not putting away criminals. I'm investigating an accidental shooting, negligence, or over-zealous police officers. And when I charge them, I don't walk from the interview room with my head held high, reeling from glory, Debruin. I walk out of that interview room the target of bitter hatred."

"So, why do you do it?" Debruin asked. "Why put yourself through all that if you don't enjoy the success?"

"I'm good at it," he replied, then inhaled loudly and swallowed hard, preparing to take the conversation deeper. "Do you ever sit with a suspect and just *know* they are guilty? You don't know how. You can't prove it, not yet anyway. But if you had to bet your house on it, or everything you own, you would call a guilty verdict?"

"It's all part of the fun."

"That's what I got from you," said Hargreaves. "All the evidence pointed at you. Your attitude stank. You had all the right answers to the wrong questions. There was so much coincidence. Yet you were so adamant of your innocence."

"You would have bet I was guilty?"

"No, the opposite. I sat down in front of you, after a chat with DSI Barnes, knowing that you were the only suspect. I tried to rile you. I tried to bring something from you that wasn't your pig-headed arrogance."

"I thought–"

"You thought wrong. I can spot a liar a mile away. That's why I'm good at what I do. I spot lies. Even if Barnes said it was you, I knew it wasn't."

Debruin said nothing. He thought of the interview room, and how Hargreaves had been so believable. It was no wonder the man was so good at his job. His role required a unique skill set.

"I spot lies, Debruin," said Hargreaves. "And that ability extends to identifying false evidence."

Debruin considered what he had said, unsure of where the conversation was heading.

"That photo of my wife was a plant, wasn't it?"

Debruin hadn't even thought about the photo since they were all on the bridge discussing the case.

"Hawes?"

"You've got a friend there. Not many people would have risked their careers for a man like you."

"Do you think he wrote those words?" Debruin was incredulous. He slowed to turn into the lane. "But TSG are watching–"

"An empty house," Hargreaves finished, and he took a deep breath, which Debruin was starting to recognise as one of the man's tells. "My wife died two years ago," he said. "Cancer. I carry that photo in my car."

Debruin stopped the car at the side of the lane, the last few minutes of conversation reeling in his mind.

"Are you saying that Hawes stole a photo from your car to plant as evidence?"

"Like I said, you've got a friend there. The moment I saw that photo I understood how much Hawes believed in you."

"But you wanted me locked up. I can spot an act as well as you can, Hargreaves, and that was no act."

"I had a choice to make. I could have arrested Hawes for corrupting the case, or I could go with it. Trust my instincts as it were."

"You chose instincts."

"We needed you back on the case. But I didn't know about Grace at that point. If I had known, maybe I would have left you both in a cell. At least that way we could have found you innocent later down the line, dropped the charges, and you could do what you have to do to save her."

"You're a strange man, Hargreaves," said Debruin, a smile finding his lips for the first time in as long as he could remember. "For an internal investigator, that's a wild stunt to pull."

"We needed you," he said with a guilty grin.

Debruin checked his rearview mirror and pulled out into the lane. He reached into the back seat as he rounded a corner, searching for anything TSG might have available as a weapon, when, out of the darkness, a figure appeared. Debruin braked hard. The car slid on the loose surface and stopped just in time. And there, leaning on the bonnet of the car, her face withered and withdrawn, and her eyes wide with fear, was Charlotte White.

FORTY-EIGHT

If the night outside was quiet, then inside the hall, where the shadows seemed blacker than black, was a vacuum. Norris stepped inside behind Harvey, and seemed familiar with the old hall that, only that morning, Blue Eyes had displayed with such pride.

Harvey knew the route, he remembered the way the corridor seemed to run around the edge of the building to the great kitchen. But he also remembered there were places where the floor had been ripped up. Places that had been visible in the daylight, but were now engulfed in the dark.

"Tread where I tread, and nowhere else," said Harvey, and Norris' reply was his silence.

Progress was slow. Every so often, Norris' sharp intake of breath would announce he had stepped on the head of a nail, or caught a sharp piece of splintered wood. But he didn't cry out. If a board creaked, Harvey would adjust his footing and ensure that Norris followed suit. And where there seemed to be no apparent way across the holes in the floor, Harvey called upon his faith in his own judgement.

"One more corner," said Harvey as they rounded the first bend.

"I remember," said Norris. "I remember it well. Shall I lead?"

He moved ahead of Harvey, his hand running alongside the cold, damp walls. He tested every step, working his way forward, and twice he turned back, sure he had made a mistake, and found a route via the other side of the corridor. By the time they rounded the last corner and Harvey's boots found the old flagstone floor of the kitchen, Norris was in full swing. He was standing at the top of the stone steps, peering down into the gloom. Waiting for Harvey to follow, as a child might wait for their father at the edge of a dark forest; keen, but frightened.

They descended together, side by side. Their footsteps were soundless, and only Norris' breathing could be heard. To Harvey's left, the corridor was lit. A string of yellow lamps like the kind that might light the entrance to a coal mine, or a construction site, hung from the right-hand wall. They cast an eerie light on the stone work, and the floors of the empty cells bore the lined shadows of the bars.

But there was no movement.

Harvey didn't want to do what he was about to do, but he must. If his plan was to succeed, then he must play his part. Norris stepped ahead of him, and Harvey placed the muzzle of Charlotte's handgun at the back of his head.

Norris stopped. His shoulders rose and fell with his breath.

"Don't hesitate," he whispered without turning.

Harvey pushed him on. Norris walked the walk of a condemned man, with slow steps, but he held his head high, and his chest was filled with pride at the idea of dying to save a life. To somehow reverse society's tainted opinion of him. Maybe he believed in God? Maybe he felt that a final selfless act would see him into some kind of paradise. Or maybe he had just had enough of the life he had led and the lies he had told, and wanted to be with his daughter. Whatever his motive, the man's strength was beyond admirable.

He stopped adjacent to the second from last cell, seeming to ache. He took deep breaths, calming his nerves, and seemed to gather every ounce of his will to take the final few steps.

He said nothing. On the far wall of the last cell, a shadow moved. Norris' destiny hung by a thread.

Before taking those final few steps, he turned to face Harvey. He uttered no words, but his eyes told a story so compelling that Harvey listened and absorbed every unspoken word. He lowered his gun, and held the man's stare. It was as if Norris was offering his gratitude. His eyes were moist and bright. They concealed nothing.

The wordless interaction was over. Each man held some kind of strange respect for the other, that even had they tried to put into words, they couldn't.

Harvey raised the gun again, a sign that it was time.

Once more, he filled his chest with all the courage he could muster. His shoulders broadened and his head, held high, rested on the muzzle of Harvey's gun.

And he stepped forward.

He did not turn his head to peer into the cell, he walked straight ahead. He stopped just three feet from the wall, and waited. Harvey held the gun in place, and turned to see what he feared the most.

Smiling, and with the sickening air of confidence that is born of greed and power, Blue Eyes stared back at him. In his hand was the weapon he had used on Giggs, and on her knees before him, her head covered in a old rotten hood, was Alice.

"Less than five minutes to spare," said Blue Eyes. "You're cutting it fine."

"Let her go, Bloom."

The man's smile broadened at the mention of his name.

"Somebody's been doing their homework."

Harvey didn't reply.

"What else did you learn?"

"Does it matter? Let her go. We had a deal."

"There are still three minutes to go, and from what I can see, you've only done half a job."

Norris closed his eyes. He understood what it meant and needed no prompting from Harvey. He dropped to his knees in front of Harvey, and lowered his head. Harvey settled the muzzle in Norris' nape, and readied himself.

"What does Spider have on *you*, then, Bloom," asked Harvey.

His smile faded, but he said nothing.

"Everyone else lives in fear. What about you?"

"You know nothing about me. Finish him."

He adjusted his stance and forced the gun into Alice's head.

"You're nothing but an old washed up convict."

"You're running out of time-"

"And you've run out of men."

"One minute," said Bloom, his breathing heavier than before.

"Where's Banks?" said Harvey. "Dead. Where's Butler? At home, I imagine. He's no longer scared of you or Spider. And everyone else? Where are they? This empire you said you had was all built on blackmail and fear. You're nothing."

"Thirty seconds. Thirty seconds and I'll do it."

"The truth is Bloom, that without Spider, you have nothing. There's no hold on you, except the fear of being a nobody. That's why you do what you do isn't it? Because you're scared of being alone. Of not being feared. I've known men like you my entire life. You're a has been. You used to be someone but now you're not. You're just a toy for Spider to play with just like the rest of them. Except all your toys have gone. You've nobody left."

"I've got these," he said, reaching into his pocket. He withdrew a small pile of photographs and waved them at Harvey. "You can't stop us. Nobody can. When one man falls, we recruit another. We've got more people lined up than you can kill in a month. You lose and your time is now up."

Harvey was silent for a few seconds. He pondered the situation he was in, the girl who was kneeling on the floor, and the man who knelt before him. How strong they were. Norris had shown such strength, and Alice. Her part was yet to be played. The photographs were only the next chapter in a saga that would never end.

"I can't do it." Harvey removed the gun from Norris' head and stared at the pattern of stones beyond. He was defeated. The gun slipped from his hand and fell to the floor. "I won't."

There was a metallic click, as Blue Eyes flicked his safety off. But Harvey was resolute.

"I'll do it," said Blue Eyes, and there was no doubt in his tone.

"Let me see her face," said Harvey. "Please. Just one last time, before you pull the trigger."

The request was aimed at Bloom's ego, and it struck with precision. A bullseye that Harvey had been counting on. Bloom's cruel grin returned. He took pleasure in revealing everything Harvey stood to lose, and tore off the bag with evident glee and malice.

Alice's hair fell down covering her face. It took a few seconds for her to blink away the darkness and focus. She looked up at Harvey from all fours, not a single tear had formed in her eye.

Harvey was motionless, expressionless and unmoved by the sight. But it wasn't his emotions he was counting on.

"Alice?" said Norris, and Harvey smiled at Blue Eyes' shocked expression.

"Father," said Alice.

FORTY-NINE

Debruin was out of the door in a heartbeat. He rushed to the front of the car where Charlotte was standing, frozen with fright.

"She's in shock," said Hargreaves.

She didn't turn to look at either one of them. Instead, her gaze was fixed somewhere way off in the dark night. Her lower lip trembled, her body was rigid, and her eyes didn't blink once.

"Charlotte," said Debruin, taking her hand. It was icy cold and limp. "Talk to me, Charlotte. You're okay now. You're safe. We've got you."

But still, she didn't respond.

Debruin removed his jacket and wrapped it around her shoulders. But she didn't respond.

"Charlotte, we found her. She's safe."

"Let's get her in the car," said Hargreaves, and he ran around Debruin to open the rear door. Debruin, rubbing her hands in his own to warm her, pulled her into a hug. But she didn't respond, even when he rubbed her back, trying to spark some kind of reaction. She just stood there, gazing.

She walked when coaxed, and even lowered herself into the

car, but she seemed to be lost, unable to react or respond to any form of communication. Debruin shut the door, and Hargreaves ran around to the passenger side. He opened the door and stopped, confused as to why Debruin hadn't budged an inch.

"Debruin, come on. We've got her. Let's get her to a hospital." He had one leg in the car when he saw the expression on Debruin's face. There were sirens in the distance. Multiple vehicles. But they were too far away to help. "Don't do it, Debruin."

"Take her," he said. "Get her out of here."

"Don't be bloody stupid. You can't go in there alone."

But Debruin was already walking. He heard Hargreaves' footsteps chasing after him and walked faster.

"Debruin, stop. Come on. Leave it to Spencer and Hawes. You heard what the gov said."

"Look at her," said Debruin. "Look at what they've done to her. Look at what they do to people. Banks, Butler, White. Even the killer. I have to stop them. I have to stop them now."

"I'm coming with you then," said Hargreaves.

"No," he said, catching Hargreaves' arm. "No. You've done enough. You've taken too many risks."

"So have you. Let them deal with it."

But Debruin had started walking again.

"Get out of here, Hargreaves," he called. "Take care of Charlotte."

"Think about Grace, you fool," called Hargreaves, and the mention of his daughter's name stirred something inside Debruin. An anger that had been building all day, simmering and spitting, ready to fire.

But he had a new-found respect for Hargreaves, enough for him to restrain the wrath he felt for those men inside that old building.

"She's all I can think about, Hargreaves," he growled. He held his stare for a moment, then with the sirens growing louder in the distance, he turned and left Hargreaves to take care of Charlotte.

Detective Inspector Mark Debruin was not a violent man. His training in the use of firearms had been limited to the requirements of programs he had attended. He had never been the type of man to train in the gym or even worry about his fitness. Over the years, he'd had reason to enter into the odd scuffle with a drunk, put a mouthy suspect back in his place, and he'd even punched another police officer in his younger years. But never was he a violent man unprovoked.

But as he walked along that narrow track toward the dark and foreboding building, he unfastened his cufflinks and tossed them on the ground; they were cheap and he hated them anyway. He passed an abandoned car that had been driven off the track, presuming Charlotte had lost control and ditched it in her panicked escape. He rolled up his sleeves to his elbows and removed his tie, tossing that away too. He approached the building as a man on a mission, heading straight for the front door, focused and angry.

But then something caught his eye.

There was a handgun on the gravel near the steps. He knew very little about guns, but he knew it was the type that TSG used. He was familiar with the slide action and safety catch. He checked around to make sure nobody was watching, as though it might have been some kind of trap. But he was alone.

With the gun in his hand and the stream of approaching blue lights barely visible on the horizon, he entered the old hall. He always carried a small, two-cell torch in his jacket pocket. But his jacket was wrapped around Charlotte's shoulders.

She needed it more.

The hall was large and dark, the type of grand entrance old buildings had, where, in the old films he enjoyed, butlers would greet guests and guide them to a lounge with a roaring fire and wood-panelled walls. He fished his keys from his pocket, on which he kept a small torch on a key chain. He'd never had the need to use it before, but it had been a gift one Christmas; a stocking filler from Julie.

Ahead of him was a widening staircase that disappeared into the gloom above. The weak torchlight showed no further than the first floor. The first exit off the hallway, and the only doorway that hadn't been barred with lengths of timber, led into a passage so narrow that if he stretched both arms out, he could feel both walls.

He was faced with the unknown. His choices were to climb the rickety old staircase, or venture into the dark and derelict hallway.

Debruin chose the hallway as the path of least resistance.

He imagined it to have once been the passage to the servants' area. He lost his footing in a few places where the floor had been torn up, but he kept a slow and steady pace, listening for voices all the while. The passage turned left and left again, and there was a dim glow in what seemed to be an old kitchen.

And faint voices.

He stepped into the kitchen that years ago, he imagined, would have been bustling with activity. There were three large island worktops, deep basins, and a floor of terracotta tiles. But on the left-hand side, disappearing beneath the house, was a flight of flagstone steps leading down into the cellar. He took the first step with caution, listening for the sound of men's voices. The stone walls below carried the sound well. Gauging the distance was almost impossible. On the last step, Debruin peered left and right. The cellar was long and thin, probably the length of the building, with small alcoves off to one side. A string of electric lamps had been hung from the wall, but the light was yellow and harsh, and it cast deep shadows. He followed the voices to his left and gasped at what he saw. He pulled back, pressing his back into the wall of the steps, and as quietly as he could, he prepared the gun to fire.

His heart was beating hard, his breathing was loud, and his pulse beat in his temples in warning, telling him how much of a fool he was being. He peered around the corner and pulled back to decipher what he had seen. But he seemed to have lost his ability to piece a scene together. Fear had hit him hard. He took the gun in his left hand and outstretched the fingers on his right. They shook; even in the strange light of the lamps, he could see them. He flexed his hand a few times, took a breath, and settled the gun in his clammy palm once more.

He peered around the corner and snatched his head back.

A man on his knees. Mature. Possibly Norris.

Another quick look.

A man standing beside him, unarmed, leather jacket.

Leather jacket. He recalled Casey's words.

The killer.

Another brief look.

They were both looking into the last alcove. But all the alcoves on the left side of the cellar had bars. They were like cells. Only they weren't designed to keep people in. He'd seen the design before. The cells each had trapdoors high up in the walls where deliveries would have been made. The bars were to prevent the staff from stealing the grain, ale, wine, or whatever was stored there.

The bars of the final alcove were open. And the two men, Norris and the killer, were talking to somebody inside. Spider maybe?

There was no way Debruin could reach them without being seen. Gun or no gun, he would leave himself exposed. Three or more against one.

He listened to what they were saying, thinking hard about

his options and considering if Hargreaves had been right to leave the job to Spencer.

"I thought you were dead," said a voice in a shocked but articulate tone.

Norris.

"I'm very much alive, Father." A female voice. His daughter?

There was a scuffle that sounded like a shoe on the flagstone.

"Don't move." A third man? Gravelled tone. A mature man. Not the killer. The killer was too young to produce that baritone voice. Ebenezer Bloom. "If you take another step, I'll kill her before your eyes."

A man whimpered. It was an agonised sound that was not born of physical pain; it was guttural, heartfelt.

"Shut him up," said Bloom. His voice boomed along the stone walls like a cannon fire.

Debruin took the opportunity to step down and rush to the far wall. With his back pressed against the stone, and the gun raised in his right hand, he took long, slow breaths.

A green light flashed on in the end cell, lighting the walls where the yellow lamps failed to reach. Debruin sidestepped closer, his heart pounding. He stopped at the first sign of movement. A large hand held a small flip-top mobile phone, like the one Debruin had seen on Barnes' desk only that morning. The man raised it in the air, moving it around in search of a signal.

And then, despite the terrible scene and Norris' wailing, there was laughter. It was the youngest of the men. His derisive chuckle was filled with the confidence of a man comfortable with his own true capabilities.

"You dare mock me?" said Bloom, lowering the phone to his side.

"You're waiting for Spider to give you the order," said the killer. His stance was wide, and his hands hung at his sides. He was ready to pounce. Like a coiled spring, he could strike in the blink of an eye.

Bloom said nothing.

"You can't do it without Spider's say so."

"There are rules," said Bloom.

Seeing an opportunity, Debruin slid his hand up the wall behind him, as far as he could reach.

"You can't do it without Spider's command because you're a nobody. Spider doesn't trust you to make a decision. You act like you have control, like you're part of something great, when all you are is a puppet."

Bloom raised the phone once more, and the green light lit the deep, dark corners of the cell. Debruin waited for his moment.

"You won't be getting an order this time, Bloom," said the killer in his mocking tone, amused at Bloom's obvious agitation. "You can wait all day for that text message to come through, but it won't come. Do you know why?"

"Why?" Bloom spat, trying his best to retain some kind of command over the situation. "What makes you so sure?"

The killer waited a few seconds, delighting in Bloom's discomfort. Debruin took a deep breath and prepared to act.

"Because she's kneeling right before you."

FIFTY

Alice looked up from where she knelt, peering through the lank hair that hung over her face, and she grimaced.

Norris, red-faced and still reeling from the sight of the girl he had abandoned to die so many years ago, stilled.

She stood, her body unfolding from the innocent victim she had played to the deadly and dastardly Spider she had become.

"Alice?" said Norris, his voice more of a whine than the strong, articulate diction he usually offered. "No. It's not true."

The soft and beautiful eyes that had smitten Harvey were narrowed, cruel, and cold, and in one of the delicate hands that had touched his face with tender patience was the little flip-top mobile phone she had used to control the devastation. The other she held palm up, waiting for Blue Eyes to give her the weapon.

He did so, astonished and bewildered.

"You faked your own abduction," said Harvey, shaking his head. "All of this is you."

"Don't be sad," she replied. "It wasn't all a lie. How did you know?"

"I worked it out at about the same time I realised you were his daughter. You should be dead by rights. Spider should have killed you. The very fact that you're still alive could only mean one thing."

"Smart and good looking," she said, and she smiled as her father shook the image of them together from his mind. "I wasn't always like this, Daddy."

"No, you weren't. You were sweet and innocent."

"And abandoned."

"I had no choice."

"You had every choice," she said. "Do you even know what I went through? Have you any idea what he did to me?"

Norris shook his head.

"Who?" said Harvey, seeing the gap in his theory. "What who did to you?"

Her mouth formed a cruel sneer and the sadness in her eyes revealed a crack in her hardened exterior.

"Spider, of course," she replied.

"But..." Norris began, breathless with the onslaught of devastating news. "But you're the Spider."

"No," she said, as she began to pace the small cell. Bloom's eyes followed her with a newfound awe, and she turned to stare back at him. "Can you imagine what it was like for me? I was abducted and used as blackmail against my weak father. I was beaten, spat on, raped, and used. By him, and one more."

She looked up at Blue Eyes, whose head cocked to one side, remembering. And suddenly, the recognition set in and his face dropped.

"That's right, Ebenezer. You remember, don't you?"

"You?" he said.

"New hair. New style. But the same old me," she said. "Can you imagine how I felt when my father abandoned me to you and him?" She referred to Spider as 'him' and seemed to spit the word from her mouth. "So, I killed him."

Norris' head dropped, as his final hopes for his daughter were quelled.

"I saw how he operated. I saw what he did and how he did it. One of the perks of spending so much time chained to the wall a few feet from where he sat, I guess. But I waited for my chance, and it came."

"How did you do it?" asked Harvey.

"He took me to the warehouse roof. He liked to gaze at his domain like a king."

"You pushed him?"

"It was all too easy. Nobody knew who he was. Even me. So, nobody knew he was missing. And when the messages still got sent, you, Bloom, did what I asked. The whole thing fell into my lap."

"Why?" said Bloom, and he began to back away toward the exit. "You could have run away. Nobody would have known."

"The old me might have," she replied. "The old me, that my father abandoned to die, and you abused, might have done. But the new me, the Spider inside of me, wanted revenge. And revenge is what I shall have."

"What?" he said, as she raised the gun to level with his chest. "What are you doing? You need me."

"Not anymore I don't," she said, and she prepared to fire, just as Norris stood up tall, his chest pumped, his withered face taut with emotion, and Harvey's gun in his hands.

"No, Alice," he said, and father and daughter locked stares for just a fleeting moment. But the moment was lost, as the string of lamps along the back wall died.

The cellar was cast into pitch darkness.

And a single gunshot fired, lighting the scene in a snapshot of horror.

The next few seconds were a blur of dark imagination, grunts of struggle, and footsteps trailing on the hard, stone floor.

Harvey dropped to his knees, feeling for where Norris had knelt. His hand touched a warm, sticky mess, and he felt hair clogged with blood.

Then a light shone from above, not green like the screen of Bloom's mobile phone, and not yellow like the string of lamps. It was bright white like torchlight, and as he turned to find the source, it blinded him.

He looked away and blinked to regain his vision. And he found the body of Ebenezer Bloom.

"You're nicked, sunshine," said a voice that was familiar in tone, and Harvey placed it.

"Detective Inspector Debruin?" he said.

"The one and only."

"I'm not the one you're looking for."

"Is that right?" said Debruin. "It's funny, because I've been onto you for six months. I've been one step ahead and one step behind the entire way. Hammersley, Slater, all of them."

"It doesn't end here," said Harvey. "It doesn't end with me."

"For me, it does."

"And Spider?"

"Not my problem anymore."

"What about all those people who were blackmailed?"

"Not my problem either."

"Are you going to let her get away?"

"She'll be picked up."

"And Norris?"

"We'll find him too."

"What about your daughter?"

Debruin was silent.

"Is your family safe?"

The man's breathing grew louder.

"You said that Spider isn't your problem anymore. How confident are you, Detective Inspector Debruin?"

He collected the pile of photographs from Blue Eye's limp grasp, then selected one. He turned and shielded his eyes from the torchlight and raised the photograph for Debruin to see. "Are you sure this isn't you, detective? Kneeling by your daughter's hospital bed?"

The man said nothing, and Harvey turned the image around for him, so Debruin could see the words that had been handwritten on the back.

You cannot run.

FIFTY-ONE

It was as if Debruin had been hit with a sledgehammer. He reeled from the blow, staggering backward. He reached for the bars to steady himself, and warm, irony bile rose from the pit of his stomach.

The killer was on him in moments. He reached for the gun, and Debruin, in his panic, dropped the torch. The light extinguished and cast them into darkness once more. But no matter how hard the killer tried, Debruin was not going to let go. He was pinned against the stone wall. The killer had one hand on his throat and the other on the weapon.

Debruin tried to aim the gun down, but the hand on his throat tightened. In his desperation, Debruin reached out and pushed at the man's face, digging his fingers into his eyes. The man's hand tightened, pinching Debruin's windpipe, and Debruin scratched at his eyes, digging deep with lungs screaming for air. He gave one final grope, and the killer let go of the gun to save his eyesight.

But by the time Debruin had recovered and held the gun aimed at chest height, searching the gloom for any sign of movement, he heard nothing, not even a breath. He saw only darkness and tricks of his mind that served little purpose other than to raise his already racing pulse.

"You can't win," said Debruin, listening for the man to offer a clue.

Hunched low, and with the fingers of his left hand splayed out before him, Debruin groped for the wall to guide him to the steps. But there was only darkness and space before him, and a cold chill, a product of his own fear, ran through his veins. All he could hear was his own breathing, shallow and laboured from his struggle with the man he had hunted for six long months.

Each step he took was a step into the unknown.

"I know you're there," he called. He waited for a reply, or for a sign that the man was close. What he didn't expect were the two hands that gripped his shoulders and forced him back into the wall.

And then he was there. In front of him. He could smell the leather of his jacket.

"Do you want to find Spider?" he asked.

Debruin said nothing. The answer was obvious.

"Do you want my help?"

"Do I need it?" said Debruin.

"Yes."

"Do you know where she's taken Norris?"

"Yes."

"You're looking for a deal. A shorter sentence?"

"No. I'm not going to prison."

Seconds passed slowly, and Debruin's pulse returned to some semblance of normal. The man was holding him by the scruff of his shirt, leaving his arms free. Debruin raised the weapon slowly. He was taking a chance so great that all his fears seemed to dance in his gut, and the bile returned with vengeance. But the man seemed not to notice. Debruin continued to lift the weapon, adjusting his grip with his finger on the trigger, until he felt the muzzle of the gun press into the man's temple.

The man didn't even flinch. Debruin felt the gun move with the man's face. He was grinning at Debruin's attempt, as if daring him to pull the trigger.

Debruin closed his eyes. He took a long, deep breath with the image of him at Grace's bedside in his mind and those three words embedded into his brain.

And he pulled the trigger.

Nothing happened. Due to the safety or the magazine, Debruin didn't know. He didn't even know if it was loaded.

"Forget about me," said the man. "It's your last chance."

Debruin swallowed. His mouth was as dry as a desert and his arms ached. He dropped the weapon to the floor in defeat.

"How can I forget about you?" he said. "I don't even know who you are."

FIFTY-TWO

The man pulled Debruin toward the steps rather than guided him. In the pitch dark, they climbed and then stopped at the entrance to the passage, where a bright, white light illuminated the scene. He shone Debruin's torch over the flooring, looked back once, as if to ask if Debruin was ready, and then he moved. He moved fast, leaping from beam to beam, and it was all Debruin could do to keep up. Twice he had to stop and wait for Debruin to catch up, shining the light on the ruined floor to help him make his way.

When they reached the hallway, Debruin ran to the two great doors and searched the landscape for a sign of Spider. But all he saw was the convoy of flashing blues approaching, less than half a mile away.

He glanced around the hallway and found the killer on the staircase, shining the light ahead of him, although the moonlight found its way through two tall and narrow windows.

"Up there?"

The man didn't reply. He waited for Debruin to follow, then ran ahead, up and up, until the winding stairs transitioned from wood to stone, and the handrail that Debruin had dragged himself up with was gone. They had reached the tower that Debruin had seen from below. Breathless, Debruin stopped the man by hanging onto his leather jacket. He flicked off the torch. There were three narrow windows around the space and the dark void below them appeared bottomless. A few steps further, at the top of the staircase, was a wooden door.

"Are you sure they're in there?" said Debruin.

The killer removed Debruin's hand from his jacket, and his face, though only half lit by pale moonlight, was hard and cold. All he would have to do is push Debruin and he would topple to his death.

Debruin stepped back, suddenly realising his folly.

But the man didn't move. He seemed comfortable with the precarious staircase, and four steps above Debruin, he appeared large, dominating the space.

"Do you know why Alice did what she did?" he asked.

"I heard," said Debruin. His throat was dry, and his leg muscles were hardened from the climb. "Because of what the men did to her, and because her father abandoned her."

He nodded.

"Do you know what happened to her mother?"

"Norris' wife? She died. I don't know how."

"She fell from their bedroom balcony."

Debruin glanced down into the gloom below. They were high enough for a fall to be fatal. He steadied himself using the stone wall.

"Do you really think she fell?" the man asked, then turned and climbed up to the landing.

Debruin followed, and as if he was leading Debruin to close the case, the killer stepped aside and opened the door, leaving Debruin with a perfect view of a circular, moonlit tower room. The remains of an old four-poster littered the right-hand space, and those tall, narrow windows marked the north, east, and west. To the south, however, to maximise the sun, was a pair of open doors. The tattered remains of sheer net curtains filled with the night breeze, and beyond them, framed in the giant moon, was Alice Valentine.

Her father was on his knees before her, his head bowed, and the gun nestled into his forehead.

Debruin stepped forward into the room, and Alice Valentine snatched her head to face him. Hues of blue danced across her face from the arrival of the convoy below. Hawes and Spencer would be there, with every TSG officer Spencer had at his command. Even Barnes and Carver would join them. But they could do nothing now except wait and hope.

"You don't have to do this, Alice," said Debruin. "He's your father."

"I've dreamed of this moment. He took everything from me."

"Look at him, Alice. Look at your father."

"He's not my father. He gave up that right when he abandoned me to a life of incarceration and abuse."

Debruin took a step forward, closing the gap to just eight feet. Alice's finger tightened on the grip and she pulled at her father's hair to lift his head.

"No closer," she screamed, and there was a hum of moans from Norris. "Stay where you are."

"You can't escape, Alice. There's nowhere to run to."

"There's always somewhere to run to," she said, and she looked down at her father's pitiful expression. "*He* ran. He ran and look what he did. He left me to rot while he hid himself away in prison." She peered down at the melee of lights and bodies below. "I'm a survivor. The moment I killed Spider, I came back. It was here that I rebuilt Spider's empire. It was here that I lived out my dreams, and it's here that I'll end the misery."

And with that closing sentence, she raised her father from his knees and forced him back onto the balustrade.

Norris, whose face sagged with exhaustion, raised his head. He stared past Debruin to settle on the killer, who observed as calmly as only a killer could. But Norris' expression was not pleading. Nor was it the face of a man who implored understanding and forgiveness.

It was an expression of thanks, silent yet sincere.

And as Alice placed the weapon between his eyes and forced him backward, until nothing but the remaining strength of the old building held him aloft, he took her in his grasp leaving her no time to fight back. Debruin launched himself at the pair, groping the air. But the balustrade gave under their weight, and even mid-launch, as the end seemed to play out in slow motion, he saw Norris close his eyes and roll backwards toward that place he longed to be, beside his wife somewhere far, far away.

Debruin landed in a heap with the upper half of his torso hanging over the edge, and he saw them below. Their bodies had separated during the fall. The body of Richard Valentine lay in an almost perfect star, as if he had embraced his final journey, exhausted of this life.

Alice Valentine had fought death every step of the way. Her body was a tangle of lank hair and broken limbs.

He reached for the remainder of the balustrade to haul himself up, but as it took his weight, the fixing gave way. In that moment when gravity seemed to pull him over the ledge, when his heart skipped a beat, and his stomach churned, he saw them. He saw Grace. He saw Julie. He saw failure. And, more importantly, he saw what failure truly meant.

A strong hand grabbed his shirt, holding him in place, and his breath seemed to fall at the shock. He was pulled back into the room where he fell onto his knees. A hand rested on his shoulder and Debruin reached for it, seeking comfort more than anything. He squeezed the hand, and, to his surprise, the hand squeezed back. Then he felt it. The ring on the finger.

He let go and turned, expecting to see the killer standing over him.

"It's over," said Hargreaves. "It's over now."

"Where is he?"

"Who?" said Hargreaves, looking behind him, confused. "It's just me."

"He was here," said Debruin. "He was right here."

Hargreaves still looked perplexed.

"The killer, Hargreaves. He was just here."

Debruin ran down the winding steps two at a time, despite the drop to one side. He launched himself into the old, grand hallway, burst through the front doors, and out into the night where the circus of uniforms was at play. He stared all around, at every face and every jacket. There was no sign of him. Even out on the lane, not a single person was in sight.

It was over. Six months of the hardest case he'd ever worked on, and all he had to show for it were two bodies, a pile of photographs, and a missing killer.

It was the voice he least wanted to hear right at that very moment that drew Debruin back to reality from that dark place inside his mind.

"Don't tell me you've lost him again, Debruin," said DI Barnes.

FIFTY-THREE

A full five days had passed when the nurse that had tended Debruin removed the drip from his arm and walked to the window of his hospital room. She pulled on the blind cord and the Venetian slats rose, allowing him a view of the ward.

Julie was standing there, beaming.

The nurse waved her hand, inviting her in, and she ran to his side to give him a hug. It was one of the hugs she used to give him, so many years ago. He pulled her closer and felt the warmth of her tears on his shoulder.

They said nothing at first, for two reasons. The first reason was that it would be days before they found out if the transplant had worked and Grace would be okay. But there was more hope than ever before, and the doctor had been positive.

The second reason they hugged for so long was...

"Thank you," she said, and Debruin's throat tightened. It was like the killer's hand had returned only, this time, the sensation could be swallowed away.

He said nothing.

She pulled away and sat by his side, examining the small plaster on his arms, one of which was from where the nurses had fed him the drugs to increase his red blood cell count. The plaster on his other arm was from where they had taken the blood. The blood that had been fed into Grace.

"It's going to work," he said. "I know it."

"Are you going back to work?"

"Maybe," he said. "Maybe not. That all depends on Grace."

Debruin knew she wouldn't argue. His health was important. Their family was important. He knew that now. It had taken him twenty years to work it out, and the biggest case of his career to fully comprehend it. Julie had known it all along.

"We'll get by," he told her, reaching for her hand. "Somehow nothing seems to matter anymore. Not Barnes. Not the killer. Not Norris. I've had time to think, Julie. It's all I've done for five days. Think."

"That's the drugs talking," she said.

"I mean it. I miss you. I miss us. This whole thing with Grace, I wouldn't wish it on my enemies. But look at us. I haven't held your hand in years, Julie."

She looked past him and frowned. He tracked her eyes to the small bedside table where the nurse had placed a tray with a jug of water and a disposable cup.

But there was also a photograph.

"What's this?" she asked, and she reached for it. "It's you and Grace. When was this taken?"

Debruin was struck dumb. Words failed him. It all seemed so long ago. It was over.

She held the photo in her hand, waiting for him to reply, but from where he was lying, he could read the three words on the back. The original three words had a thick, black line through them, and below them were three new handwritten words.

There was movement through the small window. Debruin sat up to see who it was through the slats of the blind. But the figure turned and walked away. He didn't look back. Debruin knew then. The leather jacket. The confidence in the man's stride. He'd been watching Debruin. But for how long?

"Mark, what's wrong?" said Julie, and she turned to see where he was looking. "What is it?"

Debruin could do little but smile. He lowered himself to his elbow, took the photo from Julie, and placed it on the bedside table, propped against the water jug.

It was then that a nurse knocked and entered the room. She pulled a wheelchair inside and gave them both a warm smile.

"Would you like to see Grace before she goes into theatre?" she asked.

Julie sat up, keen to go and see her daughter, but also intrigued as to what had amused Debruin. She frowned at him but squeezed his hand. There was no malice in her mannerisms.

"It was nothing," he said, thinking of those three new words. "Just a man I'm trying my hardest to forget."

"Why can't you forget him?"

He pushed himself upright to sit beside her.

"Simple," he said, squeezing her hand and offering her a smile. "Because I didn't really know him."

The End.

Also by J.D. Weston

J.D. Weston is the award-winning author and creator of Harvey Stone and Frankie Black. He was born in London, England, and after more than a decade in the Middle East, now enjoys a tranquil life in Lincolnshire with his wife.

The Harvey Stone series is a prequel series set ten years before The Stone Cold Thriller series.

With more than twenty novels to his name, the Harvey Stone series is the result of many years of storytelling, and is his finest work to date. You can find more about J.D. Weston at www.jdweston.com.

Turn the page to see his other books.

THE HARVEY STONE SERIES

Free Novella

A terrible moment in time, captured in blood.

See www.jdweston.com for details.

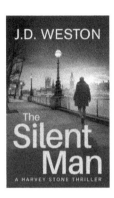

The Silent Man

To find the killer, he must lose his mind...

See www.jdweston.com for details.

The Spider's Web

To enter the spider's web, he must become the fly...

See www.jdweston.com for details.

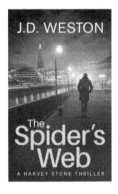

The Mercy Kill

To light the way, he must burn his past...

See www.jdweston.com for details.

The Savage Few

Coming March 2021

Join the J.D. Weston Reader Group to stay up to date on new releases, receive discounts, and get three free eBooks.

See www.jdweston.com for details.

The Stone Cold Thriller Series

Stone Cold

Stone Fury

Stone Fall

Stone Rage

Stone Free

Stone Rush

Stone Game

Stone Raid

Stone Deep

Stone Fist

Stone Army

Stone Face

The Stone Cold Box Sets

Boxset One

Boxset Two

Boxset Three

Boxset Four

Visit www.jdweston.com for details.

The Frankie Black Files

Torn in Two

Her Only Hope

Black Blood

The Frankie Black Files Boxset

Visit www.jdweston.com for details.

FREE EBOOKS FOR YOU...

As a gesture of thanks for buying this book, I'd like to invite you to the J.D. Weston Readers Group. Members of my reader group benefit from:

- A free eBook. The Inside Job - A Harvey Stone novella.
- Freebies as and when I run them.
- News of discounts from my author friends. (there's usually one or two of them running a promo at any given time).

Visit *www.jdweston.com* for details.

Milton Keynes UK
Ingram Content Group UK Ltd.
UKHW012021121023
430485UK00001B/36